42x 10/07 ✓3/08

ALSO BY ANITA BROOKNER

A Start in Life

Providence

Look at Me

Hotel du Lac

Family and Friends

A Misalliance

A Friend from England

Latecomers

Lewis Percy

Brief Lives

A Closed Eye

Fraud

Dolly

A Private View

Incidents in the Rue Laugier

Altered States

Visitors

FALLING SLOWLY

ANITA BROOKNER

Falling Slowly

–❧ A NOVEL ☙–

RANDOM HOUSE

NEW YORK

Library of Congress Cataloging-in-Publication Data

Brookner, Anita.
Falling slowly: a novel/by Anita Brookner.
p.   cm.
ISBN 0-375-50189-4
I. Title.
PR6052.R5816F27   1998   823'.914—dc21   98-12964

Random House website address: www.atrandom.com
Printed in the United States of America

2 4 6 8 9 7 5 3

First U.S. Edition

Book design by Caroline Cunningham

FALLING SLOWLY

---

*O*n her way to the London Library, Mrs Eldon, who still thought of herself as Miriam Sharpe, paused as usual to examine the pictures in the windows of the Duke Street galleries. She hoped one day to find the image she unconsciously sought, without knowing why she sought it, something to lift the spirits, to transport her on an imaginary journey, to give a hint of the transcendence which was so blatantly lacking in her everyday life of words and paper. Today there was a Dutch flower piece, badly darkened by age and varnish, and a portrait of an Elizabethan boy, snug in his ruff, his lashless eyes denoting a childhood of unchildish amusements—nothing, in short, to appeal to the vague restlessness she always felt before settling down to another silent day's work. But farther down the street, in a gallery specializing in images of the nineteenth century destined for easy consumption—girls in frills on swings, neat northern townscapes—she found something to her taste, a smoky winter scene by an artist of whom she had never heard, Eugène Laloue. It was clearly signed

at the lower left, and on the frame a small brass plate proclaimed:
'Place du Châtelet under Snow'. She looked closer, drawn in by
the dirty yellow sky, smoky where it met the roofs of the buildings, under which she could imagine herself trudging home after
a cold day. That yellow sky supplied its own illumination, although there were lights on in the buildings to the left, and even
in a shop, too small to be of much consequence but surprising in
this vaguely affluent setting. On the ground snow had been pud-
dled into water by passing feet; it dusted the tops of the street
lamps and the bench on which no one would sit. Groups of people stood waiting for the horse-drawn omnibus which could be
seen approaching in the distance. In the centre of the picture a
mother in a long black coat and a large black hat guided a
dressed-up child to the nearer pavement. All this was suitably animated. But what continued to draw the eye was the yellow sky,
lit from beneath as by a bonfire, stronger, stranger than the
human crowd below. Somewhere, in the remote distance, a flag
flew.

She stood for perhaps seven or eight minutes examining this
image, unperturbed by the jostling passers-by who barely registered in her consciousness, although they were recognizably of
the same genus as the tiny winter-clad people in the picture.
When she turned away from the window she was vaguely disconcerted to see that there was no snow on the ground and that
the sky was the colourless grey of an overcast April day. She could
not have said why the picture held such fascination for her, but
she recognized that it was the high point of a day which promised
nothing more exciting. It was not merely that the scene was of
Paris: Paris held no secrets for her. Her work involved brief but
regular visits to her agency in the rue Soufflot. These too were of
little consequence and led her to wonder where the legendary
glamour of the literary scene was to be found. She was intimidated by the decisive young women with whom she had little in

common; her work as a translator was satisfactory but it was largely routine, and in this connection she could hardly aspire to prominence. Once out of the office she marvelled at how little time had passed, leaving her free for the rest of the day.

In Laloue's picture, in which were commingled evening, homecoming, or better still homegoing, attachment (the mother with the child) and a context of belonging—for these people were confident enough not to wonder at their surroundings, not to be disconcerted by the bad weather and the fading light, and protected by that flag—she sought and partially found an assurance of a busier and more positive life than the one she knew. She doubted whether her own progress along a busy street could ever be seen as she saw the tiny figures in their urban landscape, purposeful yet unencumbered. In her mind's eye she drifted soundlessly and unobserved, even though she could quite clearly hear her heels on the pavement, could even nod to an acquaintance making for Christie's. In a few minutes she would go up the steps to the Library, make her way to the Reading Room and install herself at a table near the window. That was when real soundlessness would take over, broken only by an occasional cough and the rustle of a newspaper. This was her daily homecoming, as she had thought it to be when she was a student, as she had thought all libraries to be in those innocent days of study and application.

She could not now decide whether a library, any library, was a way out or a way in, a way out of daily life which contained too much confusion and weariness, or a way in to silent communion with true achievement, discarnate, incorporeal, couched in beautiful characters on paper, that smelt finer to her than the most recondite scents. It was somehow not her gift to be part of a crowd, which was why crowds fascinated and intimidated her. She preferred them at a distance, like the crowd in the picture, waiting for the omnibus in the trampled snow. It seemed to her that there was more silence in her own obedient days than there was in this minor scene by a minor painter. The window of the gallery had been protected by a grille. Peering through it she had felt that she was looking at an extinct species. Few passers-by gave it a second glance, from which she deduced that the picture had found its ideal spectator in herself, yet that if she were to be rich and able to buy it and hang it on the wall of her room it would immediately lose its distinctiveness, as if her own white walls were so alien that even the Place du Châtelet might be perceived as a fiction, so conclusive, so unyielding was the solitude of that room, with its unadorned bed and its faint smell of vetiver. White was the colour of virginity, or of martyrdom, as opposed to the suffused ochre of that imaginary winter afternoon. Yet when she stopped for a cup of coffee, finding herself too distrait to begin work, the picture was in the course of being removed from the window. For this she felt a certain relief, as if she were now able to glance away from some worrying spectacle. After much hesitation, she went into the gallery and asked for a catalogue. There, on an inside page, and suitably secret, was the scene, its colours only marginally different from those on the canvas. Even this was somehow appropriate, the initial experience having proved unrepeatable.

This was somehow a day on which concentration would not be possible, a day on which words must give way to images. The very idea of sitting in the Reading Room repelled her, although normally she was on quiet terms of acquiescence with the work she was employed to do, peacefully translating contemporary novels of no particular merit into English. It was not work she had actively sought; rather it had sought her. Her college tutor had remarked on her facility with languages, her ability to translate French into English and English into French, and had passed on to her a commission which he had no time or inclination to execute. It was an almost irresponsible action, but he had reached the age and stage of life when work is seen as confinement, as a check on natural impulses which perhaps have never had the chance to express themselves. She, the neophyte, with as yet no experience of this, had settled eagerly to the task. And so it had proceeded, with an ease irresistible to one with an urge to prove her worth. Money was not an immediate problem, although it was a matter of pride to prove to others that she too was a breadwinner. Now she was known for her reliability, but like most reliable people not much valued.

It did not occur to her, or rather it no longer occurred to her, to wonder what she would rather be doing; she knew that she had no particular calling. When very young she had had an amorphous love of the arts; this had dwindled over the years to a panicky relief that she had found employment of a not too onerous kind that did not oblige her to compete with more gifted contemporaries and which kept her within reasonable bounds. Perhaps the Laloue had been an echo of days when she had been ambitious for more, when Paris had seemed to her to be filled with romantic promise, rather than the humdrum workaday city that she was now obliged to visit. She had thought herself to be fitted for better things, yet time had proved otherwise.

Love was to have been the answer, yet now all considerations of love merely served to revive memories of her sister, Beatrice, whose unashamed romanticism she had always deplored. By degrees this had taught her to deplore the remnants of what subsisted of her own unconfessed longings. For it had existed, that desire to see the world as a better place, to endow all sights and sounds with significance, to reinstate the beauty of a universe now beyond her reach. She had scaled down her expectations in the name of realism, of that same exactitude that enabled her to do her work to a satisfactory standard, and to analyse without pity the circumstances that had led to such a diminution. It was not enough to accuse an unhappy childhood; most people did that. Rather there was something critical in her make-up which she did not altogether appreciate.

Memories of Beatrice continued to surface. She saw again the patient look of longing in her sister's eyes, a look that still addressed the younger woman's deeper anxieties. Then she was grateful for her unvarying task, for the qualities that made her such a steady employee and collaborator. Letters from satisfied authors, which were quite frequent, reduced her to subordinate status all over again, but this she accepted. She had long ago decided that life was possible, if not actually gratifying, if one reduced the risk. The risk remained vague, unidentified, but she knew that it existed. The preferred strategy should be one of containment. This, she knew, was faintly shocking to a temperament such as her own which had known a deep original disillusionment, but she did her best to observe it. These days she merely appreciated what could be easily managed, just as she appreciated work that was well within her grasp. Except that on this particular morning it did not seem to be; today her own activities had been reduced to their proper dimensions by art, by renewing a perception of her much younger self. It was not the reality of the Place du Châtelet that disturbed her, so much as a resurrection of the dreaming novice she still harboured, eager for unrestricted experience, before the era of blame and responsibility. Clearly it was safer and more prudent not to look in windows, not to have access to other people's worlds. The world she had grown used to would have to suffice.

When work was going badly she took a resigned view, abandoned her table in the Reading Room and went out again, ostensibly in search of more coffee, in fact to seek the animation of the streets. This was somehow disappointing, far from the vividness she craved. Such mornings—for she would never allow inactivity to encroach on the afternoons—were indeterminate; nothing had happened to change her outlook, and yet in some mysterious way she was able to pick up her daily rhythms at the price of a small delay. Such a process seemed to her miraculous, compensation for a life of meritorious activity, as if the engine of her obedience were strong enough to overcome all obstacles, or would be if only she indulged it a little. Today she was reconciled to wasting a morning. She attributed this disposition to the fact that she had slept badly, having imagined that she had heard Beatrice cry out in the night. In fact there had been no cry, and in any event it had been their mother who had been in the habit of calling her, in those last days before she had been moved to the hospital. It was Miriam who had insisted on this, for her sister's sake as much as for her own. She knew that they must get used to self-sufficiency, and in order to do this they must eschew pity and the sort of terror that another's illness brings. Their mother, for once, had not blamed her, and had seemed to revive in the presence of doctors and nurses, to die a mere eight days later, mute and unobserved, in the small hours of the morning. The outcome of this death, its legacy perhaps, was sobriety for Miriam, flightiness for Beatrice. That was the period of Beatrice's flirtations, before they decided to leave the house and begin their new life. There was no reason now for Beatrice to call out in the night; Beatrice was dead. Nevertheless something had woken her and had left her with a vestigial disquiet that for the moment at least ruled out concentration.

The London Library was now the refuge to which she repaired on most weekday mornings, although she could more easily have worked at home, where there were few distractions. But home, real home, as opposed to some fictitious home which she would know the minute she found it, was unwelcome, especially in the daytime, when she could imagine she heard the ghost of Beatrice's piano, against which she had turned a deaf ear in real life. But Beatrice had been dead for some months, and she herself was no longer a girl resigned to shouldering unwanted family burdens but to all intents and purposes a mature woman, with work to keep her occupied, and in reasonable health, reasonable beyond all expectations. If life were dull, as she had never expected it to be, she had always been stoical in the face of dullness, as if once a certain term of trial were over she would emerge a lighter, more interesting being, able to take on the world, all her fears gone. Instead she had become a connoisseur of various forms of dullness, one age succeeding another as if in some hierarchically ordered progression. Some stages were preferable to others. She had come to appreciate, even to embrace, certain years, the years spent in Beatrice's company, towards the end of her life, before her strange but so logical eclipse had put an end to their companionship, to their misunderstanding, to the strange dread that she felt even now, and would continue to feel, she supposed, for as long as memory were active. As the final repository of her sister's illness she could look back almost with nostalgia to their terminal closeness, which nothing had been allowed to disturb.

How acceptable that earlier monotony now seemed! Those careful Sunday mornings, those sedate walks round the silent streets, noting the gradual return of buds to bushes, obediently suppressing a sigh as the buds emerged so slowly, as the grey clouds sifted in the cold wind of what was still only February! The very absence of weekday noise and agitation was a balm, or was it an additional sedative? Only now did she measure the peace of that prospect. But to measure was to evaluate, to compare. Nothing prevented her from taking such a walk, on just such a Sunday, but now the very idea was hollow, leached of meaning, as everything else seemed to be. A death had occurred, and although she had dealt with it competently, with remarkably little emotion, her life and perceptions had been altered by it, as if oxygen had been withdrawn from the atmosphere, so that her steps were now as cautious as if she herself were in decline. Yet if she felt anything it was ennui, a delirium of ennui, the grey sky and the cold wind obliterating every impulse she might have felt to seek comfort in another climate, another landscape. She was free to leave but felt condemned to stay.

The monotony of her current situation was of a different order, had something shameful about it, useless; without attachments she saw her desire to please as unmotivated, unsolicited. And although this might at a pinch be counted a tribute to some residual innocence, as if she were still an eager girl in quest of friends, she knew that this was not the case. Age had invested her with new emotions—resentment, fear, sorrow—and she was shocked by her consistently ruminative mood, not previously encountered, regretting all the time now the breathless expectations of youth, which her continuance in the world had somehow put to shame. Even the brief willed peace of her former life, or that part of it that she could invoke, as if she were to swallow a sleeping pill, had vanished, to be replaced by what she imagined was a permanent scowl, though when she looked in the glass she saw only bewilderment. She had determined, so many years ago, to be good, but had somehow ended up compromised. Praised on all sides for her devotion, she felt impatience. By contrast those blameless Sunday walks were a guarantee of blamelessness. With their disappearance, her blamelessness was also mysteriously gone.

Yet she was the first to acknowledge that it had not been easy, that false equilibrium, though she almost missed the approving smiles of neighbours, even of strangers, as she accompanied her sister on their small shopping expeditions, their humble excursions. 'So devoted,' she had heard one woman remark to her companion, and had felt a preliminary spurt of horror. 'A devoted couple,' she used to hear said of her parents, yet she knew that their relationship was stormy, uneven, based on very real antagonism. Illness had united them at the end, and they had faced the world together, bringing forth sentimental tributes. And similar tributes had somehow become her due, as she had shortened her steps to accommodate Beatrice, whose poor health was known. Women admired them; men were if anything abruptly dismis-

sive, sensing an oppressively sexless world of sacrifice and obliga-
tion. They had been aware of this, could not completely ignore it.
But what was resignation in the one was something more com-
plicated in the other. They had survived their history, and besides,
they had no other choices.

Beatrice had been well named, a stately character, with a natural dignity, according to those whose knowledge of her was
based on infrequent acquaintance, and it was true that she bore
her increasing frailty with a habitual smile and shake of the head
when that Greek chorus of well-wishers and commentators enquired. It was true that the stiffness in her fingers had put paid to
a promising career as an accompanist, but the truth was not entirely served when this explanation was forthcoming. There had
been an element of willed collapse in that renunciation, a condition endemic in the family background, and rampant in her own
acceptance of the supporting role thus forced on her, the younger
sister. Or had she chosen it out of fear of contention? She remembered only too well the contentions that had shadowed the years
of growing up, or trying to grow up, her mother threatening illness, collapse, even death, if not humoured, her father all tearful
resentment, hardly a man at all, or at least not a man as dreamed
of by two wistful girls. And further back, even beyond this, there
were memories of an embittered grandmother berating her
daughter for marrying such a man, while the two girls ran up to
their bedrooms and refused to come down, thus prolonging the
dissatisfaction that was the very climate of their home. They had
learned how to protect themselves, by tacit obedience, by tacit indulgence of their mother's moods, but despite some fairly successful dissembling they had never managed to feel indifferent to
this disharmony. Only to each other could they confide their disappointment once they had knowledge of other families, picked
up from schoolfriends, who were only infrequently invited to the
house. On these occasions either the mother or the father, if he

happened to be at home, but sometimes both, would comment on
their own bad luck, although the house seemed prosperous
enough, even if the visitors were not made entirely welcome.
They were there as audience, while the girls, Beatrice and
Miriam, suffered a discomfort they were too young to identify as
moral. They longed for dignity and were not to find it.

Their respective escapes seemed to them miraculous, though
each hankered for the closeness of the other. When Beatrice won
a scholarship to the Royal College of Music, the younger girl,
Miriam, was allowed to go to university, on condition that she continue to live at home and keep her mother company. By this stage
their father was ill, and extravagantly awkward, genuine fear
shifting in his eyes, and their mother, frightened into showing a
timid support, had significant failures of control. On the street,
their arms linked, their faces wary, they were accorded an indulgent smile. Beatrice refused to be part of this drama; music supplied her with a world of feeling which she recognized as superior
to anything she had ever known in life. But she was circumspect:
no expression of pleasure, of excitement, was permitted. In any
event it would have been out of place. Their faces identified them
as sisters: they appeared well-meaning but unprotected. No one
had ever told them they were attractive, with a slightly old-
fashioned, slightly irritating appeal. Out in the world they marvelled that they were found acceptable to others, after years of
being castigated as unsatisfactory, disappointing. In a perverse but
logical manner disappointment was their inheritance. Nothing
had prepared them for a welcome.

Since there were no other family members to advise them
they had stayed in the house after their parents' deaths, a substantial suburban house on the outskirts of London, until Beatrice's
modest celebrity as an accompanist, and her own progress as a
translator, prompted their epic flight to the flat in Wilbraham
Place, prompted not so much by their own initiative as by their

friends' complaints at having to travel so far to visit them. Even so they had no thought of separating; each constituted the other's family, in a very real sense. They had been witnesses to each other's discomfiture, a condition which they could not translate for others. By their twenties, their thirties, they were popular, courted, felt themselves momentarily to be part of the effervescence around them. Those years had run their course. They had their work, they had an agreeable home, but they were a little tired of going to weddings, which to them marked the disappearance of confidantes. It was then that Miriam had succumbed to the temptation of marriage. It had not been an easy decision. She was thirty-five, an age which almost debarred her from youthful romance and its illusions. It was because she saw how dangerous such illusions could be that, wryly, she put in train certain plans of her own, searching out the candidate least likely to disappoint her. She had known him for ever, since childhood, almost. Longing, for no reason she could identify, for a safe haven, she made the necessary telephone calls. Beatrice was not consulted. As a courtship it was well outside Beatrice's experience. Besides, the outcome could not possibly alarm her, would indeed leave her intact, unslighted. The urge to protect had operated in this matter as in all the others. That it then had to be extended to her husband was something for which she had not bargained. It was some time before she perceived, and embraced, the appropriate irony.

———

CHAPTER TWO

*I*n youth Beatrice had been attractive, but what was attractive about her was not her appearance but her disposability. She entered a room with a helpless suppliant air, as if looking for a pair of broad shoulders, of strong arms to which she might entrust her evident womanliness. This attribute was imprecise, but was assumed to be powerful. Her looks were unusual, although she did not always invite flattering comparisons. Her blonde hair, almost white, was much admired by her women friends, as was the Flemish fairness of her rather broad face. She bewailed her white eyelashes, but in fact her round, unyielding, almost naked blue eyes were an accurate gauge of her character, which was romantic and unpredictable. Her piano teacher, a German, had told her that she would come into her own as a woman of forty, when others started to fade: this was a compliment not much appreciated by a girl of twenty, anxious to begin her life and already awaiting lovers. '*Saftig,*' said that same homesick German. 'He is in love with me, of course,' said Beatrice to her sister. Miriam thought that it might be true, but at the same time was inclined to put the blame on Beatrice's reading matter. Between her favoured covers men were always handsome, dashing and articulate, while women were altogether charming, as was Beatrice herself, never more so than when choosing her books, so rapt in contemplation of this ideal conjunction that she hardly had time to notice the real if imperfect men who favoured her with a speculative glance. She preferred to set the scene herself, to imagine herself always entering a room, with that look of questing obedience which she thought to be successful. 'Oh, that I might do your bidding,' said that look, 'receive your orders, supply your every need.' Such ardour sometimes drew a response, largely from men too old to be taken seriously. The homesick German was the first to be intrigued, yet even he noticed the lack of curiosity in the round birdlike blue eyes.

· Such attitudes were radically out of date, archaic even, and for that reason occasionally beguiling. While other women cultivated a deliberate childishness, and indeed looked like children in their short skirts, Beatrice covered herself with flying scarves and long necklaces, and kept her hair coiled into an elaborate structure, in itself out of date. Miriam sighed in exasperation, but 'Artists have standards,' said Beatrice. What was noticeable, somewhere slightly out of touch with that confident expectation, was a strange absence of practicality, so that as she grew older the confidence diminished, and a modicum of adult seriousness intervened, together with an expression that denoted wistfulness, with an occasional flash of exasperation.

'But what do you expect?' asked Miriam, herself exasperated by that expression. She knew the answer she would receive, having heard it several times already; it was nervous sisterly concern that made her return to the subject, and a perverse desire for an argument.

'I expect very little,' said Beatrice. 'But perhaps I am wrong.

No one can say that I am not appreciated. I am surrounded by men, unlike you, sitting there with your dictionaries.'

You are not wrong, thought the younger sister, who as a student had indulged in the usual experiments, but without great conviction. These investigations had given her little pleasure but persuaded her that she was not wasting her youth. She had thought that youth should be actively employed: in fact it had rather let her down. And for neither of them had the next chapter opened, the one that was to obliterate botched beginnings and vindicate their not quite realized maturity.

It was true that Beatrice was surrounded by men, but to Miriam's eyes they were always the same sort of men, indistinguishable, elderly, courteous, invariably foreign-born, veterans of the orchestra pit or the concert platform, who were glad of an invitation to the flat in Wilbraham Place, being lonely and ill-at-ease for most of the time. Miriam was obliged to do the honours until the moment Beatrice chose to make her entrance. This she did with a full complement of cajoling smiles, summoning, as though from unseen attendants, the bottles of whisky, of brandy (but they had already been produced) until it was time for a rehearsal, or a reprise, at the piano. Miriam knew then that she was expected to retire to her own room, and indeed had no desire to stay. Resigned to hearing the call—'Miriam! Walther is leaving!'—she would emerge to see one Walther or another kissing her sister's hand, but looking as if the interlude had not quite come up to expectations. At such times she could not avoid the impression that there was a slight alteration of the features, an infinitesimal pursing of the lips, an appeal to fellow-feeling. She understood this, but was obliged to deny the fellow-feeling. Innocence, she knew, must be protected, but for how long? And was it innocence? Beatrice was flushed, but flushed with the virtues of her own performance. 'He is in love with me, of course,' she would say, and Miriam's own lips would purse. Then they would busy themselves with the evening meal, and empathy would be restored.

'Use those dishes,' one of them might remark. 'Mother never used them.'

Yet as time went by, and they remained mysteriously isolated from the world, they began to think more sympathetically of their mother. The subject arose quite naturally on those evenings when Beatrice did not have an engagement, in the course of those same evening meals, as they lingered over cheese, or picked at grapes. They saw their mother as an exile from the land of lost content, whether or not she had ever known it, and this was a subject that gave them both pause. Was this prescience? Did they themselves begin to intuit a life of promises not kept? Superficially there was no comparison. They were healthy, and by all accounts good-looking, though differing almost comically in appearance. Beatrice, striving to identify herself as an artist (for compliments, when they came, were a little forced, or did she imagine this?), retained her long skirts and her elaborate pyramid of hair, always going to have it rebuilt if she were due at an engagement. She looked older than her years, while Miriam, short, watchful, with an expression of wary cynicism and an avowed disposition towards simple pleasures that had been only partially requited, was apparently at one with her contemporaries in clothes of the moment which she chose with care. They were in fact too careful, and inappropriately formal for one who sat at a desk all day searching for the right word or words with which to pin down a French verb. Secretly she envied those who went out and about, while she remained in the grip of her sentences. So demanding was this discipline that the words would remain with her throughout the evening. Beatrice would be unsurprised to hear her question, '*Bave?* Dribble? It doesn't seem quite right somehow.'

'Mother was lonely,' she now said.

'Who wouldn't be, married to a man like Father?'

'I think of her sometimes, sitting all the afternoon on that chintz sofa, waiting for us to come home.'

'And yet she didn't seem to love us in the way other children's mothers loved them. I always preferred to go to Anne's house, or Jean's, rather than go home.'

'She was disappointed in love.'

'Well, of course.'

'Her hopes had been too high. Like yours, Beatrice. She wanted romance, and she settled for the most unromantic man possible.'

'He couldn't help being a tax inspector.'

'It's my contention that he was deliberately unromantic, as if he wanted to punish her for being disappointed in him.'

'They hated each other, didn't they?'

'And yet they stayed together. And there were no affairs, no indiscretions. They were martyred by marriage, but they never envisaged any other sort of life.'

'I could feel sorry for Mother if only she hadn't been so defiant about being let down.'

'Virtue—if it was virtue—had turned sour, as no doubt it always does.'

'Technically, I suppose, they were good people. An awful warning.'

'I know. I blame them all the time, even now. And yet I think of Mother whiling away the afternoons, with nothing to do, in that room in which nothing ever seems to have been disarranged, so tightly was it packed together, all chintz curtains and covers, repressively creating a false impression of comfort. I once came home earlier than usual and found her sitting on that overstuffed sofa, with the *Radio Times* on her lap, just staring into space. It was desolate, somehow, yet when she saw me she looked annoyed, the way she did, you know, summoning up her grievances.'

'Will we be like that?'

'Yes,' said Miriam slowly. 'We might, if nothing happens to us. The only difference is that we have limited objectives.'

'You may have. I haven't.'

'Her needs were infinite. I see that now. She wanted a man to induct her into the fuller life. She was shy, you know. That was what reconciled her to Father: there was no need to unburden herself to him. She became incapable of that, anyway. And to do him justice he accepted it.'

'He didn't deal with it very well.'

'He probably thought all women baffling, thought it was masculine not to understand them.'

'But he was petty, pitiful.'

'He was no hero, certainly. I'm afraid, Beatrice, that he did a lot of damage. To us, I mean.'

'Yes. I know what you're thinking.'

'I'm not criticizing you. It's just that I know you. You too want an ideal man, to give you that ideal life you fantasize about.'

'Who doesn't?'

'Well, all right. But I'm more realistic than you. I'm reconciled. I know that one man couldn't give me everything I want.'

'What do you want?'

'I want to be very good at my work,' said Miriam primly, getting up from the table, and piling plates on top of one another.

'I want more than that.' Beatrice's voice was sad. 'I want love—I make no apology for that. I want the real thing. You probably think I'm quite content having my hand kissed by elderly exiles. It's they who want that, Miriam. And even they are a little confused by me. I know that. I'm not a fool. I play the social game, that's all. But I want something altogether different. I want intimacy, exclusivity, protection. My work gives me far less satisfaction than yours does.'

'Are you sure?'

'I know I do it quite well. I'm endlessly accommodating, look quite good on the platform, smile modestly when some excruciating singer beckons me forward to share her applause, meagre though it is. I told you about that, didn't I?'

'Wigmore Hall, yes.'

'I dissimulate, Miriam. I dissemble. When my arms ache, and I have to force the smile, I long to be taken care of. You make fun of the books I read, I know. You think it disgraceful that a fairly intelligent woman, in this day and age, when we're all liberated, should fall for all the old myths.'

'Tall, dark and handsome . . .'

'Quite. If Father did lasting damage, and I don't doubt that he did, it was in giving me a taste for stereotypes. Preferring stereotypes to the real thing. And I get discouraged, make no mistake. Men look so heroic on the concert platform, in their evening clothes. But you can see right through them, or rather I can. I see their sweat, smell it. I see them combing their hair. They don't live up to their roles, somehow.'

'You want a romantic hero.'

'Of course. Don't you?'

'But you've had lovers, more than I have.'

'Oh, when I was a student, yes. But they meant nothing. We were very young, almost innocent. I can hardly remember them now. None was significant. I suppose you think I'm regressing,' she said, with a look that meant that she had considered this question on her own account.

'I do, yes.'

'You may be right. And yet I feel more innocent now, as if nothing had yet happened to me.'

'I'm not a romantic, not like you. I'll probably never find the sort of person you're talking about, but it won't break my heart.'

'Are you sure?'

'I have a much stronger sense of reality than you have. I take what I can get.'

Taps were turned on, chairs were pushed back under the

table. The colloquy seemed to have ended. Yet, glancing at Beatrice, Miriam was almost shocked at the sadness of her sister's face. All at once, unbidden, the image of their mother came to mind, as she had once seen her, with the *Radio Times* unopened on her lap, not looking, not listening, and surrounded by the riotous chintz chosen to denote the joy and profusion of summer. There was one difference: their mother's expression had been querulous, distant, whereas Beatrice was genuinely yearning, her face stripped of the professional soulfulness that Miriam frequently deplored, authentic, serious beyond the limits of their recent discussion. She will be disappointed too, thought Miriam, but only if she finds the wrong sort of man. It seemed unlikely that she would find the right one, if he existed. The sort of man willing to encompass Beatrice's neediness would be kind, sympathetic, valetudinarian, even; he would not understand women, supposing them to be all alike, childish, no doubt preferring to think that way. Maybe their father had begun his married life with that primitive belief, prepared to be indulgent, but not to understand. He had been unequal to the task; his wife's sharper intelligence had discerned his weakness, which was left as his only capital, and which he then felt free to display, to exploit. A revenge tragedy, in which each partner was exculpated, blaming the other. Hideous to witness. Surely Beatrice had more sense?

'I'll finish up here,' she said, more sharply than she intended. 'Why don't you go to bed? You look tired.'

Even Beatrice's early beauty was a little dimmed, she saw. Her face had lost some of its attractive pallor; her mouth was a rueful and incongruous indicator of her unreformed childishness. For surely it was childish to believe in heroes? Childish, but inevitable, if one were on uneasy terms with reality. Miriam's heart contracted when she saw the look of wistful concentration on her sister's face as she immersed herself in her beguiling reading matter. Each time she made a vow never to look like that. At the piano

Beatrice was all smiling indulgence for the performer, her usual partner, a woman singer whom she did not like. There was a certain grimness behind that indulgence. 'One more *Mainacht* and I shall brain her,' she had said. 'And she had the audacity to ask me not to wear so much scent.' In that context grimness was appropriate. Whereas left to herself, when not practising, she sought refuge, as if growing up, becoming an adult, was something she had not truly desired.

Exasperated and alarmed at these partial confessions, Miriam shut a cupboard door more noisily than was necessary.

'Do you want a hot drink?' she called out. What else could she provide but minor indulgences, which made her uncomfortable, as if her own regard for truth were being forced aside?

'I hate these long spring evenings,' she said, as she carried a glass of hot lemon and honey into Beatrice's bedroom, larger and more profusely decorated than her own. 'I hate it when it gets dark so slowly, and yet stays cold. Light sky and cold wind: an irritating combination. Are you all right? You seemed a bit down earlier. We shouldn't go on about the past. It's bound to be upsetting.'

But Beatrice, lying in bed, seemed to have recovered herself. This was due to her consciousness of looking her best, of appearing to her advantage, her hair released, her nightdress scarcely whiter than the opaque skin of her white throat and shoulders. So would she arrange herself for her ideal lover, even if he never came.

'I do get tired, Miriam, though I try not to show it. My life isn't altogether straightforward, you know. There are professional worries. I only get second-rate singers these days.'

'They ask for you.'

'I know that, but a really good agent would do something about the situation. I've complained enough. Of course, Max is not what he was.'

'Can't you change?'

'Not really. He's on the verge of retirement, and then I suppose someone else will pick up the list. Arrangements have probably been made that I don't know about. That's one more uncertainty to add to all the others. And the truth is my fingers aren't as supple as they once were. And my arms ache. I'm bored, Miriam.'

'You're downhearted. It will pass.'

'We don't know enough people,' said Beatrice fretfully. 'Why is that?'

'Oh, people. I lost all hope of people when friends married and didn't bother to keep in touch.'

'Disappointing that, yes. But you should make more of an effort, get out more.'

'I go to the London Library.'

'That doesn't count.'

And yet it was reassuring to work in the Reading Room, and to see all those heads bent over their books. Virtue, it seemed, resided in the text; application was the key to a higher form of life.

'We could invite a few people, I suppose. We know enough for that kind of function.'

Beatrice sighed. 'Don't you get tired of making an effort? I know I do. I don't want to rely on myself all the time.'

'You want the fatal encounter, eyes meeting by chance . . .'

'It would be preferable.'

They sat in silence, listening to the sad sound of birds in the fading light. Buses, at the end of the street, were now infrequent; few footsteps could be heard. Yet somewhere people were drinking, dining, entertaining each other, on an ordinary weekday evening, released from work, eager for pleasure. Only in the flat was life becalmed, and somehow it was right, on this particular evening, after this particular exchange, that it should be so.

'Goodnight, then.'

'Goodnight. Will you sleep?'

'I doubt it. Will you?'

'Oh, I'll read for a bit,' said Beatrice, stretching out a hand for her book, her features softer now that no blame was forthcoming. Frequently her sister urged stronger reading matter on her, with varying degrees of success. Something in her rejected the promise of those attractive covers. Yet Beatrice, who was, as she thought, so beautifully attuned to men, in a way denied to Miriam, read only books about women, written by women. It hardly mattered if the subject were well-bred adultery in a rural setting, or a feisty investigation by a female detective living with her cats in San Francisco. Nodding slightly she sympathized with these women, always presented as heroines, savoured their satisfactions, their triumphs. She acquiesced in their relationships, knowing that she would do the same, would always succumb, seeing little harm in doing so. There was no calculation in this. Disarmed by fantasy, she became disarming. It was not conviction, thought Miriam; it was not even confidence. It was faith, Beatrice's substitute for invocation, less a diversion than a plea to a problematic fate, as others might make a solemn wish.

The one exception to this light, even invalid diet was *Jane Eyre,* which Beatrice read frequently, thrilling to Mr Rochester as most women did, disdaining St John Rivers, as no woman should.

'Of course it's a romantic novel,' said Miriam. 'That's why you like it.'

'That's why I'm meant to,' Beatrice would reply. And Miriam, who secretly felt the same, allowed for once that Beatrice had got it right, was in fact Charlotte Brontë's ideal reader, even wished that she too could still feel the rightness of the conclusion. But then she was not a romantic, and never failed to point this out.

'What you miss!' Beatrice would remark. 'My poor girl, what you miss!'

CHAPTER THREE

Strange how those conversations stayed with her, while those she had initially enjoyed with her husband had entirely vanished, as he had. Beatrice, dead, had more of a life even now than her insouciant husband, who had removed himself to Canada as light-heartedly as though this could not possibly affect her. Deeply offended—but in fact more annoyed than offended—she had suggested a divorce, to which he had readily acquiesced, with a deprecating charm which no longer pleased her. He was a bio-chemist; his work meant much to him. They had known each other since childhood, maybe too long; each had registered the other's eccentricities, in the days before these had become weighty, too weighty to bear. She had loved him as a brother, or as an old friend, and had therefore been unprepared for his continuing childishness, his eternal restless depthless curiosity.

His conversation had been wearisome, full of unanswerable questions. What do you think of Freud? he would ask her, or indeed any of their friends. What do you think of Picasso? Of

Napoleon? Like anyone barely educated beyond his specialization he was always slightly behind the times, a writer of letters to newspapers on subjects no longer being discussed, not much put out by a look of boredom, hastily masked, on a hitherto friendly face, because in the split second in which he was aware of a lack of interest, he would become conscious of more questions to which he was sure that someone had the answer. Hence the elusive yet insistent nature of his presence which had made her marriage tedious. His appointment in Canada had seemed a sign that they should part; she had no intention of joining him, knowing him to be too volatile to be faithful. He was no longer attractive to her, although as a boy with undisciplined hair he had awoken proprietory feelings. The trouble was that although by all accounts brilliant she could never see him as grown-up. Even after what had after all been a fairly momentous discussion of their future, or rather lack of it, even when both had discovered unacknowledged reserves of hostility, even then, after turning on his heel and leaving her, shocked, in the kitchen, he had returned after five minutes, no longer put out, sunny-tempered even, and as loquacious as ever. What did she think of Stephen Hawking? Of Jesus?

Battered by his questions, by his strange insubstantiality, she had been quite relieved to see him go. Besides, there was Beatrice, in Wilbraham Place, who needed her attention. Beatrice had never liked him. Jonathan, she called him, though he was Jon to everyone else. Miriam had sold the flat in Bramham Gardens and moved back to Wilbraham Place. Just as she had been pleased to get out of it once, she was almost pleased to get back. No, Beatrice had never liked him, although she had resented the engagement, had looked round sharply for signs of intimacy when she came home in the evenings, precipitating the alternative partnership which she had never been able to claim for herself. She had despised Jon, his elfin swagger, his apparent lack of experience, not perceiving a solipsism which could make him quite ruthless. She had rarely visited them as a married couple, so that it was up to Miriam to call in to Wilbraham Place, increasingly so, as Beatrice had become so inexplicably tired. Jonathan Eldon, who had now vanished from her life, as if his residence had only been temporary after all, as if she should have known that. Her marriage had lasted a mere five years, and now she thought of it with shame, with irritation. Back in Wilbraham Place nothing had changed, although the flat was now untidy, and her old room no longer seemed her own. A Mrs Kinsella came in to clean: she cleaned round Miriam, as if in contempt for her loss of status. Nor did Beatrice seem all that gracious, airily assigning Miriam tasks, punishing her for that initial departure. This now looked almost permanent, an awkward cohabitation, which might become a very real necessity, borne awkwardly by them both, in the absence of any cogent reason to separate.

In time Miriam had come to see her husband as insane, or at the very least emotionally illiterate. His great advantage was that he had known her parents, had not, if he gave the matter any thought, considered them crazier than his own mother, a widow, who was in love with him. It was vaguely thought a good thing that they should marry, since neither of them objected to the other, a basis for lifelong harmony, or at least adjudged so by their disaffected families. It was Beatrice who had viewed him with disfavour. On the one hand he was harmless, would not use her sister, to whom she was still close, badly; on the other hand he was inferior to her own cherished ideas of what a man should be and could therefore be relinquished without a murmur. What residual jealousy there had been had subsided. It was the state of marriage that Beatrice coveted; hence her few visits to the flat in Bramham Gardens, where the sight of a set of new saucepans, a suit laid aside ready to go to the dry-cleaners, hinted at an intimacy from which she was debarred. After their mother's death she had come more to rely on Miriam. Besides, that death had brought them closer, as if they were now free to commune with each other over their memories. In time those memories became as tenuous as Miriam's marriage was seen to be. In time Beatrice came to see herself as having the better part of the bargain: freedom, the flat in Wilbraham Place, the attention of her faithful acolytes, the not very fervent applause of the recital platform. She thought of herself as delicate, sensitive, vulnerable, identified her fatigue as evidence of her temperament, and rested in the knowledge that in one way or another Miriam would always be there—somewhere—to see to her needs.

Such symbiosis as existed was not between Miriam and her husband, of whom she was only wryly aware, as between the two sisters, who understood each other without the need to ask questions. It was the lack of questions, of everything conceived in an interrogative mode, that Miriam still found acceptable in Wilbraham Place, preferable, in fact, to all those enquiries, which were in truth entirely one-sided. Her husband always seemed genuinely disappointed when she failed to respond to his eager and somehow ill-judged curiosity. It was not that she was indifferent to the substance of his conversation; it was more serious than that. She wanted to be in receipt of information, rather than in the harassed position of giving tired résumés about the world historical figures in whom he was so interested. She did not know enough, she felt, to be educating somebody else. Unworldly, she had thought that knowledge would be revealed to her; instead she was driven back to her books, to her work, which she could do without assistance. With Beatrice she could let herself appear sombre, as if marriage were tricky, adult, not to be compared with the airy compliments that bolstered Beatrice's emotional life. She did not allude to their intimate exchanges, which were surprisingly satisfactory; a sense of decency bound her to silence. If Beatrice thought that she detected disappointment Miriam was generous

enough to allow her that, for she considered herself older and
wiser than her sister, matured by the sort of marriage judged adequate by those who had never known the fatal passion, and who
assumed that others need not know it, since they had, apparently,
no views on the matter. Beatrice considered her sister dull, conventional, but also secretive, and occasionally disliked her for just
those qualities, particularly the latter, whereas Miriam, who had
adopted a responsibility in addition to those which had been laid
down for her, for her husband seemed no more and no less than
that, merely murmured, 'I can't explain.' Unmarried, Beatrice
was an expert on marriage. Miriam's 'I can't explain' spoke vol-
umes to her, although in fact Miriam was simply tired of answering questions.

They were proud of Jon's reputed brilliance, although privately they saw no evidence of it, and in any event it was not of a
nature to benefit either of them. What he did in a white coat in a
laboratory remained a mystery; he himself regarded it as a mystery, shared only with those possessed of the same arcane knowledge. Beatrice even went so far as to deplore his ignorance of the
arts, but this proved unpopular: it was reluctantly allowed that he
was too brilliant for either of them, for if he were not too brilliant
then they must be too stupid to understand. 'My brother-in-law
the mad scientist,' Beatrice might laugh, but in one sense they
were in agreement: he was theirs. He was the man of the family,
even if he did not know it, even if he was useless at tax forms and
contracts and bills, which they were used to taking care of for
themselves. They regarded him as a child of nature, even a luxury, to be indulged as he had been indulged by his mother. He was
the male made harmless. Until his surprise announcement that he
had accepted a post in Canada they had seen no premonitory signs
of initiative on his part. The marriage ended in a fit of temper uncharacteristic of either of them. Yet Miriam had to admit, but only
to herself, that anger, or as near as he could get to showing it, be-

came him. It was only his sunny relapse into normality a moment afterwards that made her grit her teeth. 'Go, then, if that's what you want,' she had said. 'I'm staying here. We might as well divorce. That way we could meet someone else, someone more suitable.' That was when he had surprised her. 'I already have,' he said. 'She's coming with me. My lab assistant.' 'Congratulations,' she had said, still through gritted teeth.

'I'm still fond of you, but I don't think you're fond of me, are you?'

This was more character than she had bargained for. At once she felt ashamed. She had turned away, too confused to reply. There had been a moment's silence before he left the room. She went on slowly drying the breakfast dishes. But he was soon back, and eager to solicit her views on Christianity. As ever, she had no response ready, even though for once she would have given the matter some consideration, if only as a parting gift.

Those afternoons spent with Beatrice in Wilbraham Place, before Jon left for Canada, had been curative. Conversation was peaceful, inconsequential. 'Have you still got that cream jacket?' she might say, feeling only a mild interest. 'You used to wear it with that daisy-print skirt. I always liked you in that.'

'I've still got it somewhere. I must go through my things soon. Mrs Kinsella might like it for Anne Marie.'

'Oh, don't get rid of it.'

For, on the edge of an upheaval in her own life, she wanted everything to stay the same, the way it had always been. Yet there were changes, which she pretended not to see. The flat was untidy; in the bedroom clothes were laid out on the bed, as if in preparation for a holiday, an excursion.

'Are you going away?' she had enquired, alarmed, after her first sighting of these arrangements.

'Me? I never go away.'

It was true; Beatrice rarely left London unless she had to,

claiming that she would not know what she would do with herself, alone, in a foreign resort. There was something immovable about Beatrice, which was why she was so reassuring to return to. But now she was forced to concede that there was an intimation of change. Beatrice was slightly altered. The feet in the high-heeled shoes looked swollen, as did the ankles; her colour was somehow no longer transparent. They were getting older, must make provision for themselves while there was still time. She did not see that there was any urgency in this, but after Jon's departure, and before she had sold the flat in Bramham Gardens, she felt it. On the one hand it was comforting to sink into that companionable female sub-world, to watch Beatrice filing her nails, to drink tea and ruminatively smoke a cigarette, trying not to notice that the ashtray had not been emptied, for all the world as if they were two actresses on tour, marooned in some out-of-season provincial hotel, whiling away the afternoon before the evening performance, no one knowing they were there. After she had moved back (for there was no reason not to, and Beatrice's now suffused complexion, an unattractive pink under the refurbished golden hair, must have delivered a subliminal warning) she found it disconcerting to be living with a woman again, to hear her in the bathroom, to witness her briefly alarming appearance before the face she normally presented to the day was in place. With a man there was no transition: the naked face and body were quickly transformed into the clothed adult human being, with nothing to hint at frailty, at disguise, at vigilance. Men were more viable; that was why it was advisable to live with one. In the early mornings, bathed, shaved, dressed, Jon seemed normal, like any routine husband; in any event he was usually quiet until he had eaten his breakfast and scanned *The Times*. It was only afterwards that his curiosity came to life and his quite unremarkable features took on a look of boyish eagerness as he prepared to launch himself into another day of fact-seeking and opinion-sounding. His questions never concerned his wife; he never, for example, asked her what she was going to do with her day. He thought he knew the answer to that; besides, what she did was her business. She had found this very disappointing, longing to have her life taken into account.

During her mornings in the London Library she rarely thought about him, assuming that like all impervious innocents he would somehow be taken care of. It was in the course of those afternoons with Beatrice that she was conscious of the lack of a masculine presence, even that of her husband. She had no desire to involve him more than was necessary, secretly admiring his independence of her. Questioning on her part would be inappropriate; their marriage was hardly based on affinity. She had married not out of love but out of impatience, recognizing it as the next essential step. And even then she had had to work hard, had had to activate their long and almost lapsed friendship in order to bring him once more into their orbit, hers and Beatrice's. Except that she was not doing this for Beatrice. He had accepted her invitations with alacrity, having, as she suspected, few friends. They quickly fell into easy conversation, for at that stage she was anxious to answer all his questions. Beatrice discounted him: the marriage occasioned enormous surprise, even outrage, largely on aesthetic grounds. Jon simply did not look heroic enough to sleep with a woman. He was small, slight, with incongruously large hands. Beatrice, measuring him against her romantic imaginings, may have seen him more clearly than Miriam did, saw how his juvenile affability might last for thirty or forty years without undergoing any appreciable alteration. It was not his lack of gravitas that she deplored so much as his expression of sophomoric harmlessness, eternally prepared for what he called a discussion but what was in reality a questionnaire.

It was surprising, really, she thought in hindsight, that the three of them had co-existed, and had, after the initial hostilities, accepted each other so easily. Jon had had no more interest in Beatrice's life than Beatrice had in his, her early vision of him holding up a smoking test-tube doing duty for the rest of him. It was tacitly agreed that she should make mild fun of him on the rare occasions when they met. He took no notice, having always received this kind of attention. Miriam knew that he did not like Beatrice but that he was too fundamentally indifferent to give this his attention. She sensed that he despised Beatrice for her lack of sexual realism; he himself was, on occasion, feral, thought that all women were, or should be, aware of this. It was Beatrice's amuse-ment, as if he were a small boy playing at being grown-up, that annoyed him. At some level he was brutally aware that he could enlighten her, but chose not to do so. Neither of them seemed at-tractive to the other, and so their emotional lives were hidden. Miriam kept her sister's secrets, never once betrayed her fantasies, the comfort she greedily absorbed from those novels she read, in which it was always summer, in which there was a big house and no money to keep it up, and forbidden attractions were glimpsed across scrubbed pine tables in sunlit kitchens. Miriam had seen Beatrice lift her eyes from these rhapsodic descriptions to gaze out of the window at real weather—nothing like so beguiling—in the polluted setting of Sloane Square in mid-July. She could hardly blame her for preferring the other kind, or for thinking herself into the sort of landscape so fetchingly represented by the illus-tration on the jacket. Something in her own nature, which had grown sardonic after this latest disappointment, had acknowl-edged these attractions, had half-succumbed to their promise, but had rejected them as illusion, the sort of illusion she could no longer afford.

Yet even now, and however reluctantly, she understood Jon's contempt for the sort of woman Beatrice had turned into, for she no longer looked young and unprotected, seemed about to sub-side into increasingly bulky middle age. Her settled air irked Miriam; Beatrice was almost inactive, no longer in demand, not even sufficiently aware of Mrs Kinsella's hasty and inadequate attentions. There were rich pickings to be had among Beatrice's clothes; Mrs Kinsella's zeal and her exaggerated expressions of care were never more apparent than when she was able to carry home a blouse, a jacket, for her daughter Anne Marie. She was an indifferent cleaner, left taps running, liked to listen to the radio while she worked. The atmosphere had become mildly depressing, as indeed had Beatrice's company. Was she ill? Or was her indolence philosophical, as though she had come to terms with her diminishing prospects, no longer even cared much for music, was only rarely telephoned? Something in her smiling negation of a more energetic life alarmed Miriam, who was accustomed to do most of her thinking in the course of a five-mile walk, appreciating just those spoilt vistas of urban terraces that her sister so despised.

'I'd better look for another flat,' she announced. 'It's not right that we should spend so much time together like this.'

Beatrice turned a lazy head. One thick strand of her hair had slipped over her forehead; she blew it out of the way. This negligence, entirely out of character, alarmed Miriam even more. Panic made her harsh.

'And you'd better get on to Mrs Kinsella, or find someone else. This place is becoming a tip. Soon no one will want to come here.'

'But that would hardly be your problem, would it?'

'Don't let's quarrel, Beatrice. You know it makes sense.'

There was a silence, which Beatrice showed no signs of wanting to end. She was still somehow better at their rare altercations, more female, more cunning.

'I'll start looking, then,' said Miriam tiredly. The silence remained unbroken. 'I expect it will take me some time to find anything,' she offered, and then, at last, was rewarded with the ghost of a smile.

CHAPTER FOUR

In her search for a home Miriam was confronted by several quite discrete difficulties. The first was easy enough: it was the business of looking at what the estate agents thought suitable for a single woman who earned her own living, was solvent, but without collateral in terms of other properties or—perhaps more important—a man. There seemed to be many flats on the market which the agents liked rather more than she did; they had enrolled her in a world of one-bedroom conversions, with kitchens in which it was not possible to sit down, and which transported her to a mean plucky existence of looking after herself, as if she were a business girl of times gone by, wearing a beret, perhaps, and darning her stockings. She rejected them all, only retaining the one in Lower Sloane Street for further consideration. It had only one bedroom, and the kitchen could barely accommodate a small table and chair, but the living-room contained a bay window, through which she could see the Number 11 bus grinding its way to a full stop at the lights. This comforted her somewhat; she saw herself standing at the window in the evenings and gazing out like Mariana in the moated grange. And Lower Sloane Street was near enough to Wilbraham Place, so that only a ten-minute walk separated her from Beatrice. Should there be an emergency, or should the need arise, she could offer her support with a minimum of delay, though why the idea of an emergency kept insinuating itself she could not quite understand. Indeed she was only aware of the possibility that she might be needed when she half-illicitly entertained a desire to be in a different part of London altogether, somewhere higher, greener, remote from the 11 bus, somewhere with silent spaces and small inconsequential shops: Barnsbury, Fulham, Dulwich.

She might be able to afford something bigger if she moved farther out, and the idea was altogether attractive. But in fact such a move would be inconvenient, and she imagined Beatrice's hurt expression, for of course this would be interpreted as a desire to get away, as indeed it may have been, not altogether consciously, but with a sense of time running out, of possibilities receding. She did not miss her husband, but missed the sense of someone happily occupied in another room. This was not possible with Beatrice, who was rarely occupied these days, and who in any case was always waiting, to be asked how she was, for instance, and who was always—but was this her imagination?—occupying the same commanding chair.

But this image, not quite of flight, but somehow of a silent eclipse, had to do with another difficulty: the difficulty of finding a real three-dimensional home that would somehow connect with the ideal home that she had in mind. This was puzzling, for the ideal home had never existed. Home, whether in Wilbraham Place or in her parents' suburb, had somehow signified diminution, disappointment, yet if she were honest, was nearer to her mother's inviting yet excluding drawing-room, with its overstuffed sofas and the optimistic flowers on the covers, than to her last view of Beatrice's bedroom, with its discarded clothes and the slippers on their sides under a chair. Home in fact was a concept, like the grail; in both cases instant recognition would be its own reward. This home would be bathed in sunshine, the golden sunshine of evening: there would be a garden, large irregular rooms, deep colours and a bedroom of such paradisial quiet that she could hear a late bird, or an owl, or the bell on the neck of a tame cat.

This place would be unoccupied by anyone but herself, but at weekends members of a large loving family would visit: pleasing cousins, beautiful children, all of them graceful, courteous, changeless. What gave birth to this fantasy she could not imagine. She sought its origins in fiction, yet the novels she read for her work contained no such peaceable images. In fact such images pre-dated fiction, or rather were her own form of fiction; this must be what two people felt when they embarked on a happy future and were entitled to enact their heart's desire. Yet she was only one person, and could not imagine ever being endowed with such a future, with such freedom to ordain, without a restraining hand or thought to check her progress.

As for her marital home, the lugubrious flat in Bramham Gardens, she could hardly remember it, much as she could hardly remember the actual corporeal presence of her husband, who seemed to have shrunk to a small compendium of irritating habits, but whose surprisingly tuneful singing voice she still thought of with pleasure. Bramham Gardens abutted on to the Earls Court Road, which was a constant reminder of urban difficulty. Giant young men in shorts, with monstrous structures on their backs, met outside the tube station, en route to somewhere else; empty lager cans, inexpertly pitched, landed short of litter bins. This was what middle-aged disapproval must feel like, she thought, as she made her respectable apologetic way to the bus stop. And the flat had been no better, with its mournful bathroom and its exiguous dining annexe. 'What's wrong with it?' Jon had enquired, genuinely puzzled, and, 'You won't want anything bigger, I take it?' Beatrice had remarked, thus putting an end to her potential career as a mother. It had been a relief to get back to Wilbraham Place; by comparison the larger flat had seemed almost ancestral. The relief had not lasted, which was why she was now in search of something else, something new, regretting that she had not known and was now not to know a place to which it would always be pleasant to return.

Returning meant returning to her real life, with its slightly shameful freedom only modified by the thought of obligations still to come, for she did not doubt that she would be called upon to succour, sustain, protect and encourage. 'You are the sensible one,' her father had once told her, and it had become hard to maintain an independent train of thought once this burden had been laid upon her. 'I thought of you as the sensible one,' said Beatrice, not displeased, when she announced her intention of getting a divorce. 'Precisely,' she had replied, but she had been hurt. To be sensible was to be realistic, not dull, not a failure, as was implied. She knew that she had no future with Jon, for as she grew older he would grow uncannily younger, until, in his dotage (and in hers), he would still be croaking out his requests for enlightenment, looking not much different, his hair showing no signs of grey. And she would still be in Bramham Gardens, conscious of Beatrice, now helpless, waiting for her attentions in Wilbraham Place. Instead of which she felt condemned to consider the alternative option: Lower Sloane Street, with its dusty bay window and its enthusiastic accompaniment of grinding gears.

Tired, faced with the task of removing her personal belongings, her furniture to be reclaimed from store, she said to Beatrice, as Beatrice had once said to her, 'You should get out more. This sitting around is no good to you. Women don't have to decline any

more. Look at all those glamorous grandmothers putting out fit-
ness videos, or winning the battle against cancer. There are plenty
of them in that rag you read.'

'Women do decline, Miriam. They get tired.'

'Then they do something about it! They take exercise! Buy
new clothes . . .'

She wondered about this, just as the words were out of her
mouth. She had taken to scrutinizing the women on her bus in
the mornings, wondering at their ages. There was one in particular, whom she saw every day, trim, well-dressed, her full figure
artfully controlled, her hair coloured a pleasing dark blonde. She
wore pleated skirts and silky jackets: Miriam grew to recognize
the black and gold print with the yellow, the blue and green with
the black. This she liked less; it seemed to signify austerity, and on
rainy days, when the woman wore a vulgar papery blue mackin-
tosh, she withdrew her interest, feeling vaguely affronted. She
had the woman down as a Harley Street receptionist or an up-
market jeweller's assistant. She wondered what gave this woman
the courage to adorn herself every morning, to what or to whom
she went home at the end of the working day. She imagined the
homeward journey, the hair less immaculate, the feet trying to
ease themselves in the now tight shoes, the struggle to maintain
the smile, the air of interest. She followed her, in her imagination,
to the end of the line, to a street so quiet and uneventful that she
could hear her steps on the pavement. There might be a husband,
an unruly son awaiting her, but she thought not. She imagined
this woman opening a tin of soup, making herself a sandwich,
changing into slippers and settling down in front of the television.
There might be a moment of defeat, a shrug in the direction of all
the recipes cut out of the Sunday papers, until, flat-footed in her
slippers, she made for her bedroom and the task of choosing her
clothes for the following day.

She thought of her as one of those spinsters in Gissing's *The*

Odd Women, a novel she had read in her adolescence, appalled by the vision it so bleakly set out. But this was ridiculous: the woman might have a houseful of teenagers, might sigh as she heard their racket. And in any event women no longer behaved like Gissing's fearful stereotypes; indeed one hardly ever heard the word *spinster* nowadays. Yet those who remained unpartnered were still somehow suspect, their courage counting for nothing. And it took courage to contemplate the signs of ageing, to wonder on whose door she might knock if she were frightened, or ill. That was why such a woman rarely went out at night, unless with someone she knew at work. But such social contacts as she still enjoyed tended to take place over a drink, at lunchtime, or at six o'clock, and even one drink tended to send too much colour into her face. This must be watched. Therefore, this woman, who, she reminded herself, might even be a grandmother, would live a lonely, or if not lonely, a watchful life, devoting her energies to keeping up appearances, to being cheerful, so that her employer, her manager, whatever he was, might rather routinely lay a hand on her arm and exclaim, 'I don't know what we'd do without you!'

For such a woman, work, 'going into town', would be an adventure. For Miriam it no longer was. Work was simply something one did, presumably for the rest of one's life. The trouble was that as one grew older it became less gratifying, something one accomplished almost as a matter of duty. She supposed that at some point it would be appropriate to stop doing it, to hand over to someone else, almost discreetly to disappear from the field. That was what her friend Suzanne, a former fellow student, had done, had exchanged her briefcase for marriage to a man she had met through a dating agency, and was now the matriarch of his house, complete with complement of three grown-up children and her husband's mother-in-law by his first wife, and who apparently had no regrets, and a new hearty tolerant laugh to go with her situation. She got on well with the mother-in-law, drove her on shopping expeditions, had driven her over to visit Beatrice and Miriam, who had been silenced by her wealth of family references, a conversation to which they had no means of access. The visit had not been a success. They had been glad to see Suzanne, had longed for the sort of exchange to which they had been accustomed, but had been obliged to entertain the mother-in-law, who had been loquacious. The visit, for there had been only one, had been conducted to the accompaniment of much laughter, that new laughter which had something public about it. This is my new endowment, said Suzanne's laugh; it goes with realism, and also with status. French literature? I used to be fascinated, but now we are off to the Harrods sale; Mother loves Harrods. And they had been left with the feeling that the visit had only been possible because they were conveniently near Harrods, and because Mother might appreciate a cup of tea and a visit to the bathroom before the serious shopping began.

They had watched politely, their expressions neutral, as the mother-in-law heaved herself out of her armchair, her legs wide apart . . . We are among women, her attitude seemed to say; no need to put on a show. Refurbished, ready to leave, they appeared doughty, indestructible. Suzanne, who had been so delicate, had filled out, had seemed almost to enjoy her new weight, her ability to dominate a room, had clearly felt that she had conferred a favour in coming so far from Camberwell Grove (but had been coming to Harrods anyway), had looked amused at the spinsterish seemliness of the flat, implying that there was so much life going on in her large house that there was no possibility of keeping it tidy . . .

Beatrice had been subdued, politely impressed. Miriam had felt a renewed rush of love for her sister, who had behaved in so self-effacing a manner in the light of what she may have perceived as a threat to her way of thinking. They had attended

Suzanne's wedding, but had not discussed it, even with each other. The bridegroom was a man of sixty-five, his jacket buttoned tightly over a burgeoning stomach. The reception had been drowned in peals of determined laughter. Beatrice had been uncomprehending, almost stricken. Was this what happened when early fantasies were laid aside? When a mundane exchange took the place of what every woman must have secretly shaped in her mind, in her youth? Miriam could see that Beatrice was hurt, not only aesthetically, but morally as well, as if to surrender part of oneself, even the most expendable part, were an offence against nature. Miriam had merely been thankful to reach home, after all that noise, and had laid out her books with a new sense of worthiness. She had worked at home for a few days after that, aware that Beatrice might be glad of her presence. And since then work had gone on uninterrupted.

We don't know enough people, she told herself, as she fumbled for her keys. But then it is high summer and they are probably all away, the ones who used to visit. For they had once come, those women friends, had discussed their love affairs and, finding little response, had finally gone off with one another. They had been left feeling shy, inhibited. Unspoken, there lurked the suspicion that they had fallen out of the race, were no longer regarded as competition. They felt unused, despite their anxiously gained experience. So that it was almost with pleasure that they welcomed Beatrice's elderly acolytes. They were newly grateful for an opportunity to repair their dignity, a process which only seemed possible in an atmosphere of obsolete compliments. When all was said and done this company was preferable. Beatrice was soothed by it; men had not let her down, had played their part, had flattered her. Their parting kiss on her hand was reassurance that her world still turned.

As Miriam entered the flat she heard voices coming from what Beatrice called the drawing-room, the door of which was slightly ajar to reveal a broad masculine back in an armchair. This back, which she saw only briefly, struck her as brazen, as of brass, or rather of gold, shedding light, perhaps on account of the pale jacket sitting comfortably on the powerful shoulders. An equally powerful leg thrust out sideways from the chair. She could not see Beatrice, the stranger blocking her view, but she could smell her scent. As no voice summoned her she slipped into her bedroom, tidied her hair, and unfolded the *Evening Standard,* wishing that Beatrice had warned her of this visitor so that she could have had a quiet cup of coffee on the way home. This was one more reason to take the Lower Sloane Street flat, although she knew that she would never become attached to it, as surely one should become attached to one's own space. For a brief moment she regretted Bramham Gardens, and even its dining annexe: she was hungry, and dared not make a noise in the kitchen, for fear of detracting from Beatrice's presence. Kitchen noises and smells were somehow not compatible with that light-coloured, almost golden back.

After a few minutes she heard Beatrice's piano, and even Beatrice's voice accompanying it. She was singing an old song, which they both loved, *Au clair de la lune,* and her voice was tentative but pleasing. Miriam had not heard it so devoid of emotion for a long time. She waited for the performance, for that was what it seemed to be, to finish, and then went resolutely into the kitchen and filled the kettle.

'Miriam,' called Beatrice. 'Are you making coffee? Then do come and join us.'

Miriam, who had been thinking longingly of a couple of fried eggs, the consumption of which now looked to be postponed indefinitely, sighed and made her way to Beatrice's drawing-room, for she was clearly in command this evening. Beatrice looked bemused, as well she might, as the stranger unfolded his length from a chair which suddenly seemed flimsy, although it was normally one of her favourites, the chair the guest sat in. They had bought it from a second-hand shop in the Fulham Road, and had got it for a remarkably small price, since it was no longer one of a pair. The golden stranger—the light suit was now seen to be set off by a pale blue shirt—stretched out a sizeable hand and murmured, 'Simon Haggard.'

'Would you like some coffee?' she asked, her voice low, and for some reason sounding intimate.

'Yes, I should. Thank you.'

As they drank their coffee she surveyed him discreetly. Beautiful, yes, but somehow masculine as well: the word *handsome* seemed too tepid, too indefinite. She took in a tanned skin, a broken nose, a head of bronze hair, and again the broad shoulders, the powerful legs. By contrast Beatrice was uncharacteristically subdued, did little to keep the conversation civilized, and beyond saying, 'Simon has taken over from Max; he is my new agent, I suppose,' turned her head away, her profiled cheek burning.

So it was possible, then: a man could look like a hero. This did not mean that he would necessarily behave like a hero, but that much would be forgiven him. If a man looked like a hero it would be assumed that he was one. Greek gods were quite misleading, she thought, not for the first time; statues in museums could do quite a lot of mental damage.

'I heard you singing,' she remarked tamely to Beatrice. 'I haven't heard that song for a long time. How does it go on?'

Beatrice moved to the piano without alacrity, and seated herself. 'Only the last verse,' she said, as if to herself.

> *Ma chandelle est morte,*
> *Je n'ai plus de feu.*
> *Ouvre-moi ta porte,*
> *Pour l'amour de Dieu.*

The significance of these words struck Miriam with some force. She gave the stranger, whom she thought of as the stranger, for he was without precedent, a long hard look, and received a

long hard look in return. Both averted their eyes as Beatrice returned to her chair. Her presence seemed to signify to Simon
Haggard a sort of difficulty, yet surely this was only a routine
courtesy: he could not help his looks, any more than Miriam, now
conscious of her unpretentious shirt and skirt, could help hers.
Yet there was a malaise, which none of them seemed able to dispel. Miriam got up to stack their empty cups onto the tray and
made for the door, which he held open for her. It was, she saw,
eight-fifteen.

'I must be going,' he said. 'Goodbye, Miss Sharpe, Beatrice.
You'll keep in touch?' He paused. 'If there's anything you need . . .'
It was what people said after the coup de grâce.

'Yes, yes,' she replied, almost negligently. She looked dis-
tracted, queenly, Miriam saw, unlike herself, as if she had sal-
vaged some long-lost dignity. So might she have looked at the
outset of her career, when she had had ambitions to take over the
concert platform for herself.

'I'll see you out,' she said, and was conscious of his eyes on her
back as she walked to the door.

'I'm rather worried,' he murmured, catching up with her. 'I
don't think she took in what I was saying.'

'Why? What were you saying?'

'I was telling her that her contract was not being renewed.
Bookings have fallen off . . . Don't think I'm happy about this. I
hate this sort of errand. Max might have had the decency to deal
with it before he left. But as I say, I don't think she took it in.'

They were out of the flat, by the lift. 'Do you want to walk
with me a bit?' he asked.

'No, I must get back. What will happen to her now?'

'Oh, I can get her some occasional work, playing the piano for
ballet classes, that sort of thing.'

'She won't want that.'

'Miriam!' came Beatrice's voice. 'Miriam, where are you?'

'I must go,' she said hastily.

'I'll see you again, won't I?' Again the long hard look of complicity. She felt the shock, hoped that he did too.

'Perhaps,' she said, and shut the door.

Walking back down the corridor—it would need redecorating, she thought; she must see to it before she left (for now there was a point to leaving, to privacy)—she was aware of a desire for heat, light, noise, animation. She was aware of a need to make it up to Beatrice, not only for the new situation which had befallen her, but for the new situation in which she herself was somehow placed. There was no possibility, even at this stage, of turning aside.

'Attractive, isn't he?' said Beatrice with a distant smile. She did not say, 'I saw the look that passed between you,' but the information was offered, and was received in silence. 'That is how a man should look. Poor Jonathan,' she offered, by way of conclusion.

'Are you all right? What will you do?'

'I'll think about it. You won't mind clearing up, will you? I'm going to bed.' And she walked slowly, and again distractedly, from the room.

Miriam listened for tears, but heard nothing. She found herself humming the song again, requesting a door to open. Yet despite the evening's various shocks it was no longer Beatrice's door she was willing to approach.

$\mathcal{W}$hen she first saw the flat in Bryanston Square she was a little disappointed. She had expected some sort of splendour, like the court of the Sun King, at the very least a full panoply of gracious living. Instead she saw, initially, a rather large, rather dull room, with walls covered in tan hessian and incongruous and elaborate pale linen curtains, clearly devised and fashioned by a feminine hand. The bedroom too was austere, with tan and white stripes on the wallpaper and a very large bed occupying most of the space. It was quiet, or so it seemed to her, although outside the window a pneumatic drill punctured the becalmed atmosphere with its regular machine-gun rhythm. She thought fleetingly and briefly of her bedroom in Lower Sloane Street, where she slept so thankfully after her exertions. Except that after that first visit she had had a disturbing dream: she was speaking to Beatrice on the telephone, in a new lively manner to which she was glad to hear Beatrice respond. They arranged to meet, to go for a long walk. It was a Sunday afternoon in the dream, and she was eager to be out in the open air. She dressed and left the flat, only to realize, once she was halfway along some remembered street, that they had not agreed on a meeting place. This affected her with a moment's sadness, for while she could, and would, turn round and go home, Beatrice would be condemned to wander all over London in search of her. This dream, she thought, did not disturb her unduly, but she telephoned Beatrice, ascertained that she was all right, not caring to enquire too deeply, and put down the receiver with a sense of duty done. It was only later in the day that she recalled the conversation, not Beatrice's wry tones (for Beatrice knew) but her own enthusiastic manner, which contained intimations of every sort of betrayal.

But why should she feel a traitor? She was simply following impulses which turned out to be not so very random after all. If her connection with Simon Haggard was casual, or rather random as opposed to casual, that was in order, as if they were two atoms in one of her former husband's experiments, or two acquaintances destined to join, in an atmosphere of agreeable neutrality from which all moral censure was absent. Goethe had written a novel about this, she remembered; she had once urged Beatrice to read it, in order to correct her thinking, but Beatrice had found it repugnant, unwilling to contemplate unions so apparently loveless. Miriam was, she now thought, in a position to acknowledge the story's wisdom, for what she enjoyed with Simon was surely an elective affinity? She knew the relevant facts: that he was married, that he had two young children, that his wife, a don at Lady Margaret Hall, lived mainly in their house in Oxford, that he went home to Norham Gardens at the weekend, using the flat only as a base in London from which to work. He had an office in Soho Square, but found it easy to get back to the flat for lunch, which was when she visited him. Despite his busy life, with its diverse attractions, he seemed to accept her, together with the fact that she did not burden him with her doubts.

and queries. She did not know how he felt; she only knew that when they exchanged their long silent glances they were both obliged to be sincere. That sincerity was their guarantee; the word *love* had not been spoken. She did not even apply the word to herself, for she was not in love, she reasoned. It was as if something more powerful had taken over. She was not in love; she was in thrall, to Simon, to his wife, to Norham Gardens, to Bryanston Square, to the whole panorama of his life and its attributes, and this was a condition from which longing and frustration were removed. She felt as if she were reading a book, a masterpiece containing all the best fictional ingredients, written in a language she had not known she understood. She thought that he appreciated her, found her compatible with preoccupations of which he never spoke. With his naked arms around her, after a brief sleep, he seemed older, heavier; his eyes searched hers for an answering look of understanding. Then he would sigh, before a dawning smile of reminiscence replaced the older, more troubled expression.

'What have you brought?' he would ask.

'Smoked salmon,' she would answer, and, after an interval, 'Pain de campagne. Boursin. Don't go to sleep again.'

'I'm not asleep.'

'Apples. The first Cox's.'

For it was nearly autumn, and the skies were darker in the evening, when she did not see him. She went to Bryanston Square in the lunch hour, taking a picnic, for he never seemed to have any food in the house, claiming to eat out every day. It pleased her to devise little meals for him, although in every other respect she had no sentimental thoughts of domesticity. Their extraordinary conjunction, for which nothing in her life had prepared her, seemed both too abstract and too real to accommodate conventional thinking. Nor did she ask herself what the attraction was on his side. Those sincere, almost mournful gazes, when they lay in each other's arms, gave her all that she needed in the way of reassurance, and if it was reassurance without the exchange of information, or rather of further information, over and above the essential facts, she assumed it was because they had both read, or were both reading from, the same text, that they met perfectly in the same experiment.

It did not even bother her that she saw herself as slight and nondescript, for his refulgent looks did duty for both of them. She did not regret that they never went out together, were never seen as a couple. She could imagine the comments: 'What on earth does he see in her? She must be older than he is.' This was true: he was eight years her junior. But when they had eaten, and she had left him, she was aware, from glances, that her eyes were brighter, her mouth softer. It seemed to her that what they shared, that sense of being no longer strangers to each other, outweighed any more formal definition of their relationship. Even the word *relationship* seemed to her misplaced, with its smirking public overtones of possession. She felt that they were in some entirely private category, and she never doubted this. His real life, his life away from her, she discounted, preferring to relegate it to the pages she had not yet read, in the same beloved book. When they lay, facing each other, wordless, she knew all she needed to know, and even thought it appropriate that some things were unknown, or that she might in time discover them. That he was sunnily reticent, in a rather practised manner, did not disturb her. She had seen behind the reticence, discerned what was so carefully hidden. Some childishness may have lain there, or rather a nostalgia for total acceptance. She thought he knew that there were no limits to her acceptance.

She even accepted the fact that he did not always want to see her. 'I could come this evening,' she had once said, to which he had replied, 'Oh, better not. My brother's in town. He'll probably look in.' Or, 'I promised to take our au pair out to dinner. She always comes to London on her day off.' She said nothing, merely adding the brother and the au pair to the appurtenances of the

ideal family, which she was bound to admire, to enjoy. Such
riches! She thought briefly and dismissively of her own bleak
childhood home, and discarded it for ever, preferring to contemplate the house in Norham Gardens, with its noises and its casual
company, as if it had stood since the beginning of time, as if Simon
were both child and husband, as if his wife, Mary, had also always
existed, as if both were the outcome of Darwinian natural selec-
tion, the stuff of normal life. Back in the London Library, and
slightly less exalted, sobered somewhat by the inevitable aftermath of their lunchtime meetings—Simon, still naked, picking
up his telephone messages, herself in the bathroom—she thought,
contemplating the grey heads behind the newspapers, that very
few lives were in fact so endowed, that many people were lonely,
ill, that age made inroads, that much was unsought, undeserved.
At the same time she longed for him again, and when with him
she accepted what she thought of as the necessary mythology. It
was essential for him to be happy, to be as happy as he looked. Her
own part in the proceedings she took for granted.

One evening, because the September weather was so beautiful, because the day had held the last heat of summer, and because
the dusk smelt of fallen leaves, she made a sudden decision, hailed
a passing taxi, and gave directions for Bryanston Square. The
point of this decision, she thought, was to enjoy the evening, to
prolong the particular joy they had known some hours earlier. It
was almost reluctantly that she paid off the cab, feeling too reminiscent to engage in a new conversation, but when she rang the
bell, for she had no key, not thinking to ask for one, there was a
scampering sound, and when the door opened a small boy, aged
about six or seven, dressed in a white T-shirt and shorts, his feet
bare, stood there, looking at her suspiciously.

'This is Fergus,' said Simon, smiling. 'My son.'

The child was beautiful, one more love object to be added to
the list.

'Have you had your supper?' she asked.

He nodded, and she realized that she had been about to commit an error, to remind Simon that there was a fruitcake in the fancy tin that she had bought that morning in Selfridges, and that she might, for the first time, be stretching her entitlements.

'I saw a dinosaur,' the child shouted suddenly.

'Did you?' She realized she sounded awkward. Nothing in her life had prepared her for conversation with children.

'You saw a crane, Fergus. A big crane outside the window. It did look rather like a dinosaur, now that I come to think of it. And of course it was moving very slowly.'

'Dinosaurs are distinct!' shouted the child again.

'Extinct,' from the background.

'And do you know how they got to be extinct?' At last she had his attention. 'It was because the mice ate their eggs. I heard it on the wireless. The radio,' she translated for him.

He considered this, blushing deeply, bronze eyelashes lowered to suffused cheek.

'There's an exhibition at the Natural History Museum,' she offered. 'Dinosaurs of the Gobi desert. Would you like to see it?'

He nodded.

'Sally can take you tomorrow.'

'Sally,' said the child adoringly.

'Sally?'

'His nanny. They're both staying here tonight.'

Sally. Another name; an extra, no doubt.

'Why did they eat the eggs?'

'Well, I don't suppose they did, really. My guess is that they gnawed a hole in the eggs and everything inside sort of seeped out, so that the baby dinosaurs wouldn't have had anything to eat. I dare say you could find a book about it at the museum.' For it seemed important to make provision for the child as well.

Yet the encounter, for all its prettiness, somehow signified that she had lost ground. This feeling was compounded when a key turned in the lock and the door opened to reveal a young woman, Sally, presumably. She did not look like any nanny that Miriam had previously encountered. In her somewhat stereo-typed imagination *nanny* was the generic name given to the likes of Nanny Huxtable, whom Beatrice and she had shared in their extreme infancy. She remembered a stout figure in blue cotton, a watch hanging from her bosom, a hardish hat donned when she wheeled Miriam in her pram, Beatrice walking importantly by her side. By contrast Sally was about twenty-three or twenty-four, had long blonde hair, wore a silky black trouser-suit, and gave off an unmistakable aura of privilege. Simon kissed her benevolently, the child clinging to her leg.

'What time are we off tomorrow?' she enquired.

'Well, I'll be gone about eight-thirty. You'll leave some time after that, I take it.'

'Before. We want to avoid the rush.'

'I'll drive you, if you like.'

'Would you? That'd be marvellous.'

'I'll just make one or two calls, cancel one or two things.'

To which conversation, thus debarred, Miriam judged herself to be a stranger. No longer was Simon the stranger; she had taken his place.

'What about the dinosaurs?' she put in.

'Oh, he can see those another time.'

'Goodnight, then, Fergus.'

'Goodnight,' he said indifferently. 'What's your name?'

'Miriam.'

He hesitated in front of her, anxious to retain her now that she was leaving. She willed her hand not to stroke his face, imagined it clasping his bare foot.

'It was very nice to meet you,' she said. 'Goodnight, Simon. Goodnight . . .' She could not bring herself to name Sally, emerged into the cooling night in a state of confusion. Not jealousy, no, not that, but something more sorrowful, the first intimation of unwelcome reflection. She did not doubt that there was some less formal connection than that of employer and employee between Simon and the nanny. She had always imagined him making love to countless women—it was part of his endowment. The wife was perhaps too donnish to notice, or, if she noticed, too elevated to care. And the girl, in her expensive trouser-suit, looked as if she might provide the sort of sex which could be conveniently expunged from the memory, the kind that two sporting partners might share, and hurt feelings something they imagined only with distaste. She would not see him the following day, and since the following day was a Friday he would probably stay in Oxford over the weekend, so that she would be—would have to be—resigned to staying at home, no doubt with Beatrice, whom she particularly did not want to see at close quarters while she was in this state of mind. Perhaps she could arrange something for the two of them to do, visit the appalling Suzanne, for example, for the sheer pleasure of laughing together afterwards, their old intimacy restored. Simon had behaved quite naturally with Sally, she realized, his old archaic longing for total dependency quite gone. In that case, which condition did he prefer? It was her own relative taciturnity, her wordlessness in the act of love, which permitted him to reveal himself, to want more. In the rapidly cooling night she wondered whether she would always be able to maintain that silence, understood that she had made a mistake in turning up unexpectedly, resolved never to do so again.

There were more deserving cases than Simon, she reminded herself. There was Beatrice, deprived of her livelihood, and, perhaps more important, of Simon. He had telephoned her once, assuring her of his attention at all times, had given her his telephone number, but had not called again. No doubt Beatrice thought he might, that she might dial his number, just to ask how she stood with regard to possible bookings, but in fact she did nothing, perhaps pacified by the knowledge that she had glimpsed the unattainable, and thus justified all her imaginings. Perhaps the fantasy did duty for the real thing, that telephone number to give body to the thought that she might in fact summon him, but was not quite ready to do so . . . Beatrice's name was not mentioned in Bryanston Square: to do so would have meant introducing an awkwardness, a reminder of an assassination. Besides, Beatrice was behaving with uncharacteristic discretion, or so it appeared. When the two of them met, which was infrequently now that Miriam was so occupied, Beatrice assumed a lofty smile, as if she knew everything, knew indeed more than Miriam did, and talked about herself, about the clothes she was having made, about mysterious plans for the future which she might or might not divulge. 'And you?' she would ask negligently, with the ineffable smile. 'Your work going well? That's the main thing.' But frequently this enquiry came only as Miriam was about to leave. Therefore she was thankful for the enquiry, pretended a rush of work, telephoned each day in the early morning, to be treated to a leisurely monologue that had to do with Beatrice's well-being, with the previous night's dreams, with the fact that she was thinking of inviting a few people for drinks. 'They might amuse Simon,' she said. 'After all, we know the same people,' marking a point. 'Of course I miss Max dreadfully. It's not the same without him. That devotion . . .'

A hunger artist, thought Miriam, replacing the receiver. And if she were not very careful she would become one herself, revealing the strong connection between the two of them.

'I liked Fergus,' she said, on the following Wednesday, Tuesday having passed with only a telephone call. She was easy to disguise, to conceal: he merely mentioned a time, as he might do with any contact. She never telephoned him, fearing secretaries, all of them no doubt young and good-looking. This too must be concealed.

He smiled. 'Nice chap, isn't he? A pity you can't meet Daisy.'

'Daisy? Oh, your daughter.'

'Our three-year-old. We call her Daisy. Her name's really Marguerite. And she'll be the last, I'm afraid. We wanted more, but Mary says she's too old to start again.'

'Fergus looks like you.'

He smiled again, easily, without yearning. Not a hunger artist, she concluded. 'Have some more of this chicken,' she said.

'It's very good. Did you cook it yourself?'

'Of course I did.'

For he was used to the best, the most carefully prepared, having been used to it from birth, or so she assumed. It went with the loving care he must always have received, which accounted for his easy manner. She comforted herself with the knowledge of their intimacy, the only intimacy that mattered, his face buried in her neck, his quest for reassurance, for in that intimacy, although they might be momentarily separated, she knew that he had grown used to her looking after him, to her silent protection, even as he drifted into sleep.

They had had a neighbour in Wilbraham Place, a Mrs Anstruther, who had entrusted Beatrice with her spare set of keys, claiming that she was so giddy, so girlish, that she frequently forgot her own. She had looked neither giddy nor girlish: she was a woman of indeterminate age, certainly too old for the amount of make-up she habitually wore. Beatrice had hoped to make a friend of this woman, although she did not like her, did not like her powerful proprietary walk, her references to her fatigue after so many late nights. 'I'm glad I'm not paying for all those telephone calls,' she had said with a rusty laugh. She had a follower, so called by Mrs Kinsella, a doughty senior citizen with a military moustache. It was he who had once called for the keys, Mrs Anstruther clinging to his arm. 'I'm so lucky to have him,' she had confided the following day, so much luckier than either of you,

she had implied. It was the man who returned the keys. Beatrice
said that he had eyed her speculatively, wondering whether to
take a chance. This was true, but nothing came of it. Miriam had
seen him some time later emerging from Peter Jones, a woman
considerably younger than Mrs Anstruther by his side. She had
thought it wise to mention this to Beatrice, who had looked at her
in surprise. 'Do you honestly think I found him in the least attractive?' she had asked. 'I wouldn't have anything to do with
him.' From which Miriam had deduced that Mrs Anstruther had
prevailed. Thereafter references to 'my friend' were pretty constant. The keys remained, but Beatrice had said, 'I must give them
back to her. We can't be expected to be in all the time. I'll tell her
to leave them with the porter,' knowing that the porter was only
to be woken in an emergency. It was neatly done, or rather said,
for the keys were still on a hook in the kitchen. But something
must have been intuited, for Mrs Anstruther no longer troubled
them, preferring no doubt to have a spare set cut for her friend.
Miriam admired this strategy, but admired it ruefully. She deduced that Mrs Anstruther was a gangster, might solicit confidences, might enjoy sexy gossip. Therefore it was entirely proper
to smile pleasantly and to offer no information. She did not want
Beatrice's disastrous innocence wrecked by another woman. A
man would have been a different matter.

It was true that she was busy, not only in preparing Simon's
lunch, which took up most of her evenings. The chicken to be
roasted with lemons, the artichokes to be boiled, the vinaigrette to
be decanted into a screwtop jar, the whole offering to be carefully
stowed in the fridge . . . She was even busy in the London Library,
covering sheets of paper, rapidly, just wanting to finish the chapter. She worked easily, perhaps only slightly aware that the words
lacked depth, lacked her usual thought. She shrugged: people
read novels superficially, invariably remembered the wrong parts:
why should she not be superficial too? In sober moments she

promised herself to revise, to tighten, at some later date. In any event she had received no complaints. Her Paris contacts were delighted with her speed. She began to think that only speed mattered. She herself was in a constant state of speediness, as if her time were directed only to one particular moment, one particular exchange. She understood that she was living some form of apotheosis, to which the rest of life was irrelevant.

What she valued was that shared privacy, to which no one else had access and which she thought impermeable. She was glad that she had no wide circle of women friends, who would have wanted to be admitted to that privacy, who would have enjoyed talking it over, would have warned her against impermanence, would have questioned her about the wife, would have looked concerned. Women, she knew, would be there at the end, to accompany her out of this life, their mourning roles re-established. To their contemplation she would have to entrust her wasted appearance, her untended hair, as she lay in her hospital bed. They would be merciful then. But for her early middle age she desired the presence of a man, before it was almost too late. In some mysterious fashion all earlier loyalties had fallen away. Beatrice? Doing surprisingly well on her own, glad no doubt to have the flat to herself again. She thought fleetingly of Sally, who lived in Simon's house. Astute questioning had elicited the fact that Sally was his wife's niece, might conceivably be the enemy in the camp. But this too was irrelevant. The geographically distant set-up in Oxford was entirely in her favour. In fact everything was in her favour. She even knew that at some point Simon might tire of her, but her conviction that they shared something rare was enough to arm her against the future. Her reasons for living in the present were all in place.

If she regretted not seeing him in the evenings it was because she would have enjoyed emerging into the growing dark, with its festive atmosphere. She would have liked to walk a little way, down Park Lane, perhaps, to watch the couples getting out of their cars, strolling towards the lighted foyers of hotels. She pitied these couples and their routine pleasures. She would prefer the dark street, only finally aware of tiredness, reluctant to stop the taxi that would take her home. Her life was powered by her own momentum, and at last she realized that that was how life was designed. Outside agencies might until now have directed her movements; she spared a compassionate thought for those who obeyed the call of duty. A great secret had been revealed to her, and she was free.

---

CHAPTER SIX

*Q*ou must forgive me, Jacob,' smiled Beatrice, as she said good-bye to her guest.

'You were a lovely girl,' he said regretfully, as he turned away and went down the stairs.

'Take the lift,' she called, but he was already out of sight.

She had detected the note of disappointment as he had remarked on her lost beauty, as if her flushed present-day appearance had presented him with a difficulty. She had known him at the Royal College of Music; they had enjoyed a pleasant friendship, and at one time more. He had never married, had gone to live in America, had come to see her because on his rare visits to England he always looked up old friends, few of whom remembered him, or if they did, still thought of him as a spindly excitable boy, though he was now grey-haired, with a spryness that hinted at old age rather than at youth.

He thought of Beatrice as one who had kept faith with the old days; she remembered him, rather more acutely, as a companion

who had given her status in the days when it was important to as-
sert her uniqueness, or rather not to be relegated to an inquisitive
gaggle of female friends. He had made her aware of the importance that men would have in a life like hers, a life that had always
been threatened with loneliness, with only her sister for company.
In those days she had raised worshipful eyes to any man who
might adopt her, not knowing that she should be disdainful, indifferent, when she was genuinely disdainful or indifferent. She
pursed her lips ruefully when she looked back at the radiant pan-
tomimes of affection she had mustered for men who had meant
nothing to her. As she closed the door she reflected that she had
been guilty only in conveying more than she had felt. This had
been misleading, she knew; she also knew that it had not been
held against her, or not for long. If others detected a lack of
straightforwardness she was only aware of a necessary politeness,
which had led her into a more or less continuous masque of joy-
ousness, of fervent welcomes and tender farewells, had led to no
foreseeable conclusion, apart from the present one. She had become what she was always destined to be: superfluous.

Nor was it true that she lived in the past. The past had no
value for her, apart from the thankful realization that it was in
fact past. As the older girl she had witnessed more of her parents'
disaffection than her sister had, remembered all too clearly her father's frightening silences, her mother's baleful glances: nothing
overt, but everything clearly understood. She had escaped, or so
she had thought, to the congenial company of her fellow students,
but in reality she was in search of the ideal family, one which
would welcome her, protect her feelings, love her. The appeal of
men was that one of them might take her home, might introduce
her to an affectionate totality which she had never known. At the
same time, and perhaps inevitably, she began to envisage another,
or rather additional, gratification. The ideal man who was to effect this introduction would have an ideal appearance. That was

how she would know that he was ideal. His character, his worth, might hardly detain her, for she knew, or thought she knew, that most men behaved badly. Her life as a woman, when she had learned enough to be able to leave her tedious beginnings behind, would be spent enjoyably in making sure that he preferred her, came back to her, surrendered to her.

She had pictured the charm of such scenes, herself as redoubtable as a heroine in Colette, her lover or husband as rueful as a boy. She knew herself to be pleasing in an old-fashioned way, well suited to play a docile part in the loving family of her imagination, less well suited to detain an ardent or capricious lover. She knew that she lacked the ease, the assurance that a confident woman should always possess. She knew that she had always been frightened that she would be unable to seize her opportunity, if it ever came along; would be unable to make the first move, if indeed she knew what that first move should be. Therefore she smiled and was pleasant, welcomed whatever company sought her out, was surprisingly acquiescent when courted, and left behind a confused impression of accessibility and a ruinous inability to understand what was being enacted.

She had thought that music would be her life, as it had been for a time, but had grown frightened—that fear again—of her loneliness as she sat upright at the piano, smiling in the direction of the singer whom she habitually accompanied. That this singer was a woman did not assist matters. She had grown to mistrust her stark visibility on the concert platform, which contrasted with her position as a subordinate. As a beginner she had had fantasies that a discerning member of the audience would isolate her in the only manner she was able to envisage. There would follow the miraculous recognition, the bemused introduction, the acquisition of loyal loving relations . . . In time she was able to dismiss this scenario, but not altogether to forget it. She knew, in the way that faint-hearted women knew, that she needed a man's permission to be fully a woman. It was her own thoroughly undistinguished romanticism that gave this ideal man the features of a rake, an irresistible reprobate. She was not interested in honour, only in redemption.

She had not been sorry to lay aside her musical career, although her occasionally high colour betrayed the animosity she had felt towards those who had so deprived her, principally Max, whose cynical flowery manner she detected behind the decision, and also the woman singer, whose plummy indecently Welsh voice had always got on her nerves. She excused Simon Haggard from this accusation, on account of his looks. She knew that she would never see him again, knew that Miriam and he were lovers, knew all this with the ancient clairvoyance of the defeated. 'Have you met his wife?' she had delicately enquired, but her heart was not in it. There was no reason why she should ruin for Miriam a love affair which would never be hers. And yet, unerringly, she bestowed on him all the gifts of which she and her sister had been deprived: unthinking good health, intelligence, general approbation. If she allowed herself to—and she was aware that this was dangerous—she could envisage him as a son, a brother, always there to protect . . . Her imagination shied away from his capacities as a lover. In any event she saw Miriam's new secrecy as slavish, knew enough about the anxious cooking (Miriam had never been much of a cook) to be able to view the situation with distaste. She herself would have behaved differently, perhaps unaware that the age of adorable caprices was long past. In the books she favoured, but wistfully, women were unmasked, laid bare by a man who finally understood them. She knew that this was rubbish, but found the illusion so beguiling that she continued to embrace it as her own, did not realize, or perhaps failed fully to realize, that other women, even, perhaps, the women who wrote the novels, cherished the same illusion.

In her archaic mind, or rather that part of her mind that was still rooted in evolutionary prehistory, love would reveal itself in an instant. Yet she was not, she thought, entirely stupid, had learned a great deal, most of it unpalatable, thought back grimly to her family history, and of the efforts she had had to make to gain her freedom. That freedom had, she now saw, proved illusory. Emancipation, flight, had brought with them an unsleeping anxiety. If deliverance never came she thought that she might just as well not have fought her battles, cared for Miriam, inspired their move to the flat, at whose golden walls she now gazed unseeingly. The worst had now happened: she had no occupation, no protective colouring, no card of identity. The toughness that had enabled her to endure so far examined the situation. There was money in the bank, a pleasant roof over her head; she was well regarded by many who were unaware of the change in her circumstances. She had Miriam, although Miriam now had Simon, for a while, at least. When he let her down, as Beatrice had no doubt that he would, they would carry on much as they always had done, ruminatively and inescapably joined, nervily private.

She would insist that Miriam stay in Lower Sloane Street. Insensitive though she thought she may have been, with that reference to Simon's wife, she would not want Miriam at close quarters again, not want another female presence, while hers must be kept inviolate, her own longings well disguised. Miriam had always been disturbed by the sound of the piano; occasionally each had been frustrated by the proximity of the other. It was, Beatrice acknowledged, easier to live without Miriam at this juncture. In any event she felt too ashamed at her fall from grace, even from a form of prominence, to bear another's eyes watching her.

Shame and anger kept the colour high in her cheeks, would prompt her visitor that evening to tell her that she was looking well. But his eyes would be searching; his father, she remembered, had been a doctor. Indeed she had instantly known, when Jacob had first introduced her to his parents, that this haphazard household, with the collecting tin for spastics prominent by the front door, was not one in which she was keen to spend her life. He had seen it too, bore her no grudge, thinking her more delicate than she really was. Only this evening had he discerned the fact that her life had not turned out as she had wished, and had at last seen her clearly for what she was: a woman in middle age, with inadequate personal resources, and only a memory of his earlier desire to comfort her. But she was sufficiently familiar with his expression to know that once at the end of the street and out of her range he would shake his head, as if he should not have been witness to such a sight, and was even now comparing the blonde wide-eyed girl he had once known with the too gracious matron whose eyes had never quite met his in the course of the evening, and whose head habitually, instinctively, turned away from him, as if she were listening for the steps of another visitor, someone who was not himself.

Beatrice now embraced vacancy as a state to which she had always been condemned. Cautiously she began to recognize that she was glad to have time to herself, that she was no longer obliged to turn out in the evenings, just when the end of the day seemed so propitious to rumination. Her dream life had gained enormously: in sleep she revisited old friends, forgotten landscapes, embarked again on travels which had in fact been undertaken with reluctance. Work no longer constrained her; she rarely touched the piano. She was, she realized, free to come and go as she pleased, without checking her answering service. She could live like other women in this pleasant neighbourhood, meet friends for lunch (but her friends were now scattered), care for her appearance, let others wait on her. Take her ease, in short. Somewhere, beneath the shame, there dawned a wondering relief. This, she knew, was not contentment, but it might have to do duty for contentment. In time, when she was in a more objective frame of mind, she would get in touch with the few contacts who might still be useful. Yet again she might not do any of these things. There was such a condition as honourable retirement, after all. Except that it did not feel honourable, although it might have been timely.

What had necessarily passed was a kind of readiness, of preparedness. Changes were now accepted; it was also accepted that these changes would not necessarily be for the better. Youth, as a time of looking forward, was over. Nowadays she would not dare to take off her clothes for any man, although she had done so eagerly enough in the past, prompted by a desire to refute her mother's suspicious strictures. If she had had daughters, Beatrice reflected, what advice she would have given them! She would have told them that the time for display was limited, that the years would add weight, both physically and metaphorically, that a time would come when second thoughts were wiser than heedless impulses . . . She would have urged them to enjoy men, as many men as possible, before they became aware, as she was now, of the neutered state that awaited them. Therefore it was appropriate that she now be forgotten except by those who had known her when she was young. There was, somewhere in her consciousness, the luxury of a right decision, as if she alone had chosen this particular career path. At least it enabled her to contain her thoughts, to keep secret those pitiful reflections that still saddened her when she saw young people laughing together, a father holding his infant daughter by the hand. It was fathers she was willing to contemplate, as, bright of eye, they negotiated supermarket aisles, stealing proud looks at the imperious five-year-old at their side, although the five-year-old, they knew, was bored with this particular exercise, and looked forward to once more sitting primly in the car . . . Sometimes Beatrice would have to smile at the youngish man, and would be rewarded with a brief smile in return. But these smiles of complicity identified her as a mother, or perhaps a grandmother, with similar concerns. Few would see

in the matronly figure she had somehow acquired a still young
woman with unrealistic expectations.

Yet she was still attractive enough, she reckoned. By this she
meant that she was attractive enough for strangers, like the genial
Irishman who, every morning, waved his copy of the *Telegraph* at
her, and said, 'If there's no good news in this paper I'm taking it
back. All right?' 'Fine,' she would reply, charmed into this momentary well-being by his joviality. It was true what they said
about the kindness of strangers, true too that like Blanche Dubois
she had come to rely on it. Why this was so she was unsure, unwilling to examine the causes, simply accepting it as an inalienable
truth. Her doctor, whom she visited to have her blood pressure
checked, had suggested a holiday, but she knew what awaited her
if she took his advice: disorientation, of a kind, and possibly of a
depth, with which she could not easily cope. She was safer at
home, she knew, without quite knowing why she should want to
feel safe. For that reason alone it was good to know that no further services would be required of her.

This day had started inauspiciously. She had been due to meet
her dressmaker, Rachel Wise, in the fabric department at Liberty's, to choose material for a suit and a dress. She was early for
the appointment, had lingered on the hard pavement, assailed by
a sudden longing for green spaces. With a sigh she had entered
the store, remembering all at once her horror of airless rooms, had
surveyed the massed ranks of cloth with a feeling of dread. 'Now
that,' Rachel had said, fingering a bolt of orange wool, 'would
make up beautifully. With a length of that black and yellow print
for a blouse. Or that grey worsted. You could wear that with blue.
Or no, perhaps not; too dead. What about that off-white? That always looks good, particularly if you have a lunch, or a professional
meeting. What do you say? Or shall we go to John Lewis before
you make up your mind?'

'No, no,' she had murmured. 'I'll take them all.'

She hardly remembered paying, had held out her credit card with a feeling of increasing unreality, as if the fabrics had entered her lungs, making breathing difficult. For a brief moment she had wondered whether she was going to faint, wondered if she had, but only for a split second, lost consciousness.

'I'll get in touch, Rachel,' she said through numbed lips.

The next thing she was aware of was Rachel's sharp face gazing at her in perplexity through the window of the taxi.

'Are you all right?' she had asked, to which she must have replied in the affirmative. 'Don't forget your parcels, then,' said the voice, with perhaps an edge of anxiety. 'I'll wait to hear from you,' all too ready to relinquish her, until she was out of sight.

In the flat she walked slowly into the kitchen, made tea, and in due time found herself seated at the kitchen table with a cup before her. But when she took a conscientious sip the tea had felt unstable in her mouth, and a little had leaked out of the corner and run down her chin. She dabbed her face, sat still, felt a little better. When she heard Mrs Kinsella's key in the door she forced herself to stand up, behave normally. It was claustrophobia, she reasoned, her old familiar. As a girl she had had panic attacks, although she had thought she was now free of them. She resolved to say nothing to Miriam, or indeed to anyone, particularly not to her doctor. But perhaps she should ring him and make an appointment for the following week, when she was more herself.

Mrs Kinsella did not appear to notice anything untoward, but sat down with a sigh and poured herself a cup of the tea which Beatrice usually had ready for her. 'I won't do too much today,' she said. 'I'm on painkillers.' This announcement was fairly routine, served to cover her legendary inactivity. She was an envious woman, with whom it did not bode well to disagree. Those black shoes of mine, thought Beatrice; she can have those. 'I'd ask the doctor for something stronger,' Mrs Kinsella went on, lighting a cigarette. 'But then I thought, knock one devil out, knock another devil in.' She was full of these meaningless aphorisms. When she mopped her brow after one of her very rare exertions she claimed that the rush of heat, otherwise attributable to her age, was beneficial, 'worth a tenner a minute'. There was no way of getting rid of her. She had been with them for some years now, knocked about the flat singing tunelessly. 'I'm like you,' she would remark. 'Musical.' 'Just do the bathrooms then,' said Beatrice, moving cautiously towards her room. 'I'm going to write some letters. I'll see you tomorrow.' Mrs Kinsella, who was not Irish but who had been briefly married to a Liverpudlian before decamping back to her mother in Pimlico, looked offended. Beatrice trailed out and returned with the black shoes. 'These might suit you better than they do me,' she said. Mrs Kinsella, her lips pursed with annoyance, agreed. 'Treating me like a servant' were the words she would utter that evening, as her daughter kicked off her trainers and slid her feet into the shoes. 'Oh, don't go on, Mum,' Anne Marie would reply. 'These are ace. Can I have them?' For Mrs Kinsella could refuse Anne Marie nothing, which proved, perhaps, that there was a rich seam of humanity there somewhere, but that Beatrice, much less Miriam, had never been able to find it.

She rested on her bed in the afternoon, and must have slept, for the next thing she heard was the end of the shipping forecast: 'And finally Mallin Head.' Then a very brief instant of confusion until the somehow soothing last words, '. . . falling very slowly.' She was quite comfortable, thought she might stay like this, then remembered Jacob's proposed visit. There was no way of putting him off, although she supposed she might ring his parents' austere house in Hampstead and leave a message. She was unwilling to do this for several reasons, the main one being that she had uncomfortable memories of that house and of their necessary furtiveness, the father's harsh rumble on the ground floor as he dealt with patients, the possible return of the psychoanalyst mother as they were making love. Finally they had stolen up to his bedroom, somehow remaining alert to ordinary domestic sounds from below. Once they had met the father on their way out. Disconcertingly he had been all benevolent approval, reassured that his only son was gaining sexual experience, he being too busy to issue the necessary instructions. Jacob had been uneasy in his father's presence, while she had been at a loss, not knowing how to behave in the circumstances. As she prepared to slip out of the front door the father had indicated the spastics tin. Annoyed, she had fished out her purse. This was contrary to all her imaginings. And yet Jacob had loved her; of this she was quite sure. But he had not loved her in the way she had envisaged, could think of nothing more than those afternoons in his bedroom, where, truth to tell, she had been uncomfortable, aware of the people passing through on their way to the surgery, some of them quite ill . . .

She had said nothing, not wanting to be unpleasant, unaccommodating, and it had gone on for some months, until she had found the courage to tell him that they must end it. She had offered no excuse or explanation, not knowing the form of words usually offered on such occasions, but finally overwhelmed by the discomfort of it all. She smiled faintly as she remembered his crestfallen expression, remembered that she had wanted to reassure him, had finally done so, but using expressions that sounded to her unconvincing. I was unacquainted with the procedure, she thought soberly, looking at but not seeing her altered face in her dressing-table mirror. I was too unhandy.

She reminded herself that there had been others, that she had in fact lived a perfectly normal young girl's life. But something had been missing, some chivalry, some passion. Romance, that was what had been missing, and she leaned forward to the mirror to scrutinize the face which was imprinted with an unwanted stoicism. She had very early entered a state of resignation, but that resignation was undercut with longing. As it was now. Even now the sight of a beautiful face could bring it all back. Simon Haggard, at ease in his too small chair, which had threatened to crack under his weight, had inspired nothing definitive in the way of feeling, apart from a certain wistfulness. Not you, she had thought, but someone like you might have been the answer. If she had said little to him, had not been indignant, had not questioned him about her shattered prospects, it was because she had felt fear, not for her career—to that she was relatively indifferent—but for the original disenchantment dealt by inexperienced lovers who claimed too much in the way of connivance. Therefore she had perfected a whole repertory of charming invitations and gestures, had been soothed and flattered by the attentions of men who knew the rules of courtliness, of courtesy, but who were never crude enough to exact more of her. These were men who had been deprived of their homes and who were still homesick. Beatrice knew that what she had to offer was anodyne but was gratefully received.

The illusion had served its purpose. It was, after all, experience of a kind. She had been attractive then, even beautiful, but she saw, in Jacob's surprised look when she opened the door, that her looks had gone. But then so had his, although he was still slim, whereas she was not. That was why she had agreed to meet the dressmaker; many of her clothes no longer fitted. But it was better not to think of that. She was aware that she wanted nothing better than to go back to bed, but her social manners were so practised by years of hollow behaviour that she was confident that her lassitude was properly hidden. With a smile she complimented him, enquired after his career, poured his drink, realized that he might stay for the whole evening. He missed her cues as always, settled down comfortably. She remembered that he had always been content to know very little about her.

'I still love you, of course,' he was saying briskly, without a hint of sentiment. 'But I'm very happy. Meg and I have a little girl, you know. And she has a son by her first marriage. Her only marriage, I should say.'

'You never married?'

'No, we shan't bother. Let's face it, Beatrice. We're too old for marriage.'

'Yes, indeed,' she said agreeably. 'I value my independence even more these days.'

'We could have made a go of it, I suppose.'

'I doubt it. I would have bored you in the long run.'

'Well, yes, you might.' He took some time considering this. 'But you were a lovely girl.'

This remark hung in the air. She realized that in some way she had let him down. He had wanted to be flattered with reminiscence. Instead she heard herself say, 'And when do you go back to Denver?'

This, she knew, was a mistake, one which would cause her discomfort in the future. Unexpectedly he grinned at her; the ghost of their old friendship revived for a few seconds, enabling him to make his farewells without embarrassment.

'Keep in touch,' she told him. Then, inconsequentially, 'Is it nice out?'

'It is, yes. Full moon.'

'We could have taken a walk.'

He smiled again. 'Maybe we will some day.' Then, 'You must visit us when you're next in the States. Meg would love to show you round.'

'Goodbye,' she said, kissing his now familiar cheek. 'You must forgive me, Jacob. Take care.'

'You too, dear.'

'The lift . . .' she said, but he was gone. She closed the door on to his clumping steps, stood quite still, turned out the lights. In the dark she went back to her bedroom. Goodbye, she thought. Take care. And as she fell into sleep the thought recurred. Take care. Take care.

CHAPTER SEVEN

*N*either Beatrice nor Miriam had much regard for Christmas. They thought of it as a purely pagan festival: huge meals of largely unpalatable food, hot rooms, exhausted children and neglected elderly relatives for whom a family gathering was to be counted a treat. And in addition to all this indoor activity there was a deathly quiet in the deserted streets, broken only by the sound of a car trailing pop music, which faded into the distance as mournful as an elegy. They had lunched early, in defiance of tradition, on Beatrice's salmon coulibiac, did not intend to watch the Queen on television, and privately wondered how to get through the rest of the afternoon.

'I may sleep,' said Beatrice. 'You'll stay, won't you?'

'I'll go for a walk,' Miriam replied absent-mindedly, wondering why the atmosphere in the resolutely secular flat should have become imbued with the flattening significance of the day. And it was raining, a thin persistent rain that turned the grey day even more morose and threatened darkness shortly after three.

'You're not seeing Simon?' asked Beatrice, hesitating by the door, her eyelids already heavy.

'No, no, he's in Verbier. At the chalet. You go. I'll see to this.'

She was grateful for her sister's tact. She had half-expected gluttonous curiosity, such as she herself felt for the set-up in Verbier. The chalet, she knew from Simon's uninformative replies to her questions, had been in the family since Mary's grandfather had bought it in the late twenties. From this bleak statement she had constructed a fantasy of robust English aristocrats imposing their own customs on the docile Swiss. She imagined men in brown tweed Norfolk jackets and women with waved hair, content to take the air, to do a little shopping, rather a lot of gambling in nearby casinos, cigarettes tapped on silver cases, evening shoes worn out by the end of their stay. Why this picture should have formed in her mind she could not have said. She also saw these people as morally, even politically compromised, sympathetic towards Germany, from whose actresses the women had copied the lisp, the bias-cut satin, the sleek synthetic blondness, while the men remained reassuringly large, protective and, among themselves, dirty-minded. She imagined long-bonneted cars sweeping through snowy streets dotted with Christmas trees, plaid travelling rugs, flasks of martinis. Whereas the reality was both more reassuring and more ominous: Simon and Mary and the children, Sally and Sigrid the au pair, and whoever else decided to come along at the last minute. For it would all be fairly impromptu, he had laughed; sleeping-bags would be needed in case brothers, sisters, cousins decided to look them up. They would in any event be a large party, but they would be out of doors all day, and would eat out. There were excellent restaurants in the village.

Normally devoid of self-pity, or indeed of pity in general, Miriam found herself returning to these two discrete scenarios until she could perceive a strong familial connection between them. In her mind's eye Simon became the bluff dirty-minded hedonist, and Mary the decorative daughter of privilege. There was a certain uneasy excitement in these imaginings which appalled her. She had no reason to think that this was anything but a family holiday, and if she felt intrigued it was surely because she could not picture an ordinary family holiday, never having experienced one for herself. Too rancorous with disappointment to make sacrifices for their daughters, the parents had derived an odd satisfaction from sitting tight-lipped in the drawing-room, to the outward eye correct, even decorous, inwardly totting up the score of jibe and counter-jibe, neither made explicit but after long practise understood and carried on as a mind game, while the girls went up to their bedrooms and leaned moodily out of the windows. In due time they would be summoned to tea, which would be formally served, and as evening fell their parents would sigh at the waste of another day of their lives, but still, curiously, in accord on this point if not on any other. In Simon's case everything would be haphazard, accompanied by laughter, plans still fluid, skis bundled on to the roofs of the cars, a friendly neighbour waving them off. The more exactly she imagined all this the more distant Simon appeared, her connection with him more tenuous, as she felt him being reabsorbed into his proper context. She would forgive him, of course, for this defection, which, she reminded herself, was largely the work of her own longing. One always forgave fortunate people for fear of being detected as ungenerous, unworthy. And he would come back; of course he would come back, might even be glad to. She had the date of their next meeting in her diary. In her new diary it was the only space filled in.

Careless, she recognized. People like that, heavily endowed with family affections, were always careless, born to carelessness. While she had trained herself to be careful. That was the difference that inevitably divided them.

She hung up the tea-towel, washed and dried her hands, regretting the vague smell of fish, regretting even more the melancholy that accompanied all public holidays. These were days without diversion, days it was difficult to fill. In Lower Sloane Street her papers were strewn over her desk. There was no reason why she should not go home and work, thereby gaining a head start on the week. But mysteriously work had let her down. Conscientious though she was (and, she knew, would continue to be), she was now conscious of work as a vast restriction on her liberty, tying her down to one room, whereas others, it seemed, or it seemed to her on this uncomfortable day, were able to command their actions and their time. Again, but fleetingly, she thought of that healthy party in the snow. She shook her head irritably; she was well aware of the dangers of this line of thinking. But just at this moment she felt an overwhelming desire to escape, if only for a few hours. She could escape for longer, she reasoned: she could take a holiday, could go to Paris, look up old friends. But she felt dejected at the thought of the effort involved. The whole exercise would be artificial, undertaken solely so that she could offer such a holiday as conversational exchange, a bulwark against whatever Simon might reveal about his own activities. She had a strong desire to present herself as someone with friends, but knew that such friends were a fantasy, that her own mild curiosity in past friendships had caused her to be cast as confidante, and then retired when the need for confidences was past.

No one was likely to rescue her from this particular day, and from all the others like it. Yet she reminded herself that she had a source of warmth and energy in her life which had come about without the agency of friendships or introductions or any of the clumsy agencies by which conjunctions were normally effected. Once again the fact that she and Simon had so unerringly come together, without any need of explanations, convinced her that this had indeed been no accident, that they had been guided, directed, by some fate other than their own. The chill thought struck her that this random, or seemingly random procedure could just as easily divide them again when the time mysteriously allotted to their closeness was exhausted. They would know, of course, and there would be no time or occasion for recriminations. Neither would have let the other down; they would be united by the same act of recognition. It was the wordlessness of the affair that she valued. Spending all her days in the search for words or their equivalents had left her with tired eyes and a disinclination to read. Now, working with so much less attention, she could avoid the implied seriousness of what she was doing, could care for her appearance, like any cherished woman. Except that she was not quite cherished, not quite included in any plans that were being made. Except that at this holiday time she stood alone in her sister's kitchen, aware that the light was already fading, and that it was not yet half-past two.

She stood for a moment outside Beatrice's bedroom door, listening for the sound of regular breathing. 'Beatrice?' she enquired softly. 'Are you asleep?' No answer. 'I'm going out for a walk,' she said. 'I'll be back for tea.' She hesitated. 'Have a good rest,' she said. 'You deserve it. Lunch was delicious.' Then there seemed to be nothing further that she could say or do, speaking as she was into a vacancy which emphasized the general vacancy of the hour. She turned away, resolutely buckled herself into her raincoat and left the flat, easing the front door to with her key in the lock so as not to disturb the sleeping building. Outside in the street she waited for a sense of deliverance, a return of energy, but none came. A car, passing slowly along the wet road, was the only other sign of life, but even that soon disappeared.

She walked along Sloane Street, noting the lights of the Cadogan Hotel, wondering if anyone inside were having a festive time. If so they were being very quiet about it. She crossed Knightsbridge, entered the silent park. Rain fell steadily but without a sound, a mist of vapour that she could feel on her eyelashes, her lips. In the distance a man threw a ball for a dog. She made instinctively for Marble Arch, for Oxford Street, for Upper Berkeley Street, for Bryanston Square. She knew that this was masochistic and quite unprofitable, that there would be no one in the flat, whose windows she could see were tightly closed. Had there been a light on she would have been terrified, but the flat, the whole building, seemed empty, shuttered against intruders. She caught sight of herself in the brass door plate, and was so humiliated that she turned away. Bryanston Square was as deserted as Sloane Street had been, though here the rain seemed lighter, more beneficent. She began to breathe more easily, as if some suspicion had been appeased. If she had to choose between Simon in Verbier and Simon unexpectedly, mysteriously, in the flat, she would prefer him to be away, out of sight, unable to see her lingering like an orphan on his doorstep. And if the worst thing had happened and she had been discovered there she could have offered no defence of her actions. 'Hello,' she heard herself composing, in a jaunty uncharacteristic tone of voice, 'I thought I'd see what you were up to. I'm going to walk round Regent's Park. Why don't you come?' There was no way in which this could be made to sound convincing. Briefly she was glad that there were no witnesses to this evidence of bad thinking. All must be easy, unassuming, even inconsequential—that was the line to take. In that way mutuality could be assured, preserved. She knew that thinking and planning must be avoided at all costs, that she must strive for insouciance, the quality she treasured but did not possess. Anything less, or more, was doomed.

In Baker Street a pizza parlour was unaccountably open, catering to about eight people, mostly resigned Indians. A solemn Arab family passed slowly by on their way to the Sherlock Holmes Hotel. On impulse she trailed behind them, entered almost on their heels, sat down and ordered coffee. No one seemed to think this request unusual. She glanced warily around, feeling more at home in this anonymous place where her actions could not possibly be held against her. It was warm, even stuffy. A waiter brought her coffee, presented her with a bill at the same time, yet did not indicate impatience. All around her conversation was subdued, monotonous, comforting. Who came here? People from overseas, eager Americans who were valiantly proof against disappointment, Asians interested in currency exchange outlets. If she liked she could spend the afternoon here without loss of dignity, be at one with these transients, all of them downcast by the weather in the streets, the year's midnight. She could get up at her leisure and walk home again, but that return journey would take her once again into the vicinity of Bryanston Square, and she winced away from this prospect. Bryanston Square, empty, affronted her, as if she had been turned out. She was aware of colour coming into her cheeks at this thought, and resisted it. She would walk round Regent's Park and then find a taxi. She and Beatrice would have tea and perhaps listen to music. Or read. They would tell themselves that everybody else was doing the same, until increasing yawns persuaded them of the need for an early night. So had their parents passed their evenings, she reflected, and was saddened by an involuntary sympathy for that mute couple. So might she and Beatrice end up, she supposed, and again, and not for the first time, dismissed the thought.

In Baker Street it was already dark. She turned north and walked in the direction of the park, although by now there was little point in this exercise. It was simply that having started out it was necessary to proceed. There were more cars about now, a certain energy now that the evening could be deemed to have begun. Inside the park the renewed silence was unwelcome, even sinister, and to her dismay she was not the only person about. One person in particular, indistinct in the rainy dusk, seemed to be striding purposefully in her direction. She could make out little more than a bulky raincoat, similar to her own, but infinitely larger; by the size and shape she deduced that this was the figure of a particularly athletic man.

'Good evening,' she called out cheerfully, thinking this the best thing to do in the circumstances. Her heart was knocking, as if she were threatened. No one in their right mind came out for a walk in the park at this time of day, she reasoned, aware of the sound of cars passing in the distance, and wondering how to escape, if escape were to become necessary.

'Good evening,' said a light pleasant Scottish voice, as the figure slowed down and stopped in front of her.

'Merry Christmas,' she said, her voice constricted by terror.

'Merry Christmas,' replied the stranger, amused. 'Please don't be frightened; I'm not an axe murderer. If I stopped so abruptly it's because I'm sure I've seen you somewhere before.'

'I don't think . . .'

'St James's Square? The London Library? You usually turn up just as I'm leaving. About four, four-thirty. Tom Rivers,' he said, holding out a hand.

'I know that name. Why do I know it? Oh, Miriam Sharpe, or rather Eldon. Either. How do you do?'

'I'm a journalist.' He mentioned a Sunday paper, one of the ones she rarely took. 'Chatham House is useful. And the Library, sometimes.'

'You're a foreign correspondent, aren't you?'

'More of a political historian, I like to think.'

'Weren't you on television?'

'For my sins. Do you particularly like this park? It's rather damp. Would you like tea or a drink or something?'

'I'd very much like to get out of here,' she said. 'I can't think why it seemed such a good idea. I just felt like a walk.'

'That's what I thought. I didn't like it much either. I'm sorry if I frightened you.'

She smiled, aware of her hair misted by the rain. Now that she could see him more clearly she felt dreamily reassured, his bulk no longer threatening, even a protection against the growing dark. He had a pleasant quizzical face which promised interest, sympathy. He would no doubt appeal to women; men of that size and shape, with pleasant manners, and an equally pleasant directness of approach, would be on every hostess's list. If hostesses still existed. He would also be pleasantly frustrating, she thought, able to deflect unwanted interest with the very real excuse of an urgent assignment. She focused once again on his steady smile, which had her in its sights.

'I really ought to be getting home,' she said. 'My sister is expecting me. I don't want to worry her.'

'Do you want a taxi?'

'Yes, I do.'

'So do I. I'm going to the office, I'm afraid.'

'Oh, poor you.'

'I don't mind. I loathe Christmas.'

'Oh, so do I.'

They laughed, turned gratefully away from the murky park, walked back in the direction of Baker Street.

'Here's one,' he said, raising a long arm.

'Are you sure you don't want it?'

'No, no.' He hesitated, held out his hand. 'I'll look out for you in St James's Square. At the Library. Or, better still, I'll give you a ring. Are you in the book?'

'I'm in a rented flat at the moment.'

'What's your number, then?'

She gave him the Lower Sloane Street number, knowing that she was perfectly safe. He did not write it down, which seemed to guarantee her safety. Except that he was probably trained to file away information. She shrugged. What did it matter? She thought of Simon with a rush of love and affection, thought of the diary in her bag, thought of the date of their next meeting. Suddenly she could not wait to get home.

When she was safe in the taxi she saw that the afternoon seemed to have a point, if only an incongruous one. She was quite

sure that she had never seen the man before, although he had obviously seen her. Rivers, he said his name was; she was vaguely
aware that she knew it. But she was cold now, conscious of her
damp hair, almost anxious to be back in the flat. Rivers would do
for an anecdote, she thought, something almost amusing to offer,
in exchange for her good lunch, an anecdote it might be useful to
employ on a dull afternoon.

She found Beatrice working at her tapestry, a particularly
hideous piece depicting a vase of orange flowers on a beige
ground.

'You'll never finish that,' she observed.

'No, I shan't,' agreed her sister.

'Why, if I may ask, did you start it? Did you think we had a
dozen chair seats to be covered?'

'I thought this was what unoccupied ladies did.'

'They may have done once. Nowadays they go to the gym.
What will you do with it?'

'I thought it would make a nice present for Mrs Kinsella,' said
Beatrice pleasantly. They grinned at each other. 'Have you had
tea?'

'I'll put the kettle on. Did anyone phone?' she said carelessly.

'Oddly enough, yes. Max, from Monaco. Having a perfectly
horrible time, from the sound of his voice. I heard him out, heard
about the beautiful weather, the oysters he had for lunch . . . Then
he shocked me by saying that he missed London.'

'Oh? Why? I thought he was longing for retirement.'

'Exactly what I pointed out. Then he said it wasn't what he
was used to, wished he'd kept the house in London instead of
buying what sounded like a very noisy flat. He said he thought he
might sell and move back.'

Beatrice sounded pleased at this evidence of Max's discomfiture, as well she might. 'He seemed anxious to have news from
home, even asked about you.'

'He can't stand me.'

'I know. That's what alerted me to the fact that he must be lonely.'

With a complacent glance at her buckled tapestry, Beatrice stuck her needle into a marigold, smoothed back her hair and said, 'There's a cake in the tin, if you want it. How was your walk?'

'Well, an extraordinary thing happened. Picture the scene. I'm in the middle of Regent's Park; it's almost dark, and suddenly a figure looms out of the mist and makes straight for me.'

Shocked, Beatrice looked up, her eyes reproving. 'You avoided him, I hope.'

'He introduced himself. Rivers. Tom Rivers. Said he was a journalist. Said he'd been on television.'

'I'd have remembered. What did he say?'

'Oh, nothing much.' Miriam turned away, slightly annoyed. The life seemed to have gone out of the anecdote, which had had its value mainly as a reward for Beatrice's lonely afternoon. Suddenly, in her mind's eye, she saw lighted windows, heard healthy laughter, heard water running in baths and showers. She almost wished an accident on Simon, one of those comical broken legs one saw hobbling off the plane, until she reasoned that she, in fact, were this to happen, would suffer more than he did.

'I hope you're not going to make a habit of encountering strangers in remote places,' said Beatrice. 'Though at your age I can't see why not.'

'Quite. Anything on television this evening?'

'Not a thing, as usual. Why? Were you thinking of going back to your flat?'

She said 'your flat' as if it were not quite real, as if it were merely the sort of aberration over which it behoved her to maintain a tactful silence, implying that this unreal flat of Miriam's was mainly the scene of indecent fumblings, though in fact Simon had never visited it. In Lower Sloane Street only anxious cooking took place, the results to be conveyed in plastic containers in a Selfridges bag which bumped against her briefcase. But what did this matter? What did any of the details matter? Her reward outweighed any temporary loss of dignity.

'So Max is thinking of coming back?' she said.

'It looks like it.'

When the clock struck the half-hour both instinctively looked at their watches. 'Do you remember that story—I can't remember who it's by—about the man whose wife has been told to rest, and who keeps looking at his watch as if he can visualize what his mistress is doing in Paris?'

'Colette. *Chambre d'Hôtel.*'

'That's right. And the woman who tells the story is dispatched to Paris with a note for her, but really to find out what she's up to.'

'And finds she's gone off with a lover.'

'How does it end?'

'I don't remember. I only know that Colette comes out of it best. The onlooker, I suppose, seeing most of the game.'

'There must be some compensation for being an onlooker,' said Beatrice. 'The role is not always an enviable one.'

They digested this in silence. Finally Miriam collected their cups, said, 'I'll do these, and then I'll be off. You won't mind?'

'You look tired,' said Beatrice sharply. 'Are you all right?'

'Quite all right. I'll ring you in the morning.'

The rain had stopped, she noticed. In the street the evening was almost pleasant, quiet, damp, windless. She looked back on her day with shame, the fantasies stronger than the reality. And she had dealt ungraciously with that man; she should have accepted his offer of a drink, but in truth he had annoyed her by breaking into her train of thought. But that train of thought had been unattractive, she now realized, based on an unwelcome comparison between the cold dark park and the scene of light and laughter she had so successfully—too successfully—conjured up. She knew that this form of primal scene would recur to torment her, cursed herself for an imagination which had never troubled her in the past, so that Beatrice had often complained of her morose realism, yet this imagination had delivered, detail perfect, an ideal image in which pain and an almost perverse delight were commingled. She knew that she would return to that scene in inconvenient moments, before sleep, in the course of other blank afternoons. The reality might be quite different, even boring. Surely she herself, with her sensible working life, her independence, and her habitual scepticism, should be proof against such imagined scenes. But that was the point: scepticism, and indeed independence, and if she were not very careful, her habits of work, had been overturned by Simon, who thus appeared in the guise of an anomaly. She shrank from the implications of this. Her real, her normal life, was something she would later resume, if necessary. It would see her into a respectable old age, at a time when the life of the body took on a different meaning. She imagined that otherwise unimaginable future, saw her future body as hollow, all sentient organs in abeyance, dematerialized. In those circumstances it might be genuinely interesting to apply herself to the latest Prix Goncourt, for what other diversions would she have?

Across the street a lone figure was looking into the lighted windows of Peter Jones, but she could spare no more sympathy. No work tonight, she thought; the day had left her feeling unworthy, as if she had fallen below her usual standards. Tomorrow she would apply herself. Tomorrow she would be very careful. She would need to be, she reflected, for she had so nearly let disorder into her life, and it would be disorder rather than any outer agency that would destroy her.

$\mathcal{M}$ax Gruber raised his hat to the flight attendant, settled it more firmly on his head and prepared to take his first grateful step back onto English soil, even if the soil were only that of Heathrow. He was, he thought, a landlocked person: that open sea had done him no good at all, had afflicted him with something like nausea, even though he was not on it. The confusion of his last days in Monaco, when he had surrendered the flat at a ridiculous price to a film producer who would only use it for three months of the year, filled him with distress and a sort of shame. The money did not matter; what had mattered was the homesickness, and a vast store of memories which had shocked and bewildered him by their persuasiveness. He had discovered the price of exile: recovered childhood. And now even the sight of the airport building disturbed him, although his panic had subsided somewhat during the flight. He would have to look for somewhere to live, but now it seemed to him that all homes were temporary in comparison with his original home. At the age of seventy-five he suddenly missed his mother and father.

He had been born in Cologne, although rumour, which he did nothing to dispel, had him growing up in Vienna or Budapest. By the same token his father had not been a musician but a music teacher whose own instrument was the violin. His fine manners, his incessant flattery, had given Max a genuine old-style European aura, which he cultivated; few knew of the underlying cynicism which regarded his progress as nugatory, misleading. If he thought back now it was to his first home in England, a tall house over a shop in Kentish Town, which the family had acquired piecemeal as money came through from Germany, first the two upper storeys, and then the shop itself, from which his father, dispossessed of pupils, was forced to make a living. The shop sold watches and clocks, and occasional novelties such as perpetual calendars on silver mounts and silver ashtrays in the shape of hearts, clubs, diamonds and spades. These were surprisingly popular, and once they had installed a fellow refugee in the back room they could undertake repairs. They lived modestly, his parents, his sister and brother, but managed to recapture something of their original comfort. They were polite and cheerful, had few friends, but had each other.

Beyond Kentish Town lay Cologne, their Sunday drives to Bonn to contemplate the statue of Beethoven, their summer holidays in Baden-Baden, sedate family walks along the Lichtenthalerallee, the cup of coffee in the Casino gardens, where the orchestra played . . . And his mother, with her silk dresses and lace collars, his father sporting a summer panama hat, his beautiful little sister as serious as a grown woman. Women no longer behaved like that, and their disappearance was one of the sources of his grief. His brother, Michael, and his sister, Adela—Addie—had worked in the shop, while their mother rested upstairs in the cold rooms of this strange English house. When their father died Michael had taken over the shop, releasing Addie, who took singing lessons and hoped for a career on the stage. This had come to nothing, but Max himself had been fortunate in obtaining a job in a theatrical agency, where his excellent manners and ceaseless efficiency had earned him a good name. It helped that his immediate superior had died six months later, so that Max could offer an intimate knowledge—always respectful, always unassuming—of the business in hand. From then on it was simply a matter of waiting until everybody else died. He had never doubted that in due time the agency would be his, and in due time it was.

He was known for his radiant bonhomie, which did something to mitigate the impression given by his extreme ugliness. His short stature and his permanently brown irregular features, his sparse hair and huge hands, marked him out as the sort of physical type which his one-time friends in Cologne were intent on eradicating. Hence the flight to England, where he was regarded with indifference and a sort of amusement. But he was observant, sharp-witted, as only those denied physical beauty learn to be. Their mother lived long enough to see him established, and died happy in the knowledge that her children were safe, Michael on hand downstairs in the shop, Addie still living at home, Max as often as not sleeping in a room above the office, but telephoning several times a day to see that she wanted nothing. By common consent they sold the building, goodwill and all, after their mother's death; it made a surprising amount of money, which enabled them to disperse to flats of their own, Addie to Edgware Road, Michael to Bayswater and Max, who was paying himself a decent salary, to Hampstead. They did this in the happy anticipation of love affairs, of which they never spoke, as if their mother might be listening. But every Sunday they met for lunch in Michael's flat and talked about the old days. Addie cherished her two brothers, as their mother had done, examined their cupboards and larders to see if they were eating properly, ran over if either of them had a cold or indigestion, did them more good than any doctor, they assured her. And it was true. Such love, such beneficence, linked them with the past, with an unbroken heritage of lavish kindliness. In this they were conscious of their good fortune.

But they never married. This was a source of bewilderment to them individually, but not of unhappiness. Such matters were not discussed; it was assumed that each had some private arrangement, as was the case. For Michael and Addie such arrangements were of long standing, a hotel manageress in one case, a retired businessman in the other. These affairs were placid, undemonstrative, *heimlich,* not the stuff of excited conversation. Max was different; Max was a womanizer, had a succession of unsuitable companions intrigued by his exuberance and his generosity. This suited him well enough but left his vestigial heartache untouched. He wanted a woman like his mother, his sister, but where to find her? At the same time he was sexually voracious, and shrewd enough to know that one did not have affairs with such women, only to discard them afterwards. He avoided sentimental women, although he responded to them. He knew that one slept with a sentimental woman at one's peril. His sister treated him like a lovable boy, which was the sort of attention that he craved, but he discovered that few women were so unselfish. He got used to parting with rather a lot of money after each affair, but did so thankfully, if ruefully. The disappointment that this created was concealed by a worldliness that was both assumed and genuine.

And now Addie was in a nursing-home, and Michael, still in the same Bayswater flat, was a bent but fit old man who occupied his time by taking long walks and playing bridge in a nearby club. On the glass and brass table in his living-room stood two nests of those silver ashtrays in the shape of hearts, spades, clubs and diamonds that he had brought from the shop, not so much for sentimental reasons but because he liked them, thought them genuinely decorative. Max laughed, but indulgently, when he saw them; Addie scrutinized them for dust, gave them a quick polish.

Michael, at seventy-eight, was the most durable of the three of them, went to visit Addie in the nursing-home every day, chatted amiably with the ex-businessman ex-lover who also looked in, then took the bus home again. He was regarded with some affection in the neighbourhood because he gave no trouble and seemed to want nothing; he had few friends apart from his bridge-playing cronies, but nodded in greeting to a fair number of people. Michael at least had grown old in the approved manner, thought Max, unlike himself. He seemed, in what he supposed was old age, to have acceded to a vast regret, the latest manifestation of which was this Monaco folly. As if he could have survived so far from home! To a lifetime of enjoyable travel he had said an almost relieved farewell. He would now live like Michael, if necessary, be an amiable crabbed bachelor, his former glory forgotten. He had enjoyed his profession until his always persuasive skills, his flattery—usually sincere—began to bore him. Then he knew it was time to go. The future was entrusted to his partner, and to the new younger man, Haggard, useful with tricky women clients, his charms there to soften the blow, or to exaggerate the—rarely—good news.

This brought him uncomfortably back to the matter of Beatrice Sharpe, who caused him some retrospective embarrassment. He had, he saw, made a grave error: he had shrugged her off as if she were one of the unimportant women with whom he had affairs, whereas, he now realized, she belonged to the alternative category. If she were to be compared with anyone it would be with those who were to be respected, like Addie, like his mother. He should have spoken gently to her, patted her hand, mentioned his age, so that she would have been instantly alight with sympathy. She was foolish, of course; that sort of protected woman invariably was. She assumed that she knew him better than he knew himself, which was not, could not be true. How could any woman appreciate his consciously deployed charm other than those women who gave in through curiosity, for a while? Poor Beatrice had deserved better, which was why he had, at the end, avoided her.

Between the permissive and the impermissive a line was drawn, no less discernible for being invisible. All that was now changed; in matters of sex women had learned from men to take the initiative, to demand satisfaction. But like many people of his generation Max regretted the old order (although the other had served him well enough); something archaic in him desired women to be modest and protected, though experience had told him that those who were did not advance very far, unless they met and married men who were equally virginal. But what woman would want a man like that? Men, if they were to be men, had to lose their innocence, and to lose it sooner rather than later, and women had to make difficult choices, less difficult now, he supposed, when each sex knew what the other was up to. In Monaco, with nothing to do, he had pondered these questions, found himself looking out almost eagerly for the elderly couple who sat and drank coffee every morning in the café near to his flat. They looked contented, as he himself had never felt contented, not noticeably infirm, although the man offered the woman his arm as they turned to leave . . . What else could they be but man and wife? In that moment, every morning, as he saw them make their stately way, arm in arm, out of his range, he felt fear, as if his life, his popular, successful, crowded life, had left him bereft, had deprived him of a peaceful domestic existence, with an excellent professional reputation his only reward.

He loved the world, loved even this grey damp crowded place, was prepared to give it his most expert backing, as he had so many times for so many ventures in the past. Except that that past was now almost out of date. He had enjoyed more friendships than his siblings, had travelled more widely, had been possessed by more enthusiasms, genuine and otherwise, and yet after each adventure he preferred to go home alone. Home was a hallowed place, filled with ancestral memories: photographs of his parents were prominent on his bedside table. Women who visited his house were disappointed in the conventional furnishings, the thick patterned carpets, the crowded sofas, the footstools. They were not encouraged to stay. He would drive them home, and usually spend the night with them. In his mind home meant order, innocence. If his home remained inviolate he felt above board. That was perhaps why he was such an accomplished visitor, looking in after work with a compliment, a flower, delighted to be welcomed, even more delighted to be welcomed with ceremony.

For this he had to award Beatrice Sharpe full marks. Her wide-eyed greeting, almost parodic, pleased him by its stateliness, although he perceived that she was sexually ignorant. She knew the rules; had she been older she would have been more than acceptable as one of the friends who visited on Friday evenings in Cologne, or took tea with his mother. The younger sister was a different matter, cold, shrewd, an unwelcome contrast to Beatrice's softness and sympathy. He and she understood each other perfectly when they mimicked affection, devotion. Because he considered Beatrice unawakened he knew that he was safe, ran no risk. He was perceptive enough to know that Beatrice discounted him because of his unsatisfactory appearance, but did not hold it against her. After all, she could know nothing of his successes and excesses, may even have thought of him as disqualified by his ugliness. She was a romantic, he could see that, and therefore to be treated gently. Few men, he assured himself, would take the trouble, but at the end he had failed to take the necessary trouble himself, cynically concluding that a good-looking stranger would do the unwelcome business of easing her out of an overcrowded profession just as efficiently, while at the same time ensuring her a brief moment of gratification. The incident would have hardened her; he knew that too. Neglect is not easily forgiven. But it had not been neglect, rather a sudden mournful cessation of enthusiasm for the task in hand. He had felt his age, quite suddenly, never having been particularly conscious of it before, had decided to spare himself unnecessary difficulties, yet had run into more, in the shape of Monaco and the awful plate-glass flat that let in the sun at all times of day. It had seemed easier to go than to stay, and he knew that the only way to go was to go quickly. Few people, he thought, would be able to say with certainty what had become of him, fewer still would attempt to find out.

Get a grip, he told himself, as the English did. The phrase had convulsed him with mirth when he had first heard it, and he had only to say, gruffly, 'Get a grip, Michael,' for his elder brother's solemn face to relax into a smile. Now it was a reminder to stay alert, to fit in. But in fact he felt more German these days, hankered after German food, roast goose, fish in aspic, a simple supper of smoked meats, pale tea in fragile Japanese cups, like the ones in the cabinet at home. There was little of that on offer in the expensive restaurants he had been used to frequent, and in Monaco, in the hotel in which he had first taken up residence, his stomach had been revolted by the stagy cuisine. Cooking for himself was even more of a problem, and he had had to rely on the local *traiteur,* had eaten too many dubious pâtés and terrines which he always feared might poison him. This had some bearing on his decision to return to England, although there was no one to cook for him in England now that Addie was in the nursing-home. She too had reverted to type, conversed with the other ladies, had her hair done regularly, enjoyed an occasional game of cards. Or so he supposed. His money, fortunately, guaranteed her decent company: decent company, in these matters, did not come cheap. And Michael seemed quite content to live on brown rice and raw apricots, extolled the virtues of his rudimentary diet, which indeed seemed to keep him fit. In summer he walked the streets in an old pair of shorts and an aertex shirt, vowed he had never felt better. Yet he looked like the old man he had turned into, seemed grimly pleased to have grown old so successfully, looked back to the old days, perhaps, only in Addie's company. Darling Addie, cherished daughter, photographed as a child with ethereal, almost transparent eyes, now probably a reserved matron, on good nodding terms with everyone, much esteemed by the staff... Addie, he thought, would be glad to see him. Most of the visiting had been left to the laconic Michael, while he, Max, had gone on being enthusiastic to strangers. He had been all hilarity, when what he yearned for was a quiet Sunday evening in his old home, with his sister playing the piano, and his mother's face smooth with contentment.

He retrieved his luggage and joined the queue for taxis. An unwelcoming time of the year, late winter, and no sign of spring. Briefly, he regretted the sun. Even more unsettling was the fact that he had no home to go to, would have to stay with Michael in his flat off the Bayswater Road. Michael was not known for his sense of comfort, would almost invariably keep the heating switched low, or indeed not switched on at all. In one of Michael's kitchen cupboards he had once counted ten screwtop jars full of nails, the purpose of which was never revealed. He would make the best of it, of course, would look for something as soon as the agencies opened on the following morning. He half-hoped that there might be an empty flat in Michael's building, which would save a lot of trouble. This one he would barely furnish; he knew he had no taste, had always relied on Harrods in the past. This flat would have bare white walls and the minimum of furniture, a good table and chairs, a good bed. After all, he did not intend to entertain.

'So,' Max said heartily, as he put his bags down in Michael's hallway. '*Nu?*' he had nearly said, but in fact he only said this to

English clients, who thought it quaint. He then stepped forward
and embraced his brother, who slowly responded.

'You've had lunch?'

'On the plane.'

'Then we'd better get off. Addie knows you're coming.'

'What have you got there?'

'Cakes. She loves cakes. I take them every day, for her tea.'

'You're well placed for taxis here,' he remarked, replacing his
signature Tyrolean hat.

'I usually take the bus. It's only half an hour.'

He shrugged. 'If you like.' For, he remembered, he had also
sold his car. 'I'm quite rich, you know,' he said sharply.

'Good,' was the reply. 'Pity it's raining. You won't see the park
at its best.'

From the bus London looked mournful, as he remembered it
from Sundays past. This homecoming was not as he had pictured
it. He was tired, irritable; he wanted a hot bath. The bus itself was
crowded, the passengers brooding and morose. He had not
wanted this excursion. He had wanted a welcome of sorts, as he
was used to being welcomed by those who had formerly solicited
his company, his bustling competence. Now at last he knew that
those days would never come again, that he was just another old
man whom nobody knew. He had until now avoided such reflections. Even Monaco had served his purpose in this, since the life
he had lived there was factitious, almost without importance.
Now, in his damp overcoat and his jaunty hat, he came face to face
with the facts of age, of anonymity. He had few friends who were
not convinced of their own importance, and in any case what
would he say to them? He would sound querulous, plaintive; they
would be shocked, would shake their heads when he left, would
think him sadly diminished, as indeed he was. His memories
faded in the light of this new reality, new to him, at any rate,
though not to Michael, who was looking out of the window as if

the scene were of more than passing interest. But Michael had always managed without company, lived stoically, no longer looked to life for romance, if indeed he ever had. Max became aware of a vast difference between them, whereas on the plane he had had an overwhelming image of closeness. And Addie might not have forgiven him for his long absence, might, out of pique, treat him like a stranger, when what he wanted was to be admitted once again to her devotion. He was uneasily aware of outsider status, the rich absent brother whose money paid for her comforts but whose life went on elsewhere, in a place which held no interest for her. Her reality now was one room, her company that of strangers. He might even be forced to accept these conditions for himself one day. And no doubt Michael would visit him, and bring him little treats, but with a look of scepticism on his face, as if the long absent brother had hardly deserved them.

The nursing-home was reassuring, or would have been if not for an underlying smell of age and—dare he think it?—incontinence. The first thing he noticed about Addie was that she looked exactly like his mother. The second thing he noticed was that she did not rise from her chair to greet him. As he leaned over her to kiss her he noticed gratefully that she smelt only of scent. He cursed himself for having brought no offering; he should have filled a bag at the airport. She looked presentable, even decorative, except that the dress she wore was of viscose, for easy cleaning. On the back of the door hung an ugly pink dressing-gown, quite uncharacteristic of her fastidious taste. Visited in her flat in Edgware Road he had always found her lovingly pleased to see him. Now, however, she seemed more interested in Michael's box of cakes.

He was puzzled by her apparent indifference, had thought she would understand why he had wanted to spend his retirement in the sun. But apparently he was not to be forgiven, and they were not to reminisce about the old days. He wondered if she were losing her memory, if she were in fact ill, turned away for a

moment, his face convulsed with shock. Her decision to enter the
nursing-home had originally seemed a matter of convenience
pure and simple; she knew one or two of the women there, and
the upkeep of the flat had become too much for her after her elderly maid had retired. He had thought this rational, sensible at
the time. Now he was not so sure. What if she had detected a hidden menace and had said nothing of it to him? He had gladly dis-
bursed monies, had been relieved that she would be cared for, had
not suspected that there was anything amiss. But she had still not
moved from her chair, had expressed no interest in him. He was
appalled at this dereliction, searched her face for a clue to her feelings, but she was placid, almost tranquil. She held the box of cakes
in her hands, waited for Michael to ring the bell for tea . . .

But she was only seventy-three, he reasoned; there was no
need for this surrender. He should have insisted that she stay in
the flat, should have found staff for her, nurses, if necessary. This
was what he was good at, the deploying of services, arrangements.
Despite himself he felt a twinge of resentment. Was this how they
thought of him, as one whose money would ease their difficulties?
It was true that they had never asked him for anything, but then
they had never needed to; he thought ahead for them. Just as he
had telephoned his mother two or three times a day when he was
a young man, to discover what she needed, he had anticipated
other needs, had carried over that faculty into his professional life.
He thought of his busy office, of the telephones ringing, of his
own good humour, of the secretaries spoiling him, and then with
a wrench faced the reality of this room, of the ugly pink dressing-
gown hanging on the back of the door (it should have been in the
bathroom, he realized, as it would have been at home), and of the
sight of Addie complacently eating her way through Michael's
cakes, a crumb at the side of her mouth. When her head drooped
forward he ran to the bell, alarmed. A nurse appeared, the first
person in uniform he had seen. 'She's a little tired today,' said the

nurse cheerfully, removing the box from Addie's hands. 'Say goodbye now, dear.' Addie roused herself, smiled dreamily. 'Max!' she said. 'Give me a kiss.' As if he had just come in.

They said nothing on the way home, until he broke the silence. 'Is she ill?' he asked fearfully.

'Alzheimer's,' replied Michael. 'Nothing to be done. But you saw for yourself, she's quite happy. She's in the best place.'

'She hardly knew me.'

'Well, she hasn't seen you for some time, has she?'

The reproach—but it was hardly a reproach—hung in the air. What has happened to my life, thought Max; how has it ended so quickly, so abruptly? Tomorrow he must look for a flat as soon as possible, must move into an hotel if necessary. But he no longer had the panache, the self-sufficiency for hotel living; he saw himself walking the streets until such time as he could decently go back to his room. Michael might even be hurt, although, being Michael, would say nothing. Yet his feelings too must be taken into account. Apparently he had given offence by leaving, and yet it had seemed the appropriate thing to do. And stylish; he owed it to himself to continue to behave with style. He had always pictured himself with a vast audience of admirers. Perhaps it was the audience that was missing? Without witnesses how would he continue to be Max?

For their dinner, in deference to his brother's gourmet tastes, Michael produced a dish of pasta with a little cheese grated over it. Max ate it humbly. His one anxiety was to have done with this terrible day, to lie in bed, returned to his own imaginings. Those fragile Japanese cups in the china cabinet, the statue of Beethoven, the Casino gardens . . . The bedroom was chilly but tiredness soon overcame him. Tomorrow he would put everything right: was he not good at that? The flat first of all; in his own four walls everything would seem more normal. A home, he realized, had been in his thoughts all along. He had merely been mistaken in thinking of the homes he had lost. The future was what mattered now, while he still had some hold on it.

On impulse, the following day, after Michael had gone to his club to play bridge, Max picked up the receiver, made a few calls, was momentarily restored to his laughing joking self. Then he made the call he had been intending to make all along.

'Beatrice? It's Max here. How are you? Are you at home this evening? I'll look in, shall I? No, no, nothing to eat. Just a chat about old times. Until this evening, then. Goodbye, dear.'

CHAPTER NINE

'Darling,' she said experimentally, but he was asleep and did not hear.

After a minute she was glad of this. She was afraid of being thought intemperate. On the way to Bryanston Square she had picked up a bunch of anemones, as an adjunct to the asparagus quiche she had bought earlier. This had seemed to her inadequate, unappetizing, and would have to be eaten cold as there was no time or opportunity to prepare the meal properly. With a nagging sense of haste she wished she could for once have dispensed with these arrangements. When she presented the flowers, with a carefully mock affectionate gesture, he had raised an eyebrow, smiled quizzically, and said, 'I don't think we have any vases here.' The flowers lay on the kitchen table, together with the food. She knew that they would still be there when she left.

This gesture had been totally out of character, and therefore unwelcome. She knew, or rather was aware, that to be acceptable she had to obey certain rules, to stay within certain limits. And yet she wanted to endow him in some way, to let him know that he had shown her a life she had never known, in comparison with which the restrictions of their affair had no importance. The formality into which she had learned to retreat now seemed to her regrettable, no longer in order. Yet that was the moral stance she had taken all her life, an essential protection against alarm, in a life which until now had delivered few treats. But this was where common sense broke down. In default of that moral stance she had, she thought, little to offer. If he continued to appreciate her it was because she withheld so much, and into that category came endearments as well as judgements. She was aware of vast inadequacies, but on her side, not on his. He had only to mention his family of brothers and close cousins, usually in the context of something hilarious they had said or done, some journey one of them had made, some celebration that had taken place, for her to feel sad that it was not possible for her to respond appropriately, for she had no one whose words or actions gave her own a certain weightiness. Not for the first time she felt discomfort on behalf of the poor remnants of her own past. Her parents she no longer considered with anything other than a tired irony. What was much worse was that Beatrice, whom she loved, was beginning to resemble their mother, not only physically, in certain gestures, but in her refusal to regulate her own disappointments. Obstinately sitting in the flat all day, more or less idle, Beatrice seemed determined to let time pass without incident, whereas Miriam knew that this danger above all was to be avoided.

What she loved about Simon was his pleasure, his natural effervescence. After a life of minimal satisfactions she discovered, marvelling, that it was possible to be confident, expectant, at ease. Or rather that it was possible for Simon to be all of these things. If one is unaware of fatality it is possible to delight in happy accidents. That was her status, and it suited him perfectly. She supposed that she was an ideal mistress, tactfully present, just as tactfully absent; she also knew that the condition of a mistress was somehow subject to deterioration, that there came a time when reproaches would be aired, or an unseemly curiosity would surface. She was tormented by thoughts of what she did not, could not know: his life away from her. His work she did not take seriously, for it posed no threat. It was his leisure that was so markedly different from her own. Indeed she hardly had any leisure these days; when not at the Library she was involved in a semblance of domesticity, devising light meals that could be easily transported and eaten hastily after they had repaired their disorder. She was naturally fastidious, and a brief shower seemed inadequate preparation for an afternoon of sober study.

Except that sober study was hardly the order of the day, had been overtaken by an inordinate restlessness which applied to almost everything, and, by extension, to everyone, including, sometimes, Simon himself. When a stranger had greeted her in St James's Square and had looked puzzled when his greeting was not immediately registered, it had taken her several seconds to realize that it was the man in the park, Rivers, who was both smiling and frowning at her. Ashamed, she had turned back to him and apologized, had smiled herself, had blamed her absentmindedness. 'Work, you know,' she had offered as an excuse, but it was not true. However untrue, she knew that he would accept it, simply because he lived in a normal world with a normal timetable, in which work was the principal interest of the day. She had detected no waywardness in his pleasant features, nothing to suggest a life bounded by one particular and wholly significant other. In this she measured their incompatibility, without ever knowing a thing about him other than his name.

She was conscious of his eyes on her back, shrugged off his attention irritably, almost ran up the stairs to the Reading Room. Quite simply no other man could compare; there was no room in her life for more than one person. She was in no doubt that this situation was extremely dangerous. She accepted the fact that she was marked for life, and at the same time deplored such insights, tried to work up some criticism of Simon's insouciance, his acceptance of her extremely careful planning—of which he knew nothing, she reminded herself—of the restrictions under which she was obliged to manoeuvre. If he loved her it was because she fitted in with his arrangements; if he loved her it was because she pressed his face against her throat when he felt rueful, out of favour. She knew that these moments were authentic, that in such a charmed life they would feel unbearable. Nothing would have prepared him for regret, bewilderment; his sunny nature was its own defence. She also knew never to speak of such matters, to let the moment pass, and when she judged that it had passed to be as practical and as noncommittal as ever, to vanish, always tactfully, to the bathroom, and to repair to the kitchen to prepare her offering. How sad these moments seemed, when the rules of good behaviour had once more to be observed! Nor did she crave expressions of sentiment, of attachment. She was aware that her feelings ran higher than his own, and therefore must be masked. To offend his sense of ease would be fatal, yet sometimes, in the course of a sleepless night, she would be aware of a whole repertory of hurt feelings, of which she was ashamed. There was no possible reason for him to feel guilty, or for her to feel resentful. What they enjoyed belonged to that category that was not susceptible to argument, to rationalization. This was the very negation of a love affair such as the world approves and which conducts its business beneath indulgent eyes; this was not the sort of affair that leads to an honourable estate. Rather it was its opposite: essentially lawless. Even if she knew him only in one circumstance her knowledge of that circumstance was total. In this she knew she could not be deceived.

And yet there was deception, she was forced to remind herself; he was married. She had seen his son, remembered his little bare feet which she had wanted to touch. If she was free of guilt in this respect she was not free of longing. She imagined him, at the weekends, going home to a friendly house, being met by excited children perhaps, whereas she, on her own, was often puzzled by her solitude. Strange to feel so solitary when her life was so full. Surely the time for such feeling had been before she met him, when she was an untouched observer of other people's follies, and of her own. How diligently she had carried out her tasks, her duties, even her marital duties; none had touched her. Now she was aware of a stream of feeling biding its time until it chose to overflow, if not for Simon's benefit then for another's. She would have to marry again, she saw, in order to preserve this love affair in its strange entirety. Her future husband would benefit from her lack of curiosity about him, for she did not expect ever to love again. Perhaps, she reflected, she wanted the world's approval. Clandestinity, the clandestinity she cherished, had its drawbacks.

But to have to get to know another man, to learn about him with the same fascinated scrutiny, was somehow out of the question. That scrutiny was in the present circumstances more often than not frustrated. She felt an immense and inconvenient curiosity about his life at home, how it was conducted. There was nothing prurient about this. She wanted to know what the rooms of his house were like, what food they ate, whether his parents were still alive. At this point she was conscious of a craven gratitude to her own parents for being unavailable for comparison. She was sure that in any contest his parents would feature as shining and forthright characters, while her own would be imprinted with signs of venality, whereas in fact they had been a pleasant-looking couple before their decline. Nevertheless heredity created dispositions, expectations, and hers had always erred on the side of watchfulness, of wariness. Unable or unwilling to trust, she had conducted her life prudently. She could see no such signs in Simon. She had fallen in love with her exact opposite, one whose approach was, by blessed design, ludic. She had him to thank for an insight to which she had never before been a party. If this were a game it was at least a game in which they were both engaged.

Simon, who woke as easily as he slept, stretched out a hand for his watch, looked at it briefly, said 'Crikey,' then settled back, his arms above his head. She loved to look at him in such moments, which were rare, to admire his beauty, while at the same time adopting a neutral, even critical expression. In a moment, she knew, he would be ready to resume his ordinary life. Except that he did not seem anxious to move, or even to turn to her, to nestle into her neck. She missed that gesture, his unique acknowledgement of her role in a life she could hardly imagine, but would do nothing to solicit it. She sensed an absence in him, wondered if her bunch of flowers had made him irritable, as if she had offered a clumsy tribute in lieu of her usual tact. This would need care. At the same time she thought of her quiche, which they were clearly not going to eat. She would dispose of it without a word, take it home again. This struck her as an unwelcome departure from the norm. She reached over him for his watch, saw with a start that it was after half-past three, that she must have dozed herself, although she was usually preternaturally alert. He put an arm round her, pressed her shoulder briefly, then swung his legs over the side of the bed, and sat there, his head lowered.

'What is it?' she said. 'Is something wrong?'

He turned to face her, a puzzled smile on his face. 'Shall we have some tea?' he said. 'You don't have to rush off, do you?' And he got up, stood in the middle of the floor, brooding.

'Tea,' she said. 'What a good idea. You get dressed. Unless . . . ?'

'Yes, I'd better get dressed,' he agreed. 'Do you want to go first? In the bathroom, I mean.'

'Just give me a minute. Then I'll be in the kitchen.'

In the kitchen she bundled both flowers and food into her Selfridges bag, stowed it in the hall behind her briefcase, went back and made the tea, aware of clothes pulled on too hastily, aware of disorder, of alarm. She sat down, poured herself a cup of tea, drank it too quickly, choked, wiped her mouth, and took her slopped saucer to the sink. Did he mean her to stay? The urgency of the early afternoon had leaked away, into this interval for which there was no precedent. She regretted their normal recovery, hated the bad light in this north-facing kitchen, promised herself that she would cancel the rest of the day, would go straight home, if that was what he wanted her to do. Yet he was in no hurry, it seemed, was not checking his answering service, was, if she could judge it correctly, making one single muffled call. She had no idea how to behave in these changed circumstances, willed her features to remain grave, attentive, as if she were to hear bad news, and would have to deal with it correctly. I should have brought a cake, she thought, or some biscuits; he must be hungry by now.

There was something in his voice on the telephone, which she could only just hear, that disturbed her: it was deliberately low, informal, as if he were speaking to someone he knew so well that there was no need for introductory remarks. She knew, with a lover's fatal instinct, that he was talking to his wife and that this tone was self-explanatory. Yet when he came into the kitchen he was smiling with disarming courtesy, the badge of his kind. She summoned up the same expression, looked at him pleasantly, and poured him a cup of tea.

'You're not going to the office this afternoon?' she asked.

'No, I'm going to Oxford. I've taken a few days' leave.'

'Oh?'

He sat down. 'The thing is, Mary's not too well.'

'Oh, I'm so sorry. What's wrong?'

'I don't know exactly. Something female that I'm thought not to know about. She's bleeding,' he said, his smile faltering for an instant.

'That could be nothing. Break-through bleeding, it's called.' The thought struck her. 'Is she pregnant?'

'She thought she was, and then this started.'

'What does the doctor say?'

'Oh, he's an old friend. He doesn't seem to be worried.' He looked at her. 'Do you know about these things?'

'Not really. I seem to have everything still in place. And I've never been pregnant.'

'How have you managed that?'

'I'm not at all sure. Maybe I can't have children.'

All at once, and for all time, she knew that this was true, and that she had never faced the truth before, had never needed to. The idea of having a child by Jonathan had been out of the question. He was such a child himself that he had never envisaged fatherhood, and had not paid enough attention to his wife to wonder whether she might also be a potential mother. She had at the time been grateful for this, as if he were expendable. Now she began to wonder, thought of the child Fergus, of her longing to clasp his foot, to beguile him, to win him over. She had thought the reason for this was simple: she loved his father. Now she was brought up against the fact that Fergus had a mother, that his mother was still fertile. As she was not.

She was sensible enough to know that this was still a good thing, but grieved to realize that there was no future in her way of life. And, at her age, no present either, for with a child one had a hold on life that was not within her grasp. Motherhood made women into complacent tigers, whereas she could only admire, enquire. She had always been a recipient for confidences, but latterly had been a recipient for confidences about her friends' children. Was this why she avoided them? Having nothing of the same nature to offer in exchange had left her at a loss. She had blamed the friends' tactlessness, had been offended by their lack of reciprocal interest in her life, her activities. Now she wondered if they had sensed her condition, had seen in her slight taut body and her discreet and careful clothes a singularity that they had been spared. She had thought she had detected a certain irritation, a certain resentment at her appearance. What she had taken for resentment was in fact contempt. You are not one of us, said their eyes; you do not slop around untidily, push your hair back behind your ears, dress in the first thing that comes to hand. You do not shop for cornflakes, fish fingers, baked beans. You will not get fat. You do not take family holidays, the car loaded with junk. You only carry a briefcase, look astonishingly young, yet you must be what? getting on, anyway. Too late for you, then. You will just have to make do with the rest of your life, with only yourself for company. And that husband of yours, he was a disappointment too, wasn't he? So tell me, which one of you was unable, no, incapable? You don't mind my asking, do you? After all we are old friends.

This conversation had only taken place once, but it had marked her. She had avoided the erstwhile friend after that, had even remarked to Beatrice on how terrible poor Alexandra had looked, remembering her as a neat schoolgirl with a ponytail, suddenly wondering whether their friendship had always been so slight, or whether it had been broken off all at once. She had been momentarily proud of her appearance, had dressed even more carefully, and yet the incident continued to rankle until time had finally taken care of it. And now it appeared that Mary may have been pregnant: at least that was Simon's natural assumption. Her mind shied away from the implications of this, her own part in these matters reduced to nothing.

One feels no jealousy for a woman who may be sick, only for one who may have been pregnant. She had known that there was something wrong with this afternoon, even before that low voice on the telephone confirmed her unease. Yet even now his face was not tragic; perhaps a little more serious than usual, but not noticeably so.

'Is she in hospital?' she asked, pouring him more tea.

'No, no, nothing like that. She's been told to stay in bed for a bit. She'll be fine.'

'How long will you be away?'

'Oh, a week, ten days. I don't really know.'

'You'll let me know?'

'Of course. I'll give you a ring.'

He looked at her properly, saw her drawn face, and in a moment was by her side, his face buried in her hair.

'Will you still want me?' she managed.

'More than ever,' he said.

With a deep sigh, as if she had been crying for hours, she said, 'Tell me about Mary.'

'Oh, well, we go back a long way, Mary and I. It may be her age, of course. She's older than I am. Forty. That's a bit early, isn't it?'

'I'm sure it's possible.'

She stroked his bronze hair, a gesture she only permitted herself occasionally. She no longer wanted to know about his life at home, away from her; that fantasy had been laid to rest. Now, if she wished, she could imagine it in all its naked intimacy. She had been like a child, dreaming of a happy family. The idea had seemed harmless, as if she were reading a children's story. It was an image which only now convinced her that the players of this particular game were adults, herself unwillingly included.

'Then I'll wait to hear from you,' she said, putting the cups in the sink.

'Leave that. I'll send Sigrid up tomorrow to put the place to rights, change the sheets and so on. You'll be all right?'

'Oh, yes,' she said lightly. 'I'm always all right.'

'You are, aren't you?' he said, his serious expression lifting. 'How do you do it?'

'Why did this happen?'

'Why did what happen?'

'Us.'

He shrugged. 'I don't know. I only know that it did happen and I'm glad of it.'

'You don't perceive a conflict of interests?'

'You think like a woman. Men don't, on the whole.'

No word of love had been exchanged, yet she knew that the unspoken thought was there, that this was not the time to articulate it. If there were to be mutual confessions, of the kind that had never passed between them, then they could only take place if and when they came together again. Until that time she must remain within her role, burdensome as it now appeared to her.

'Try to telephone me,' she said. 'Even before you come back.'

'I will.'

'Won't they miss you at the office?'

'Oh, they're very understanding. My immediate boss is an old family friend. He's always been fond of Mary.'

In his world, she thought, everything connected with everything else. Someone was always there to smooth one's way, in an unearthly form of kinship. She only knew the agency as Max's creation, heard of it only through Beatrice. Now it appeared that it was part of Simon's extended family. Poor hand-kissing Max shrank immediately in importance, was probably tolerated as an amusing outsider who gave himself the airs of an impresario. With Max removed, no doubt by that same old family friend, the business could be conducted in the proper English manner, with full weight given to holidays, long lunches, visits to the tailor, and leaves of absence. She felt a pang of pity for Max, whom she had always disliked, and who thought he was retiring because of his age. He had probably been eased out, had thought of his age only when, bewildered, he had received so many concerned enquiries about his health, had consequently felt unwelcome, had rallied in order to invite everyone to a grand farewell party at the Festival Hall, and then disappeared. Beatrice had gone to that party looking resplendent, not noticeably stricken at the thought of losing Max, simply beguiled by the idea of the party. Beatrice too had her childish moments. It was even doubtful whether she genuinely missed him, whether anyone did. She spared a moment of fellow feeling for Max, like herself dispossessed. In his case there would be an ancient conspiracy theory in place, in her case merely an uncomfortable void. At this particular moment she thought her case the more extreme. Max had managed a resounding departure. That was not within her power. She knew that it would be wiser, as well as more elegant, to take her leave, rather than content herself with evenings by the telephone, as if she were a lovesick girl. She had been a lovesick girl too often twenty years ago. Even then she had never been the first to break it off.

'I'll run you home,' he said, picking up his keys.

'No, no, you get off. You're busier than I am.' She smiled at him. In that moment she felt only love and trust.

'Are you sure?'

'Quite sure.'

She moved forward and kissed him on both cheeks. He put a hand round her head and kissed her hard on the lips.

'Don't forget me,' she said.

'As if.' He kissed her again, and she knew that the affair—the love of her life—was not yet a thing of the past.

But this mood was not sustained once she was out on the street. She walked to the nearest rubbish bin and deposited her plastic bag. She felt, above all, bewilderment, as if without him she did not know how to proceed. Her map was all unmarked, her timetable quite empty. She had never been so aware that they were going to separate homes, that the whole width of darkening London was no longer a measure of distance but a symbolic enclave: beyond it she did not know the lie of the land. She hoped he would not drive too fast, wished, as never before, that she were permitted access to his every action. He had not looked noticeably altered from his former self when they had said goodbye, had looked durable, impatient, even slyly reminiscent, in a way that both comforted and shocked her. He would soon seek to be happy in his own way, whether she were there or not. She knew as much, as she seemed to know everything on this fateful day. His wife, for whom he clearly had the most faithful affection, would know this as well, but would be able to rely on what united them—equality, the sort of closeness she could not emulate. She saw them as part of the same family, in more ways than one, as if they were siblings, and incest the most natural thing in the world. She was, quite simply, an anomaly, blessedly independent, with no ties, and apparently always available.

She stopped to look at her reflection in the window of Marks and Spencer. She saw the sort of neat active outline that enabled her to pass unnoticed in a crowd. Shoppers eddied around her: doors slid open onto harassed women carrying several plastic bags, like the one she had carried earlier. She thought that she could still smell the asparagus quiche on her hands, but surely this was impossible? She went into the store, remembering that she had no food at home. Immediately she, who knew the place intimately, lost her bearings, found herself surrounded by children's shoes and anoraks. Cold meat, she thought tiredly, salad, but could imagine herself eating neither.

In front of her, at the check-out, was a tall pretty girl in her late twenties. The thought came unbidden: she would suit him. Horrified, she wondered if she were now condemned to imagine his desires when she was not there to share them. What they enacted could be enacted by anyone; all that distinguished her from other partners was her silence, her lack of importunity. She did not see this as an advantage. At the end of the day she could not make that telephone call, become incorporated into his world. Exhausted now, she imagined herself as an old lady, in a room somewhere, with no visitors. In that children's book she had imagined herself reading, all endings were happy endings, and only the wicked received their just desserts. She knew that this was not a fate reserved for the wicked, knew too that she was not really a wicked woman, but one whose instincts made her want to surrender her isolation, and to share what wholeness she still possessed.

How had she, a not unintelligent woman in the late twentieth century, when women were supposed to know everything, come to this? But her part was clear; she was committed. She would manage, somehow; there was no sense in which she would be found wanting. She would go home, have a hot bath, wash her hair. And then she would go to bed, and begin her period of waiting. And no one but herself would know what it cost.

———————

CHAPTER TEN

*Y*ou're looking well,' they both lied.

'There are three stages in life,' said Max, rubbing his hands and following Beatrice into the drawing-room. 'Youth, middle age and "You're looking well." Margaret not here?'

'Miriam. No, she's got her own flat now.'

She was grateful for Miriam's absence, for the absence of her usual sardonic gaze. Max, in this new incarnation, was hardly a flattering acquisition, although he had come back, she reminded herself. But he had come back diminished, and moreover wearing an ill-fitting pair of blue jeans, which, together with the Tyrolean hat, had filled her with dismay when she had opened the door to him. Nor did she think he looked well. His face, which bore only a vestige of his habitual crowd-pleasing manner, was both seamed and rubbery, the brownish circles under his eyes more pronounced. Deprived of his official functions he seemed unimportant, as if only work had lent him distinction. But had it been distinction? He had been a fixer, an operator, running be-

tween disparate parties like a matchmaker, with only the dignity
of office lending him a certain eminence. He had been immaculate, scented always with eau de cologne, persuasive, but what had
been truly persuasive about him was his sudden sweet smile of
pleasure when the deal was finalized.

She knew that she had not ranked high in his own professional hierarchy, had accepted her removal with surprising fortitude, a fortitude that was apparently denied him—but then he
had so clearly thought of himself as irreplaceable. He was following hard on her heels, anxious to forgo the preliminaries, to be
seated, with a drink in his hand and the olives within reach, so
that he could start to tell her about his immense disappointment,
the disappointment of a homecoming from which all signs of welcome had been missing. From there he would pass lovingly to
reminiscences of his young years, of his happy home, of his life before the exodus, and even of the house in Kentish Town, where
they had all been so united, his family against the world. That was
what was lost: unity. During the past weeks, once he was installed
in an adequate but unsympathetic service flat in Chelsea, he had
thought of Beatrice not as a woman but as the ideal person to
whom he might recount his life story. He had thought he might
write an account of it, had even bought a loose-leaf notebook at
Ryman's, but then it occurred to him that what the world expected from him was a fully fledged biography, with details of the
illustrious persons he had known, whereas he desired to recall
sweet small incidents, family dignity, unassuming love. No pub-
lisher would be interested in such a thing; refugees' stories were
all too common. The notebook was empty, although he had
thought of a title: *The Statue of Beethoven.* But on the whole it was
too much trouble, and probably too late. Besides, it was easier
simply to talk, and Chelsea was so close. He could now walk to
Wilbraham Place, and did so frequently, sometimes bringing a
bottle of champagne, although he had never known Beatrice to

drink anything stronger than Perrier water. He enjoyed the champagne, enjoyed his comfortable chair (the chairs in his flat were all too small), enjoyed the undemanding female company. It was often quite late when he left, but Beatrice did not seem to mind.

But he did not think she looked well. She looked as though some fundamental alteration had taken place, one of those significant shifts that mark the passage from one age to another. She had put on weight; that at least was evident, and her legs, which had been so elegant, were now thickened. But it was her face that was different, he concluded, eyeing her covertly. The china white complexion was now unclear, even slightly suffused, the round innocent eyes held a hint of judgement, of some withheld amusement. Momentarily he felt ashamed of his frequent visits, as if she might have guessed that he had few friends left. His bottle of champagne, of which he drank two glasses, was a propitiatory gift, to allay suspicion that he was not being universally fêted. He supposed that she threw the rest away, gave no thought to the bottles piling up by her innocent dustbin.

On the face of it they were two old friends who had once had much in common and who even now understood each other perfectly. He discounted the discrepancy in their ages; once past a certain point he considered women ageless. He really considered them sexless. If they had not married, if they were not known to have lovers, they might as well, he thought, be old women. Beyond desire and its complications there stretched a limitless plateau which would know no accidents until death supervened. His eyes, still practised in these matters, discerned that Beatrice was a woman without a man in her life, although she displayed none of the signs of deprivation which had always offended him. She was expertly made up—perhaps a little too much so, but, he reminded himself, the skin altered with age—expertly coiffed, and smelling of some light lemony scent which pleased him. If a woman wore too much scent he deduced that she was trying too hard. Over the years he had learned to identify all the major brands, but never offered any, thinking a woman's adornment her own business. Beatrice, now plump, pleased him by her almost familial resemblance to a German woman. The hair was still blonde, though considerably helped now, he supposed, the expression discreet, worldly. Surely he remembered it as more naïve, unprotected? That had been her most charming attribute, but of course naïveté was out of place in one of her years. How old was she? Fifty, or thereabouts, he supposed. That shocked him slightly. He had known her as a girl, an innocent, had never made love to her for that reason. His experience would have removed her innocence, and something had held him back, some respect, that and the younger sister's watchful eye. He congratulated Beatrice silently on her maturity, congratulated himself for having left her intact all those years ago, when she had been so much more enticing. Those expectant eyes might have attracted men, but not for long. He supposed that a number of men, like himself, had shaken their heads, and had walked away.

He thought that she must possess some experience, otherwise she would not be surveying him with such scepticism. At least he supposed that it was scepticism; it might have been amusement, but he did not want to think about that. Her lovers would have been undistinguished, he assumed, not dangerous like himself, and therefore compromised. Whoever they had been, and he was convinced that they all belonged in the past, they had not conquered her, had not left their mark on her. He remembered her as a girl who loved love stories, and who had only been offered simulacra. At least that was what he deduced. He had always had sympathy for women, knowing how hard it was for men to take them seriously. Taking them seriously meant sacrificing one's liberty, even one's thoughts, which would henceforth be anxious. He had taken walks in London since his return to England (there was little else to do) and on Sundays had witnessed family outings with amazement. These people were young, yet they were complacent, as if the main part of their lives were concluded, and the badly behaved children accompanying them were their certificate of good behaviour. Beatrice, at least, had never succumbed to that vulgar temptation, although there could have been few inducements to remain unpartnered. A woman like that, vulnerable, would suffer on her own; she would miss a man's attentions, miss everything about a man except his sexual curiosity. In fact with such a woman a man would feel little curiosity, knowing that beneath the obedience and the flattery lay something rueful, untouched. She had conquered her disappointment, for he did not doubt that she was disappointed. Soon, if she were not very careful, she would reflect some of the younger sister's cynicism. He did not want that to happen.

Appreciatively he looked round the drawing-room, which she had made so attractive. The pale yellow walls, the darker yellow silk curtains, the Indian red of their armchairs, were a pleasant contrast to his pallid service flat, with its slit of a kitchen and damp bathroom. At least his towels were always damp, as, he feared, were some of his clothes. He had taken the flat in a hurry, maddened by his brother's minimal interest in any sort of comfort. He had been hungry for days, until he had discovered a small café which did breakfasts. After muesli and weak tea with Michael he could tuck in to croissants and coffee as warm and sweet as mother's milk, before emerging reluctantly to face the day. Looking for a flat had been a form of tourism; he had settled on one rather than on any of the others because of a moment of discouragement, and because his feet were tired. He had always had it in mind to move on, to find something more permanent. The advantage of his present horrible flat was that there was furniture of a rudimentary kind and a porter behind a desk at the entrance.

Any thought he may have had of looking up old friends was quickly abandoned; no one should see how he was now living. In fact the unwelcome thought struck him that he was now more of an exile than he had been in any of his previous manifestations. Whereas this flat, on the other hand, would suit him perfectly. He thought he might even manage with Beatrice there, unless of course she could be persuaded to go and live with her sister. If not they might be able to come to some arrangement. He wondered whether he could avoid marrying her. He was not a marrying man, considered his family background as celibate, despite the arrangements that he and Michael and Addie had enjoyed. But that was because no one had measured up . . . At his age he felt a mild distaste for sex, felt returned to a prelapsarian inactivity which did not displease him. Marriage would have no meaning unless it were a contract thoroughly understood by both parties. He thought that he might make Beatrice amenable to this, explaining that he would offer his protection in return for her services. He rather regretted the necessity for this, but his surroundings were so pleasant that he thought the difficulties could be overcome.

And the sister had moved out. That was the major difficulty removed, though he did not doubt that he could have relocated her himself. She could have had his service flat, he thought, until he remembered that she had already found a flat of her own. Surprising, that: obviously a man involved. He had always suspected her of arrangements similar to his own. Similar, that is, to his past arrangements. Now, he reminded himself, he was on the verge of quite another.

Beatrice was quite aware of what was passing through Max's mind. He intended her to take the place of his sister, Addie, of whose sad deterioration she had heard rather too much. She did not care for stories of other people's illnesses these days, being slightly preoccupied with her own health. She had had another of those frightening absences this very evening, shortly before Max's arrival. She had been at her dressing-table, looking into the glass, when for a moment she had seen two reflections. She had carefully put down the earring in her right hand but had misjudged the distance; the earring had fallen onto the floor. She had sat still as a stone until her vision cleared. Then, with a great effort (but her heart was beating strongly, too strongly), she had stayed there until she saw her familiar face again, not noticeably altered. She had blushed, a dark burning blush, as if she had been caught out in some agonizing misdemeanour.

It had even been quite reassuring to know that Max was coming. If she were ill he would know what to do, as she did not. She did not particularly want to see him, least of all to listen to his reminiscences. But she had to admit that there was some prestige in having him as a regular visitor. 'Celebrating again,' had observed the ever-vigilant but otherwise disappointing Mrs Anstruther, as she deposited yet another empty champagne bottle. That was Max's only value to her these days, although like most women of her old-fashioned type she liked to think of a man's presence, however inattentive he may have been, as an advantage. She had noted his eyes appraising the flat, knew that he found it to his liking, wondered what it would be like if he were to move in. She could hardly suggest it, nor did she really desire it. It was simply that she had come to realize and to understand the lure of convention, of turning the tables on Mrs Anstruther and her kind, for she would of course insist on marriage, which had always eluded her. She had once considered her life to be too picturesque for any routine coupling, such as that which her sister had known with her unlamented husband, had thought she was destined for some kind of stardom, until reality had put in a late appearance in her life. But latterly she had understood that women such as herself, brooding, unschooled, did not have too many choices, that clever women saw compromise as reasonable, unless they were fortunate enough to marry when they were young and ardent.

She had been ardent herself, until she was rather forcibly reminded that she was no longer young, had sought to ally herself with the heroines of novels rather than with the practical business of finding a partner, still preferred stories in which a long ordeal is crowned with a happy outcome. Of her failed expectations only her sister knew, and characteristically blamed her choice of reading. But Miriam's face had remained closed, weary, throughout the years of her marriage (five! How had she lasted that long? thought Beatrice, with an access of sympathy), which merely confirmed her suspicion that a loveless marriage was worth exactly as much or as little as her own hopes, failed, certainly, but still intact.

And if anything were to go wrong Max would certainly look after her. He would be forced to, but in addition he had a background of genuine family obligations, a sort of family decency which would win through, however reluctantly. As against this there was a certain peace in living alone, in not having to conceal or subdue certain intimate noises, in walking about without shoes when her mysteriously swollen feet pained her . . . She would be condemned to keeping up appearances, when appearances even now were a burden. On the other hand they could go on holiday. She had never felt comfortable when travelling alone, thought it unfair that she should have to carry a bag, stand in queues, conduct all the wearisome business unassisted, and in the end so desolate that fine buildings, majestic scenery were as nothing compared with her discomfort at sitting at a table for two and explaining that she was on her own, while the extra covers were removed and the exaggeratedly long wait for food condemned her to polite inactivity.

He could take her back to France. Maybe he could take another flat, might even be able to relieve the film producer of the original flat in Monaco. He might not want to do any of this, of

course, but perhaps it was time that her own wishes were to prevail. She had seen women of her physical type, still impressive, become even more decorative when they were in a position to issue
orders, to voice desires. She had a distinct vision of them both,
whiling away idle days in the south of France, Max old, gloomy,
but resigned, herself cynical, frivolous, and—at last—unfeeling.

She longed to be relieved of the burden of feeling she had carried for so many years, her hopes of love all gone, manhandled or
ignored by men with whom she had been timidly obsessed, and
who had passed her over for some other woman, or rather girl, for
she had been a girl herself then. She still could not believe her lack
of success, though she had participated obediently in many minor
adventures. But she had never deluded herself, and at last she
knew that she would have to fall into the compromise that she
was beginning to glimpse. It would be fairly unbecoming, like all
compromises, but she would gain dignity in the eyes of the world.

They would live abroad, she decided; she had had enough of
filling the days in London. And he was her only hope. No matter
that he would want to settle down here, in Wilbraham Place.
Miriam could move back, and so could she, when she was a
widow, as she had no doubt she would be. That was another attraction. Max could fulfil his masculine function by providing her
with an escort, a status. And then she could leave his body behind,
in Monaco, if necessary, and come home to a chorus of approval,
the approval that she had been used to at the beginning of her career and which was now so conspicuously lacking. And he knew
her, that was an added advantage, had known her when she was
young. Now was the time for him to enact the devotion he had always protested he felt for her, and which she had never taken seriously.

'Addie was such a lovely girl,' he was saying, having dealt
with the matter of Beatrice, or rather having postponed it for future consideration. Time was on his side; there was no need to

rush matters. It was not as if either of them were going anywhere. He would simply get her into the habit of looking forward to his visits, which he would increase, until he looked in (he still thought of it as 'looking in') every evening. Then he would stay away for a week or two, a tactic which had always proved successful in the past. He did not doubt that she would miss him, would become alarmed, would wonder if she had paid him too little attention, for women of Beatrice's type always blamed themselves. Then he would press his advantage, would suggest a merger of some kind, an amalgamation of both their assets. And no need to look for a place to live, or to discuss money, of which, presumably, they both had enough. Since his travelling days were over he would fill his time agreeably in this city which had long been his home, would take reminiscent walks, while Beatrice occupied her days with the hairdresser or the dressmaker, might start to invite a few friends again, since he knew that she would always be an excellent hostess. And when the time came (but not yet!) she would undoubtedly nurse him with care, would see that he never lacked comfort, would not deteriorate. His health was good; he felt like a young man. And almost gleeful, as if he had glimpsed the solution to all his problems.

'My uncle August, our uncle I should say, kept an apartment here, you know, in George Street, for when he came over on business. He was a family hero, or rather legend, because he lived in such a lordly manner, servants and such. And a white silk scarf with his dinner jacket. Many ladies. August Gruber was a famous ladies' man. And yet I think he was in love with my mother, who smilingly kept him at arms' length. Women knew how to do that in those days. They seem to have lost the art.'

'Maybe they were glad to lose it,' said Beatrice sombrely.

'You're not serious?'

'Quite serious. Women employ other arts these days, Max. They take what they want.'

'You sound quite regretful,' he said with surprise, bringing his attention to bear on her for a moment. 'But of course you are joking. I'm sure you have nothing to regret!' He laughed comfortably, thinking he was paying her a compliment.

'I know women better than you do, Max. Do help yourself, by the way,' she said, indicating the three-quarters empty dish of olives.

'Thank you. I know women too, Beatrice. Don't forget . . .'

'Oh, of course, you are a man,' she said negligently. It was as if she had said that she had momentarily forgotten that he was a man. He refused to meet her eye, suspecting that he might discover something inimical there. He had no intention of entering into a discussion about men and women, having discovered from past experience that this usually led to hostilities. It was a pity that she still had views on such matters, when she was past the age when such views could be stimulating.

Beatrice rather wished that he would leave. She was tired now; indeed she was always tired by his reminiscences, which served to reduce her to his audience. She would be better off in bed, reading *Jane Eyre* for the eighth or ninth time, and urging Jane silently not to settle for St John Rivers, when she was so clearly imprinted for life with the image of another man. Not that Mr Rochester was a better man, far from it; he was worse in every respect. That was the point. Jane clearly knew the value of a reprobate in a woman's life, and thus won the approbation of every woman reader. She had never known one herself, although she suspected that like Miriam she would succumb immediately if one were ever to be drawn into her orbit. Or rather she into his. She hoped there was a way out for Miriam, who might turn her back on feeling if things went wrong, as they surely would. She telephoned as frequently as ever, but gave little news of herself. Beatrice suspected that there was little to give. Curiously enough she had mentioned someone called Rivers, the man in the park, as she thought of him. He had asked her out for a drink, for lunch, but so far she had heard nothing more. If Miriam could be persuaded to look on him more kindly than Jane had looked on her Mr Rivers then something might be saved. But Beatrice knew that in this matter Miriam was like herself, though she denied it. Mr Rochester, preferably undamaged, would be the one she would seek out, would not even have to seek out, for men of Mr Rochester's stamp arrange matters to their own satisfaction. That, in a world of half-hearted pursuits, was their particular virtue.

Apart from her necessary participation in urging Jane on to her apotheosis there was the little matter of her health to be considered, which she could only do safely when she was in bed. Feeling quite well now, aided no doubt by a rush of impatience and practicality, she dismissed that strange brief attack as a moment of inattention, or rather of disorientation. There was no need to panic; it had only lasted a few minutes. This was an additional reason to make changes, to put her health into someone else's care. Her gift to Miriam would be to keep her in ignorance. Maybe she too would die in Monaco, which would spare Miriam the tiresome necessity of having to take charge. Monaco might be an unsympathetic setting for such an eventuality; she would insist that they move to Nice, where there was a British library. She could see herself quite clearly walking down the rue de France, with Max trailing glumly behind her. She would become another sort of woman there, demanding, self-indulgent, making up for all the polite eager days when she had asked for nothing but to be overwhelmed and taken into somebody's care. No man had answered the challenge, though she had never seen herself as a challenge, leaving that role to the sparky cruel women she read about in the magazines at the hairdresser's. How they honed their skills, these women, knew what to do both in and out of bed, were told what to wear, where to go, how to proceed, in short! She had never had these skills, had simply turned beseeching eyes on one unavailable lover or another. Her innocent expectations had been the challenge, one to which few were likely to respond. And she was no longer young, when her eyes had been at their best. She reminded men of their mothers, their sisters, as indeed she was doing at this very moment.

'Why did you never marry?' she asked, bringing matters back to the present.

He reflected. 'I lived for pleasure,' he said finally. 'I had a young man's urges well into middle age. I loved the start of the thing, hated the thought of denying myself. And I knew how to please. I discovered that my looks were no handicap. I felt like a king,' he said, soberly now. 'I felt I had carte blanche.'

She saw him for the first time as an eager ugly young man, refining on his expertise, hardly able to believe his luck. And having been lucky, unwilling to renounce a gift that must have seemed innate, as if at any minute his looks might reclaim him, relegate him to the ranks of the unsought. He had learned to supplement his gifts with extravagance, with generosity, and always with naked impetuosity. Now he was an old man, with an old man's consideration for his health, his welfare. But just as she was now unlikely to benefit from any man's impetuosity she felt at last that she was able to envisage the way ahead.

'So you settled for a series of affairs,' she said.

He smiled. 'I didn't settle for anything, Beatrice. I took what I wanted.'

'Were you never lonely?'

'Oh, of course I was lonely. Sometimes I went back to my house and wondered about that. But then I would get on the telephone and sooner or later the game was on again.'

'You never missed anyone?'

'What I missed was all in the past.'

There was a brief silence. 'And you? You never married either.'

'No I never married. I was too needy. I wanted love.'

'Ah, yes. Love.' His tone was polite, as if they were discussing an illness. 'And now?'

'Now I am much more sensible,' she said briskly. 'Now I too live in the present. It's not a bad life, I suppose. Dull, of course. But at least I'm free. That is quite an advantage.'

'It is,' he agreed, ignoring the desolation that was part of his own freedom. 'You can always count on me, Beatrice,' he said, perceiving her sadness.

'I know I can. Dear Max.'

They were back in their roles, after having come dangerously near to self-exposure. He was devoted, and she was susceptible. That was the way to proceed, unless both wished to go deeper, as they so nearly had this evening. This way was better. He stood up, took both her hands.

'We've had a good talk, haven't we?'

'Very good.'

'I'll look in again, shall I? What are your plans?'

'Oh, I'm fairly flexible. Give me a ring. What is it?'

'My hat. What did you do with my hat?'

'It's in the hall. But surely you don't need it? It's nearly May, after all.'

'I shall buy myself a panama. Father had one. Did I tell you?'

'Yes, you did.'

'Goodnight then, dear.'

'You must have a meal next time you come.'

His face brightened. 'I'd like that.'

'I'll roast a chicken. We can eat it cold.'

'How will you cook it?' he asked hungrily, being condemned to eating out.

'I'll stuff it with lemons. And make a rice salad with lemon juice and herbs.'

He kissed her fingers. 'I shall look forward to that.'

It was a terrible thing to deprive a man of his work, his contacts, she thought, as she washed up the glasses, even worse than it was for a woman. Max, whom she liked to remember as prestigious, was now futile, living the life of any old-age pensioner. She imagined him trotting out in the morning, in his now dreadful clothes, and after breakfast wondering how to fill the day. As she did. And yet her life, unlike his, had a strange consistency, perhaps because she did not dwell on the past. She could hardly imagine herself now, in her black dress, smiling discreetly behind the piano. Now she thought of the future, of that absurd vision of sauntering through the streets of Nice, with Max at her side. Yet something united them: the urge to disappear, as if in disgrace. To judge from Max's experience this did not work. At least it had not worked for him. But she too had tired of her empty days, grateful to them only for submitting her to no future tests. She had surrendered entirely to changed circumstances, been written off by her friends. Indignation, long buried, struggled to the surface. She did not hold Max responsible for this, but rather the audience, that unseen audience whose criticisms—unheard, totally imaginary—had for so long existed at the back of her mind. It would be no bad thing to spring a surprise. And maybe respect would come at last. Respect: that was the thing, and she now knew how to acquire it.

---

CHAPTER ELEVEN

*M*iriam had a terrible dream. She dreamt that she had offended Simon in so naked, so direct, so personal a manner that he would never speak to her again. As proof of this she was presented with a book which opened at a photograph of him looking noble and disapproving. The book was written in praise of his achievements, of which she knew nothing. She supposed that these achievements had to do with his life in Oxford. She was working in some kind of office in which she was markedly unpopular. So unpopular was she that from time to time it was decreed by her fellow workers that she go to France for the day. This she did, choosing not one of the Channel ports but a small town in the centre of France which was unfamiliar to her. Its name, which she saw on a signpost, was Colombier something: Colombier le Neuf, or even Colombier le Vieux. As soon as she was there she had to make the return journey in order to get back to the office, but there were no trains. The area was somehow cordoned off, owing to the presence of national television studios: she could see vast cranes and banks of lights, but no people. She supposed that this was because she had arrived on a Monday, when everything was closed.

She knew that she had to get back because some kind of office party was due to take place in the evening, and for which she was already dressed, in a white rayon suit with a cumbersome skirt. Arriving too early for the party she was met with the usual disapproval. Silently, tight-lipped, one of her colleagues placed the book containing Simon's photograph in front of her. She spent the rest of the dream, and what seemed like the rest of the night, contemplating his severe handsome face. The face now seemed to radiate a look of disdain, but from time to time someone would sidle up, look over her shoulder, and express admiration. She alone did not know him in this guise. When she woke up she wondered how much she had ever known him, whether he were in fact some sort of hero. This seemed likely. In that case her own status was, and always had been, that of a lowly office worker who would not naturally come into contact with so exalted a being. This impression, together with the dream, of which she remembered every detail, persisted into the following day.

She knew why this was. She had heard nothing from him for three, no, she reminded herself, nearly four weeks. From this she deduced that Mary was seriously ill, was bleeding to death, had cancer, that Simon was devotedly at her bedside, was consoling the children. Perhaps she was already dead—but there had been no notice in *The Times,* which she scrutinized every day. Death seemed so normal, so routine in those columns, that she lingered over them, fascinated by the children, grandchildren, sisters and brothers the deceased left behind. Always there was reference to the devoted wife or husband, now bereft, and details of the funeral, 'at which all are welcome'. Through Directory Enquiries she had obtained the number of the house in Norham Gardens, but knew that she would never use it. The most she could do was leave a message on his answering machine in Bryanston Square. The problem was what sort of a message to leave. Her own anxiety would seem out of place compared to what his must be. The idea came to her that it would be in order for her to signal her own absence, and, perhaps guided by the dream, she resolved to go to Paris for a few days.

There was no reason for her to do this. She had had no work for the past few weeks and would have none until November, when the literary prizes were announced. On the other hand she kept a room there, in the Avenue des Ternes, and might just as well while away time in the Avenue des Ternes as in Lower Sloane Street, along which the buses seemed to grind more noisily than ever in this dusty undecided summer. But in fact the whole reason for going to Paris, in which she would be equally unoccupied, was so that she could leave an airy but sober message on Simon's answering machine, as if there had been no silence, merely mutual preoccupation which had kept them out of contact for a while. That preoccupation would, of course, be soon ended.

She took some time composing this message. In the end all she said was: 'In Paris. Back on the 28th.' Even to her own ears the message sounded unconvincing. To give it some validity she would indeed have to absent herself, maybe bring back something typical, cheese or wine, signal some sort of cosmopolitanism, with droll stories of her neighbours in the Avenue des Ternes. He would be amused, as always, would lose the severe look he had had in the imaginary photograph and which she had never seen in real life, and they would have recaptured their original intimacy through the sole agency of her having gone to Paris. This seemed to her eminently reasonable.

It did not seem so to Beatrice, whom she was obliged to attend the following day. Beatrice was at her dressing-table, trying on and discarding necklaces and earrings, peering forward to smooth her eyebrows, stretching her mouth to apply a swathe of lipstick. Beatrice appeared to be rehearsing for some sort of audition, as if she were being called upon to play a part, even a leading role, in some scenario which she was improvising, as it were, in her dressing-room.

'You're going with St John Rivers, I take it,' she said finally, capping her lipstick.

'Please don't call him that, Beatrice. His name is Tom, and I hardly know him.'

'Pity,' said Beatrice, glancing approvingly at her three-quarter profile. 'Have you time for coffee?'

Humbly she followed Beatrice into the kitchen, humbly accepted a cup of coffee. She felt as if she were back in that imaginary office, with those disapproving colleagues. She had never worked in an office, had often wished to do so, thinking they must be convivial places, filled with pot plants and collegiate female chatter, though the only office she knew was that of her agency in Paris, staffed by disdainful immaculate girls who rarely met her eye because they were staring at their computer screens, and displaying few signs of conviviality. She imagined these girls, who must have been born adult, sweeping out to lunch, to dinner, on the arms of ever-changing escorts and complaining about their domestic obligations while downing glass after glass of wine and never getting drunk. Although her work was by all accounts excellent she always felt timid when handing it over, largely for some extraneous reason, such as a sudden realization that her skirt was too long or that her hair needed cutting. Catherine or Eliane would appraise her in one swift scan, say, *'Chic. On va être content,'* take the manuscript from her, and the exchange would be completed. She realized that the cumbersome white skirt she had worn in the dream was a reflection of all the garments suddenly perceived as unsuitable under the searchlight of the French gaze, although when she had left home she had been quite content with her appearance, and indeed, once out in the street, she met with glances which were far from actively disapproving. She resolved, as always, to do better, but was, as always, unsure as to how this improvement might be effected.

She was still unsure. She had spent her few weeks of inactivity in searching for new clothes, renewing herself in some more modish image. This too had proved unsatisfactory. She had bought a jacket and two light dresses, neither of which found favour with Beatrice. Even now she tried to hide as much of herself as possible behind the kitchen table, aware that her new olive green shift would be creased when she stood up. She would travel in it, she supposed; if she could get the creases out. In time she might look in to the office in the rue Soufflot, just to wish them a cheery 'Bonjour,' and to remind them of her existence. This was otiose, she knew; she would be met with blank looks from behind the computers, to which eyes would return a second later. She would then be free to spend the time exactly as she wished, which was to count the hours until returning home. Her loveless marriage had had one advantage: it had made her meticulous in the exercise of her duties. It now seemed to her that her life had been all duty, that even this artificial journey to Paris was a duty, and the reason she was undertaking it was simply that she would feel uncomfortable if caught out in a lie, though it would be a harmless lie and would cause confusion to no one but herself.

'That colour doesn't suit you,' said Beatrice. 'You need something light, white or cream.'

But the skirt in the dream had been white, and had impeded her walk. Her legs, she saw now, as if she were unrolling a film of her dream, had been covered in unbecoming dark stockings, with several snagged threads. On her feet she had worn an old pair of black shoes, like those kept in the hall cupboard by Mrs Kinsella. All attempts to persuade her to carry these with her in her holdall had failed, and they remained in the hall cupboard, together with her spare cardigan and headscarf. Beatrice had had to remove certain articles of her own, as if they might be affronted—as she herself certainly was—by possible identification with Mrs Kinsella's effects. Visitors' overcoats now had to be laid on Beatrice's bed. Hats (but nobody but Max wore a hat these days) could be left on the hall table.

'So tell me about your Mr Rivers,' she was now saying. 'Is he—how shall I put it?—courting you? Favouring you with his attentions?' Miriam, glumly, supposed that he was. Twice he had nonchalantly entered the Reading Room and taken her off to lunch. Obeying an impulse dating from her early adolescence, when their mother had schooled both girls in the arts of discouragement, she had tried to dissuade him, but was forced to follow him outside the Reading Room in order to do this. A slight twitch of a newspaper had informed her that silence was in order.

'I am really grateful to you for this lunch,' she had said on the last occasion. 'I was awfully hungry. But I don't want you to get the wrong idea.'

'What idea would that be?' he had asked, smiling.

'That I am a decent person. I am quite underhand, really. Pedantic, disagreeable.'

He laughed, his pleasant face radiating genuine amusement. 'And how did you become all of these things?' he asked. 'Was it your cruel husband? Women usually blame men, don't they? At least the women I know do.'

'Oh, my husband was quite innocent. Anyway I've practically forgotten about him. You see? That's hardly the sort of remark a decent woman would make. No,' she said, suddenly serious. 'I think it was being left alone again. I think I told you that he went to Canada? I didn't miss him, but without him my life was somehow no longer a matter of record. Does that sound stupid?'

He shook his head, his expression as serious as her own.

'The days went by, and I felt they had no significance. No markers. I had to get on with them by myself. And my thoughts were not good company.'

'That's why you were walking in the rain on Christmas Day?'

But she remembered glancing up at the windows in Bryanston Square, felt shame and anguish, looked at her watch, exclaimed at the time, and said she must get back.

'All right,' he said quietly. 'But you're going to tell me about it one day, you know. When will you let me take you out to dinner?'

She was grateful to him for his gentleness, which she had not expected from one so well set up, so ruddy-faced, so generally at ease. She could see that he was attractive to women, although she herself was not attracted. She appreciated him as a harmonious feature of the landscape, but felt no curiosity or desire to know him further. All physical feelings belonged to her knowledge of Simon, to memories of his naked figure striding unselfconsciously round the bedroom, as he picked up the telephone and reconnected himself with the outside world. At the same time she felt an edge of animosity. She was newly aware that he had not telephoned, that she had no news of him and that she was unfair in concentrating on her own reactions when in Oxford a tragic scenario may have been unfolding, that the house in Norham Gardens might be hushed, alien, invaded by nurses, that children might be bewildered, and Simon harassed and impotent, as she had never seen him. She even envied poor Mary such moments of intimacy as surely must pass between them, castigated herself for her monstrous reactions, and realized that she would have to go to Paris if only to annul her own feelings of shame. When she returned she would surely be a better person, as receptive to his life and what she knew of it as she had ever been. In this way she thought that the least she could do was to go away, for his sake if not her own.

'I'll be back at the weekend,' she told Beatrice. 'I'll ring up when I get there. Though I don't like to use her phone too much.'

'I don't see why not,' said Beatrice. 'You practically pay for the thing, don't you?'

The arrangement in the Avenue des Ternes was a mutually profitable one. She paid a minimal annual rent for what was in reality the run of a substantial flat. The woman from whom she rented the room looked on her as an assurance against burglars, malefactors, and any representatives of an official body alerted by the *gardienne*. She was an elderly eccentric, with relatives in Egypt and Turkey, whom she visited on a regular basis, fearless in every respect except one: that her son, with whom she had fallen out long ago, and who had gone to the bad, might emerge from the latest in a series of prison sentences, and come home. Miriam had been instructed as to how to deal with this. She was to present herself as the new owner, returned to France only recently after her husband's death in a foreign posting. She was to say that she had no idea where Mme Bertin had gone, but had heard that she was no longer in the country.

The son had in fact once turned up, and had not been easily routed. He had lounged against the jamb of the open front door for some fifteen minutes, looking suitably disreputable, until steps had been heard coming up the stairs, at which he had unexpectedly detached himself and disappeared. She deduced from this that someone was looking for him, and told Mme Bertin so when she next returned from Cairo. '*Tant mieux,*' said Mme Bertin, removing her large felt hat and giving it a knock or two. Her ancient lips had worked reflectively, but within half an hour she was on the telephone to a cousin in Davos and promising her a visit. Miriam assumed that she would be welcome precisely because the son was an object of excited speculation among those safely removed from any possibility of his reappearance, and because Mme Bertin was so peripatetic that she would soon be on her way. Money was handed over to the *gardienne,* a purely business arrangement, rather like paying the rent. Mme Bertin explained Miriam away as her late husband's niece. This deceived no one.

The apartment in the Avenue des Ternes was dustily appointed, in a way which did not detain Miriam's interest. She was aware of spindly pieces of furniture in an unvisited salon, but generally kept to her own room, where she now supposed she could hole up for a few days. Apart from this she had no idea how she was to spend her time, but time without the possibility of seeing Simon did not much matter. She suspected that Beatrice was aware of this, but Beatrice in her new incarnation, as if she herself were planning to move on, chose not to dwell on it. They kissed abstractedly and parted with mutual admonitions to take care. This too was felt by Miriam to be inadequate, but she was grateful not to be asked further questions. She went home and put a few things into a small bag, feeling at a loss without her ordinary tasks to occupy her. The telephone message was what counted. The rest was unimportant.

It was the silence that was so insupportable, not so much the breaking of their usual connection as the breaking of any connection at all. He had never been out of contact for so long, had previously always warned her if he had to leave London. In vain she summoned up that picture of a household in disarray, but by force of repetition this image was losing its potency. And her inability to sustain the silence was beginning to tell on her. Outwardly as controlled as ever, she had started to suffer small accidents, had snagged a finger badly on the wire of a supermarket basket, had stubbed her foot on the kerb in Sloane Street. These injuries were symbolic of her new disarray, all the more worrying in that they were only noticeable by herself: the bleeding finger, the bruised foot . . . Both were slow to heal. And there was another problem. A new tenant had moved into the flat next door, an Italian woman who left bags of rubbish on the landing, and when gently guided to the dustbins in the courtyard laughingly agreed and did the same thing all over again. The possibility that she might have to move if she wanted to avoid this daily detritus was becoming very real, as was the impossibility of looking for another flat. She could move back to Wilbraham Place, of course, but Beatrice might not be happy about this. Beatrice, she sensed, wished for the time being to be unobserved, and although this had suited her in the recent past it no longer did so. Those long hours without occupation would have been agreeably filled by a familiar presence. As it was she wished for company, and had failed to find it. No suggestion had come from Beatrice, and she was so unsure of her welcome anywhere that she would not venture it herself.

These thoughts occupied her so completely that she reached the Gare du Nord without being aware of the journey. She took the Metro to St-Germain-des-Prés with her last ticket, and wondered whether this was symbolic. Once she was separated from Simon by distance as well as by time she felt worse rather than better, realized anew that this whole enterprise had been artificial, an error. She went into a small restaurant in the rue Saint-Benoît and ordered a tomato and mozzarella salad and a bottle of water. The arrangement on her plate, when it arrived, was sparse, not to say ironic. This was another change. She remembered from her student days that she could rely on this place for substantial though slapdash meals and that it had been popular with young people like herself. Now the only other diners seemed to be Japanese. And as well as being hungry she was sure that she had lost weight. That perhaps was why her new clothes failed to fit her properly. She felt alarmed, out of sorts, knew she could not quite face the silence of the flat in the Avenue des Ternes, resolved in that moment to return to London on an evening train. No one would know, no one would blame her. She would eat her lunch, take a walk in the Luxembourg Gardens, and then change her ticket and go home unobserved.

The resolution calmed her, though she knew it was deplorable. That it was correct was proved by her renewed sense of purpose once she was out in the air. For the first time she was indifferent to the blandishments of the city she had always loved.

The weather was grey, mild, overcast. The summer exchange of inhabitants for tourists had not yet taken place, yet there was an impalpable slackening of pace, of attention, as if families were counting the days until they could get in the car and head south or east. Catherine and Eliane and their kind would in due course be revealed as normal people, obedient wives, harassed mothers; habitual quarrels and gratifications would replace austere professional performances. She abandoned the thought of visiting the rue Soufflot, just as she had abandoned the Avenue des Ternes. Both suddenly seemed to belong to a past phase of her existence. Resignedly she dragged an iron chair on to the terrace in the Luxembourg Gardens. That was where the mothers sat, while their children ran off to play. Occasionally a wheeled infant would attract admiration from a normally tight-lipped populace. *'Minou, Minou,'* an exceptionally outgoing character might murmur. The baby would gaze back with the same indifferent French stare. No currying favour there!

She wished that she had brought something to read, but books no longer detained her in the same way. As girls she and Beatrice had read voraciously, seeking alternatives to their restricted lives. As she thought back to those silent days her heart constricted with sympathy. What chance had she and Beatrice had of applying their piecemeal insights, their imperfect information? Simultaneously exalted and repressed, they were disabled for the conduct of ordinary life, as lived by more fortunate women. And their parents must have laboured under the same handicap, so that what was passed on was ignorance, until the innocence that had once pertained was spoiled by disappointment. The daughters had done their best, had embraced the world eagerly, too eagerly, failed to make simple connections or even to exercise a choice. Her own marriage had been effected by a desperate resolution which no longer took love into account. Until nine months ago she had not known true love, and because of that she was marked for life. That was the tragedy of her situation, and no amount of valiant reason would prevail in the light of this alarming fact.

To be marked for life . . . To remain for ever alert for the sight of a particular figure, the turn of a particular head. She knew that this was to be her fate, whether she saw him again or not. Frightened by the idea that the mystery of his silence might never be solved by something so simple as an explanation, face to face, she nevertheless felt that the moment for such an explanation had already passed. Time had taken care of it: to return to the original cause would now be redundant. If, given the opportunity, she persisted in asking questions, he would look puzzled, irritated, as if he had already given an explanation, or explanations, to others, in answer to kindly and legitimate enquiries. She suddenly wondered whether she had given him both telephone numbers. Beatrice would certainly take a message, but it was just as well that she had not prepared Beatrice for such an eventuality. Once innocent, she must now feign innocence. 'Did anyone call?' she would ask in due course. 'I left this number while I was away. You don't mind, do you?' And Beatrice would not mind, as long as she had no inkling of these machinations. For to offend Beatrice's good faith as well as her own would be unthinkable. She began to perceive fissures in the natural order. That order was, or should be, composed of expectation and fulfilment. Surely it was not in the interest of the Almighty, or whatever prime mover one promoted as a substitute, to recreate chaos out of order?

It was past midsummer day; from now on the light would fade a little earlier each evening. The sky above her, in the Luxembourg Gardens, was still grey, undisturbed, but the mothers were packing up and leaving, their children summoned back from the distant playground. Although no dramatic change was visible, a smell of cut grass, which she had not previously noticed, stole towards her, alerting her to the arrival of fresher air. When the park had emptied she made her way back to the busy streets, had to wait a long time for coffee to be brought, and at last, spurred by the imminence of departure, was able to behave like an ordinary visitor, rather than as an exile. She bought a couple of books, which would take their place on the pile by her bedside, and perhaps at some time in the future, when this enormous upheaval had been put aside, she would have the patience to read.

When she knew she must make her way to the station she picked up the bag which she had carried about with her all day, and was able to envisage the thought of her silent return with a modicum of impatience. Though it might be shabby it would mean wasting no more time, although time was the one commodity which she had in abundance. On the train, calmed, as always, by the journey, by the silence of the evening landscape, by the lights that appeared and disappeared, by another train passing with a whine in the opposite direction, she was even able to give a thought to Tom Rivers. How tolerable the day would have been if spent in his company, how agreeable the indeterminate hours! He was sweet-natured, undemanding, seemed genuinely interested in her life, seemed to regard her as a piece of research he might one day decide to undertake seriously. And she had asked him so few questions about himself, feeling preoccupied even in his company. And he had sought her out. He was a temptation which she might one day be too tired to resist. But until that day her life was unfinished business, which she alone would have to tolerate. She wondered who was the first to frame the concept of suffering in silence. At Waterloo, her usual neutral smile in place, the usual courtesies offered and accepted, the usual immaculate appearance adjusted, she took her first steps into a world in which she perceived the possibility of being denied essential information, a world in which silence was a commonplace, and absence a foregone conclusion.

CHAPTER TWELVE

*B*eatrice, strolling round the beauty counters in Harrods, which she did more and more frequently ('Why don't you go to a museum?' asked Miriam. 'The National Gallery?'), watched as a woman was lowered to a chair by an assistant and felt a sympathetic trembling in her own throat as the woman tried to apologize and failed. A collapse of some sort, a faint: no doubt a commonplace. Fortunately they knew how to deal with it. The assistant knelt by the woman's chair, murmuring consolingly. Then suddenly the woman's head went back and her legs spread untidily. Beatrice watched, unable to look away, as now two assistants attempted to hide her from public view, while a third, behind the counter, picked up a telephone to summon help. In due course two uniformed men picked up the chair, with the woman still spreadeagled on it, and carried it somewhere out of sight. She would be taken away, and when she recovered—if she recovered—she would be aware only that she had felt unwell. The unaesthetic aftermath, the rescue operation, would be obliterated.

Beatrice had no doubt that an ambulance was already on its way, was perhaps being directed to a side door. Incredibly, very few people seemed to have noticed this incident. Sales of perfume were proceeding normally: advice was being given on moisturisers and foundations. The girls, so glossily unreal in their confected beauty, were perhaps more animated than usual, but expert at concealing what tremors they might have felt behind capable smiles. Later, in the staff-room, they might speculate on the woman's fate, but without anguish. They were young; nothing similar could happen to them.

Beatrice, who took some time to collect herself, who lingered, as if putting herself under Harrods's protection, felt dismay at having witnessed such a terrible loss of dignity. Her own unsteadiness she attributed to some malign form of identification. She had felt at one with that unknown woman, had understood intimately what was happening to her, had seen it, or imagined it, all before. Her mother had had similar episodes, had emerged from them bewildered, had gone about her business shakily, as if soliciting forgiveness for her brief loss of autonomy. For it was always more or less brief, and she was only marginally aware. She was certainly unaware of its significance. Beatrice remembered with shame that she had fled from the room, unable to bear intimations of disaster. It was Miriam who had dealt with these crises, Miriam who had insisted on a proper investigation in hospital—*tests* being the operative word—Miriam who had over-ridden the doctor and insisted on a private room. Beatrice still did not know how she had managed this. Their mother had lost all independence as soon as she was installed in the hospital bed, had initially asked when she could go home, then lost interest in the answers. 'They are going to do some tests,' she had told Beatrice, who had steeled herself to visit every day. But there was no time for tests, in which she retained an illusory confidence. Briefly she became another woman, lavished endearments on the nurses, took Beatrice's hand and whispered to her such details of the nurses' lives as she had been able to gather, always with a strange schoolgirlish glee. It was almost as if she had been relieved of her adulthood, of the strange world in which two sexes were active and in which she herself had achieved so little. In the nursery atmosphere she seemed to experience an odd peace. A final stroke killed her a mere eight days later.

Thinking back Beatrice found this fate more unbearable than she had at the time. Her own legs were still unsteady; the sight of that unknown woman's head, the careful bluish-grey hair now dishevelled, bobbing helplessly on a uniformed shoulder, had filled her with a brief alarm which connected with her own situation, though she could not have immediately said why this should be so. But she had always been sensitive, she reasoned, had indeed proclaimed her sensitivity to anyone who would listen to her. 'I am a vulnerable person,' she would say, half noticing but ignoring the sceptical look with which Miriam favoured this remark. But it was true, had always been true. Illness must be kept at arms' length; no rumour of it must be allowed to reach her. Disasters must be concealed from her. Sometimes the television news made her tremble; an appeal from stricken parents could reduce her to tears. That was why her idle life was a form of protection against the world's assaults; that was why she tolerated it so easily. Beatrice knew this, but thought that no one else might. To accede to a life of virtual inactivity after the grotesque prominence of the concert platform was incomprehensible to most. Mrs Anstruther, whom she had reluctantly invited one afternoon for a cup of tea, had overdone the sympathy. 'It must be terrible for you, sitting here all day, now that your career is finished. I couldn't imagine it for myself.'

'A quiet life suits me now,' Beatrice had replied. 'The stresses were very great, you know. And I am a very sensitive person.'

'Oh, so am I,' said Mrs Anstruther enthusiastically, helping herself to a biscuit. 'It's a mixed blessing, isn't it?'

As she grew older Beatrice grew more frightened. She was

unpartnered; few people expressed an interest. This position had been slightly reclaimed of late by Max's visits, but the audience was still missing. The wretched Mrs Anstruther was her only witness, and had been invited to tea for that equally wretched reason. There was some virtue then in that alternative scenario she had created: a slightly raffish life on the Riviera, under a brilliant sun, on a balcony, with nothing to do beyond taking a siesta and waking up in time to bathe and change for dinner. A little gambling, perhaps; she had no objection to that, and it might amuse Max, who had not so far entered her calculations. Hastily, she made provision for him. He could stroll, perform small tasks; he could wear his panama hat. He would be bored, of course, but then so would she. Her ennui would have something self-indulgent about it; she would reflect on her disappointments, the main disappointment being Max himself, instead of that stranger whom she no longer expected to meet. That she, who was so filled with passionate feeling, should be so cheated, was still a wonder to her. What should have happened had not happened. Fiction was better at arranging such matters.

Some time ago she had tried to substitute irony for longing, and had almost succeeded. That was why this alternative life so nearly appealed to her. It would furnish her with splendid opportunities for the sarcasm she had always kept hidden. She would spare no one. Those who thought of her as a compliant and anxious character would be surprised by her sharp tongue, her barbed observations. These would be given legitimacy by her own immense stupefaction at having been left out of the race, of having to make do with second best. It was only right therefore that the second best should be fairly spectacular, should have something showy about it, that rumours should reach one-time friends at home. And it would not last for ever, or need not. This part was vague to her; she did not quite go so far as to envisage a further freedom. She only knew that in some vital way she would have

rescued her reputation. Women were always being urged to re-
cover their self-esteem—at least they were in the newspaper she
read. She would be doing this for her self-esteem. Self-esteem apparently was its own reward. That too would suit her well
enough. She had been resigned for far too long.

And then the sun, the sun! She craved it as though it was still
winter in London, but in fact it was the end of a humid July, the
sky undecided, rain sprinkling down every so often, and what
heat there was damp and uncomfortable. That was why she had
so little energy, why that poor woman had been overcome. She
shied away from the thought of the woman's careful dressing that
morning, of the feet slipped into the elegant shoes, one of which
had fallen off, of the underwear suddenly, grotesquely, on display.
The woman's skirt had ridden up, to reveal several inches of a
white slip, such as only women of her age wore these days: that
fussy border of nylon lace had put her definitively into a different
category from the kind girls assisting her, their pretty faces intent
on their task. The staff no doubt had instructions, knew how to
cope with emergencies. As she did not. She could only look on
helplessly, immersed in her own sense of dread.

Suddenly the mingled perfumes, even now being dabbed on
to wrists, seemed to her intolerable, and she made for the nearest
exit, found herself in the fruit and vegetable department, looked
round carefully as though calculating her needs, lingered until
she judged herself steady enough for the street. She had intended
to buy some made-up dish for her lunch, but lunch now seemed
unwelcome. She had eggs at home, would make an omelette.
Then she would perhaps have a rest; the incident with the faint-
ing woman had upset her. That was why the sun's embrace
seemed so imperative. She would be becalmed, if not entirely safe
(no one was safe). And she would be protected, if anything were
to go wrong. Max was suddenly very dear to her, in this new role
of which he was totally unaware. She would do her best to make

him happy, that is to say to make him comfortable. Happiness was no longer an issue. They were both in that uncertain time which succeeds the beautiful impulses of youth, the hungry curiosity of middle age. This was not maturity so much as anti-climax. She had not been warned about this, but had to accept its reality, rather earlier than she had anticipated. She was still, on her better days, an agreeable-looking woman, but behind the careful façade she was aware of defeat. Her good years were past. She had had a revelation, not of fulfilment but of escape, and she had had the sense to recognize it for what it was. For that, surely, she deserved some compensation.

Miriam could come out for holidays. No, that was clearly un-realistic; Miriam and Max had never got on. Her poor sister, whom she suspected of being unhappy . . . She had telephoned on her return from Paris but had stayed largely out of sight. That was how Beatrice knew of her unhappiness. She mentally as-signed Miriam to that Rivers person, in the hope that he would take care of her. He had taken her out to dinner a few times, but all she would say, when asked if she had enjoyed herself, was, 'Yes, it was pleasant.' There had been a set to her lips which Be-atrice had not liked. She knew that she too was about to incur op-probrium. But she had to save her own life, for no one had so far shown any signs of wanting to do it for her. She would miss her little sister (the fantasy now taking on the hard-edged appearance of reality). Something was owing to Miriam. Beatrice longed to bring a smile of approval to her face. Miriam had suggested that she go to a museum. That, then, was what she would do. She would then invite Miriam to supper, and discourse intelligently, objectively, for once. The days of recalling their youth were over. Or perhaps had not yet truly arrived.

It hardly signified that Max had been absent for a week or two. Her plans for him over-rode such paltry considerations. She was experienced enough to know that this was a tactic put in place to secure her wandering attention, though she was never unmannerly enough to let any hint of this escape her. She considered such a course of action puerile, although she would express concern when he reappeared, as she knew he would. Momentarily she was glad that she was too old to take him seriously, was content to relegate him to a jokey stereotype of the kind that had never held much interest for her. She would have to take seriously a facile explanation, would suggest a holiday out of sheer unselfish concern. He would be unwilling, she knew, only enjoyed his own company within the limits of a well-defined day. She would remind him tactfully of his past triumphs, watch the pleased smile return to his face, but at the end of the evening would remark that it was too early for him to live in the past, would sigh, would say that it always seemed to be raining these days, that summer, such as it was, would soon be over, that the long dark nights would soon begin . . . And he would be vaguely unsettled by such thoughts, as she intended him to be. She would feel her own will turn to steel as he looked downcast. She would urge him to take care of himself, as if he were on the brink of disintegration. And the next evening they spent together she would be all smiles, all reassurance. What was he thinking of, to be so preoccupied with his health? He was in the pink of condition. Boredom: that was his problem. And she would leave the matter there. She found this idea liberating, as if after a lifetime of more or less good behaviour she had glimpsed a whole range of new techniques.

As she approached Wilbraham Place she saw the elongated figure of Anne Marie Kinsella detach itself from the entrance to her building, lift an arm in greeting. A faint 'Hi' acknowledged her presence.

'Why, Anne Marie! I wasn't expecting you. Is anything the matter?'

'Mum said to tell you she won't be in this week. She's bad with her back.'

'Oh, I'm so sorry. Do come in.'

'And to remind you that we're going on holiday next week.'

'Oh, yes. Majorca, your mother told me.'

'That's right.'

'So you'll take her holiday money home with you. You are still living at home, aren't you?'

'For the moment. I'm thinking of moving in with my boyfriend.'

'Oh, how nice,' said Beatrice helplessly. She was not used to the codes that governed young people. 'Would you like a cup of tea? Something to eat?'

'No thanks, I'm on a diet.'

The girl was about sixteen, she reckoned, remembered from Mrs Kinsella's conversation that she had just left school. Yet her hair was already dyed, an unconvincing blonde, and her dress, black and tight, created an impression of streetwise competence. Unfortunately she had inherited her mother's sturdy legs.

'Do sit down and tell me about yourself. Are you sure you won't have a cup of tea?' She herself was badly in need of one, although the girl's smooth face and sprawling ease were something of a comfort after the decrepitude she had earlier witnessed in Harrods. 'What are your plans, now that you've left school? I've got that right, haven't I? Your mother said you wanted to be a nurse.'

'Yeah, I did, till I found out how long it would take. I've got a smashing job, though, in the record shop. I used to work there on Saturdays, then they said they'd take me on permanently. On trial, like.'

'And you're pleased about that?'

'I am, yeah.'

'Are you going to Majorca with your mother?'

'Well,' said the girl handsomely. 'Since it's the last time. I'll be going with Geoff after that. And since she hasn't got a feller.'

'Yes, I see,' said Beatrice, who did. 'Well, I'm sure you'll both have a good time. I shan't see her for three weeks, then. Give her my best wishes.' She rather balked at sending her love. 'And her money, of course,' handing over a discreet envelope.

'Here's one you prepared earlier, eh?' said Anne Marie, stowing the envelope away in a large black gamekeeper's bag.

'I beg your pardon? Oh, I see. How clever of you.'

She was desperate for the girl to go, so that she could make herself a cup of tea and relax for half an hour. Anne Marie did not take the hint: indeed no hint had been given. Beatrice shrank from saying that she was busy, knowing that this would cut no ice with Anne Marie, who was now quite comfortably settled and looking around her in an appraising but far from conciliatory manner.

'You've got a lot of books,' she said.

'They're mostly my sister's. She used to live with me.'

'Yeah, Mum told me.'

'We both read a lot. Do you like reading?'

'Well, I don't get a lot of time, what with school and the shop and all. We did *Pride and Prejudice* at school.' She made a face.

'Did you like that?'

'Well, it was better on the telly, wasn't it?'

'I expect you watch quite a lot, don't you?'

'We watch videos mostly. I only watched *Pride and Prejudice* because of school.'

'It's a lovely story, isn't it?' said Beatrice.

'It's okay. Old-fashioned, though.'

'If you're going home,' said Beatrice, standing up in a gracious but resolute manner, 'I can give you a lift in my taxi. It's Tachbrook Street, isn't it? Then I can take the taxi on to the Tate.'

That was what she had half-promised Miriam. The Tate was nearer than the National Gallery. And in any case she had no preference for either, not ever having made a habit of dropping in to renew acquaintance with a particular favourite. She was, if

anything, afraid of art, resenting the huge events, the magnani-
mous gestures, the whole cultural apparatus pictured, encapsu-
lated and endlessly repeated in the high inimical rooms. The steps
that led up to museums made her feel humble, unworthy; she was
not at home with admiration, preferred, these days, a world in
which cynicism was allowed. Even when young, dragged to an
exhibition by Miriam, she would feel uneasy, as if those penetrat-
ing portraits served only to undermine those like herself who had
an undeveloped sense of their own identity. And she had all the
wrong reactions, was profoundly sorry for the Virgin, whose destiny was being revealed to her by the angel, wanted only to rally
the saints, to give them a sense of life's urgency, to tell the cruci-
fied Christ that there were other deaths to be mourned. She said
nothing of this to Miriam, although Miriam sensed her agitation.
The only time they had ever coincided was when Miriam, point-
ing to a Dutch picture of a lazy servant dozing off in a littered
kitchen, said, 'Oh, look. There's Mrs Kinsella.' She had been
grateful for that remark, for having art, which was so frighten-
ingly separate, brought into contact with her own ordinary life.
Therefore, for Miriam's sake, if not for her own, she would go to
the Tate.

She shepherded Anne Marie, who was still enough of a child
to allow herself to be directed, into a taxi, and resigned herself to
an afternoon of duty. She would have preferred to stay in the taxi,
to ask it to take her on a little tour, but she had never done such a
thing, and now seemed an odd time to start. She was, as she so frequently said, a vulnerable person, one who preferred being at
home, and preferably in bed. Briefly a limitless sun-struck cor-
niche flashed across her mind's eye, and she wondered whether
she had made the right decision, whether in fact she need imple-
ment it. The beauty of certain fantasies was that they needed no
reality to structure them. Her future life in the south of France
was already perfect, complete. Why run the risk of translating it

into the stuff of every day? But in fact the arguments in its favour remained the same; the whole adventure was in the nature of a vindication of her present existence, a rebuke to those who had forgotten her. As for Max, his part in the affair had always been a minor one: she had no real use for a man past his prime. He was essential only as a companion, for she did not think she would survive on her own. She needed routine, familiarity, to combat loneliness. Even Anne Marie, sitting beside her in her funereal black, was a comfort. She was quite sorry when the girl left her in Tachbrook Street, found herself leaning forward to wave to her as she turned to unlock her front door, was rewarded by a lifted hand and a brief smile. Her own smile was slow to fade. Yet she was not particularly fond of the girl, any more than she was fond of her mother. It was just that youth was the essential component; without its presence the day lost some point. Belatedly she saw that her current fantasy, and even all her previous ones, were at fault. Adults in their various guises could not deliver what the young delivered. Her own longed-for transformation was without merit, she now saw. This frightened her. Without the consolation of that project what would become of her? There had been a certain energy in those brutal imaginings. Without them she was reduced once again to idleness, worthlessness, loss of meaning. This was somehow not to be borne.

Yet fear followed her up the steps of the Tate. Inside the building, in the great echoing halls littered with what she took to be broken pieces of sculpture, fear turned to dread. This was somehow going to prove too much for her. With an aching heart, as if she had been newly separated from everything she loved, she turned off at random into one of the endless galleries, sank down onto a bench and looked about her with despair, wondering what she was bidden to appreciate. There were few people about, which was just as well, since she would rather ignore the pictures unwitnessed. The rare spectators were young, students, she sup-

posed, with heavy packs on their backs. She would rather have
looked at the students than at the pictures, but that was not why
she was here. She was here to please Miriam, to entertain her with
an account of an afternoon spent intelligently, rather than of time
wasted. In that moment she longed to do something for Miriam,
who was not happy. Tears filled her eyes at the thought of
Miriam's unhappiness. A warder, hands clasped behind his back,
observed her curiously. She got up, moved towards the nearest
picture, assumed a reflective expression. 'A Ship between two
Headlands,' said the label. 'J.M.W. Turner.'

But she could make out neither ship nor headlands. What she
saw in front of her was chaos, or perhaps Creation, before it had
fully emerged. Perhaps they were the same thing. She saw a
serene aqueous void of impalpable shapes. The sun was rising,
that was certain, as it might have done on that distant first day, before the human drama was enacted. The colours were miraculous: blue shaded into yellow, yellow somehow contained blue.
The effect was of majesty, of serenity, and yes, now she could see
the ghost ship gliding through the water, which was hardly water,
which was evanescence, towards her. Dazed, she returned to her
seat. From this vantage point the picture was different. Close to
she had felt incorporated into that magical void, as if she too were
present on that primeval morning. But seated on the bench she
saw the picture as less reassuring, perceived a swirling rhythm
that her eyes had not appreciated, for a moment dizzily apprehended that there was no solid ground, no place for rest. This was
organic movement in its entirety: ships and headlands were neither real nor relevant. She glanced fearfully round the gallery,
saw some conventional canvases which were without interest, although she was grateful for their recognizable shapes. But what
she had seen drew her eyes again, and again her eyes misted with
tears. If this was paradise, this golden light, this ship becalmed on
an immaterial sea, then she saw quite clearly her pitiful fallen

condition. If she could scarcely bear this for herself how could she bear it for Miriam? And there was something else, something even more agonizing to confront. The picture now seemed to her to have lost its immobility, to be involved in some surreptitious circular rotation. For a moment—but she had lost track of time—the void represented was the exact embodiment of the void inside her own head.

The same warder who had had her in his sights earlier informed her that the gallery was about to close. 'Are you all right, Madam?' he asked, seeing her haggard face. She summoned her last energies, attempted a smile and retraced her steps down the echoing sculpture halls, which she now perceived as a sort of graveyard. She caught a taxi, managed to spare a glance at the unlovely river, as far removed from the ecstatic Turner as it was possible to be, wondered why she felt so little relief at being returned to reality. She was still sorrowful, filled with an almost terminal clairvoyance. She had been wrong to put her faith in that poor vision of hers. It lacked beauty, just as her thoughts did. Yet it, they, must have had a purpose. It might simply be that her life was intolerable, in which case it was only sensible to change it. But the cruelty—that, surely, was out of character? Would it not be possible to leave, but to leave in an open-hearted manner, for Max's benefit, for Miriam's? For she did not see how she was to continue as she was, a petty, idle, confused woman. She would like to redeem herself before it was too late. The adventure in the south of France might go ahead—it still seemed indicated—but like the picture viewed from a different distance its meaning had changed. What she must now embrace was not escape but exile. That experience in the gallery: she thought of it as the abyss. There had been others. She would seek a last solace in the sun, and if possible celebrate what was left to her. But she would act leniently. Now when she looked at this projected exile, shorn of its self-important embellishments, she saw that it could still be accomplished, but easefully, and with due care for her companion. She thought of Max, who would be homesick. She would be homesick herself. But was this not a condition of living in the present? And for those like herself, denied the painter's radiance, would it not be as well to sigh, and pick up the burden once again, and, once again, try even harder to arrive at acceptance?

'Yes, I went to the Tate,' she said later that evening, when Miriam telephoned. 'Yes, lovely. You don't mind if I have an early night, do you? I'll see you at the weekend, won't I? Yes, fine. Goodnight, then. Take care.' And replaced the receiver gently, so as not to disturb Miriam any further.

CHAPTER THIRTEEN

The thing is,' said Miriam, 'I feel I am here under false pretences.'

'Oh, do stop saying that. You are here because I asked you to be here. I hope you're hungry.'

'I'm always hungry. I suppose it's because I'm such a limited cook. But you're right. I'm being rather rude. Do tell me about yourself.'

'Women always say that when they're anxious to please. Are you anxious to please, Miriam?'

'Well, I'm not averse to trying. And I am interested.'

'Well, I was born, grew up, went to school, university, taught for a bit, and then got a job. I work mainly for the BBC. And I work a bit on my own. Politics fascinate me, the history of government, and so on. Have you decided what you want to eat?'

'Fish, I think. Turbot. And are you now or have you ever been married?'

'Ah, that sort of information usually comes later, doesn't it?

But yes, since you ask, I was married briefly, soon after I left Oxford. We were both too young. What is it one says on these occasions? It didn't work out.'

'And since then?'

'You mean is my mistress at home waiting for me? I have of course told her I'm working late. No, nothing like that. And you? You strike me as rather solitary.'

'I've become so, certainly. I suppose I could say that my marriage didn't work out either. It really didn't. Jon was meant for another kind of woman entirely. Or perhaps for no woman at all. I wanted to be married, you see. I thought it would be easier than it turned out to be. But I felt guilty because in the end I didn't like him very much.' She smiled briefly. 'Mine is not a success story. I live on my own. I work steadily. I do the sort of work that takes no account of weekends. I suppose yours is like that too?'

He nodded. 'I don't mind that. I feel I'm still a student. But I think you do.'

'Yes, I do. I'm a very reliable worker, always have been. But lately I've begun to realize that I don't want to work any more.'

'What do you want to do?'

'I want to live a normal life, get up late on Sundays, read the papers. I daren't read too much because it might interfere with the text I'm working on. I want to go out for walks, spend a morning shopping, that sort of thing.'

'You could come out for walks with me.'

'I'd like that. But I don't get a lot of free time. Isn't that absurd? I'm entirely autonomous, can make my own hours, and yet I feel constrained to sit down every morning at seven so that I can put in a couple of hours before going to the Library. I could stay at home all day, of course. But I don't think I could stand my own company.'

He watched a shadow darken her face, and regretted it. She had been looking pretty, animated, her colour high. He wanted to know more, but sensed that he was on delicate ground.

'Why don't you care for your own company, Miriam?'

'It seems undernourished. Impoverished. I have no ties, you see, except for my sister. I love my sister, but we don't want to live together, even to see each other very much. Have you any sisters?'

'No, alas. One brother: he's a farmer. We get on very well. I'm rather fond of my own company, though.'

'Are you? How extraordinary. And have you no ties?'

'Several mistresses, of course. They club together to buy me little luxuries.'

She looked at him cautiously. He laughed. 'Your expression! No, I'm alone, but it suits me. I might have to go abroad at short notice, you see. Here's your fish. Do you think you'll like that?'

'It looks delicious.' After a minute, 'It is delicious. What a nice place. Do you know it well?'

'Pretty well, yes.'

'You bring your mistresses here, I expect.'

'It's useful for meeting colleagues, or interviewing Trades Unionists. And I like a good meal.'

She thought he looked as if he did. He was broad-shouldered, with a large but elegant head. His face looked Roman, or as she imagined Romans to have looked, with a thin slightly curved nose, a firm mouth, eyes shrewd, assessing, as if he were about to go to the Senate or the Colosseum—either would be acceptable; he would not be averse to a little bloodletting. Yet he had himself well in hand, appeared certain of his place in the world, was a stranger to deference, anxiety, self-doubt. He had arranged this evening to suit her, had waited patiently until she had run out of excuses, and then had calmly told her that he would meet her at the restaurant at seven-thirty. 'I take it you don't want me to pick you up?'

'No, of course not. Do men still do that?'

'I believe some of them do, yes.' Now he said, 'You were obviously telling the truth when you said you were hungry. What would you like to follow?'

'Tarte Tatin, I think.'

'I'll have the same. Excuse me a minute, would you? There's a man over there who is pretending he hasn't seen me. We have to have a meeting, and he knows I'm going to ask awkward questions. I shan't be a minute. Will you be all right?'

'I'll be fine. What could possibly happen to me?'

She drank a glass of wine and came to the conclusion that she was enjoying herself. This restaurant in Covent Garden, which she did not know, obviously aimed at the higher end of the market. There were no mobile phones, no men with unsuitable companions, no familiarity with the waiters. All was decorous, gentlemanly, like an exclusive club. She thought it typical that a man like Tom Rivers—easily masculine, easily in control—would choose this place rather than somewhere smarter, more frivolous, more feminine. She leaned back in her chair, tried to glance discreetly at his broad back bending over a distant table, ranged contentedly round the room, and then saw Simon, sitting in a corner, with a girl. Even as she looked, she saw his hand reach out to stroke the girl's hair. He was smiling lazily. The girl, meek, her eyes cast down, like a heifer, was beautiful. She submitted to having her hair stroked as if it were something she expected, as if being caressed in a public place were an everyday occurrence. Simon, one elbow on the table, his hand propping up his chin, totally absorbed, his other hand fingering a strand of the girl's long hair, was apparently oblivious to everything and everyone else. Miriam hastily averted her eyes as Tom Rivers joined her.

'What's the matter?' he said. 'You look as if you've seen a ghost.'

'I thought I saw someone I knew,' she said. 'But I was wrong.' She applied her fork valiantly to the glutinous slice of tart on her plate, congratulated herself on showing so little emotion and sat back with as much composure as she could still manage. 'I'm sorry, Tom, a sudden wave of tiredness. Shall we go? Or rather shall I go? I'm really rather anxious to get home.'

He watched her narrowly. He was annoyed; she could see that. She had spoiled his evening. This precipitate departure was unmannerly, altogether deplorable. Yet unless she left soon she did not see how she was to behave in a rational manner. She knew that in days, years to come she would see that hand reach out to stroke the long hair, knew that this scene, almost a primal scene, would never be explained to her, for who would explain it? It was self-explanatory, needed no further gloss.

She was aware that her plate was being removed, that the bill was being paid.

'I take it you didn't want to wait for coffee?' he said stiffly.

'I'm sorry, Tom.' There was nothing else she could say.

In the street, by the open door of the taxi, the engine running, she held out her hand, then reached up to kiss his cheek. He caught her face in both hands, and said, 'I want to kiss you properly, but I have a feeling this is not the time. What happened in there? Were you upset because I left you?'

'No, no,' she said distractedly.

'But something happened, didn't it?'

'Another time, Tom.' She had nearly called him Simon.

'Promise me that there will be another time.'

'Yes, I promise.'

For he was the better man; of that there was no doubt. More adult, more subtle too. He had not interrogated her, as he might well have done, did not rebuff her simplistic excuses. He had looked genuinely concerned, curious, but was too polite to enquire further. He released her face, gave her a brief kiss on the cheek, and said, 'So I can telephone you between seven and nine in the morning, then?'

'Please do. Goodnight, Tom,' and vanished inside the taxi. 'Lower Sloane Street,' she managed to say, expecting to cry, to collapse. But in fact she did neither, sat stonily upright, as if she might never speak again. To whom could she offer an explanation of her behaviour? Not to Tom Rivers, who had every right to

feel aggrieved; not to Beatrice, who was all politeness, who would
never in her life commit such a solecism. A sense of shame now
overlaid her shock: she felt as if the entire restaurant had witnessed her confusion. She was at least sure that Simon had not
seen her. This was just as well, as she had almost stumbled on the
way out. Tom had taken her arm, had steadied her. Somewhere
in her mind was a sense of true gratitude. He was kind. She might
need his kindness, but not yet, not while illness threatened,
breakdown. These must first be dealt with.

In fact once she reached the flat she felt devoid of the anger
she had half expected. She felt consternation, a retrospective embarrassment, as if she had been a gullible girl, willing to be taken
in by someone with a superior ease of manner, like King
Cophetua and the beggar maid. But in the picture, from which
most people know the story, the beggar maid looks stunned, not
by her good fortune but by her inability to overcome her original
lowly condition. Those who are born lowly do not rally quickly to
a change of fortune. She felt, no, she knew, that she must always
have demonstrated an unappealing humility. But her wordless acquiescence had pleased Simon; of that she was quite sure. He was
light-minded, but she had been part of that light-mindedness,
that almost casual desire which had seduced her by its effortlessness. The effortlessness had been contagious for a time; now she
saw that she had acted out of character. She was a serious person.
His great gift to her had been to make her feel as inconsequential
as she somehow knew that he did, had always done. His life was
satisfactory, regulated; but he had no real needs. His charm
should have warned her that this was a man who did not lie
awake at nights tormented by moral problems. Briefly she remembered her sense of him in the chalet at Verbier, her intuition
of a lax, self-indulgent, slightly scabrous character lazily taking
his ease, while she walked through the gloom of a December afternoon, trying to forget that it was Christmas. She had looked up

at his window, half fearful of seeing him. This image was burned onto her retina. In some ways she would be relieved if there were no further meetings. She had been revealed to herself as a suppliant, whereas his only failing was a trouble-free partiality from which, she reminded herself, she had benefited. He had thought that the act of love needed no explanation, no glossary. So that any explanation would be redundant. It would be altogether sensible to forget the whole matter. Besides, it was now divested of any significance. And she was too old to continue to take it seriously.

When the telephone rang she assumed it was Rivers, who in his nice way would be worried about her. She picked up the receiver with a sigh, faced with the possibility of summoning up reassurance, politeness, a convincing explanation.

'Miriam.'

'Simon.'

'I saw you.'

'You saw me leaving, I expect.'

'I didn't know you knew Rivers.'

'Because of course you do know him.'

'His brother farms near an uncle of mine.'

'What was it you wanted, Simon? You've been out of touch for quite a long time.'

'I have, haven't I? Sorry, sorry. But I knew we'd meet up again sooner or later.'

'She's very beautiful, your girlfriend.'

'Patience? Yes, she is lovely, isn't she? If I weren't a happily married man . . .' He gave a mock heavy sigh.

'And Mary?'

'Mary? She's fine. It was a false alarm. But that'll be it, I'm afraid. No more little Haggards.'

'Do you feel anything at all?' she asked curiously.

There was a silence, which neither felt able to break.

'I did, you know,' he said finally.

'I did too. I still do.'

There was a further silence. When it seemed as if there were nothing more to say she replaced the receiver. She knew that there would be no further calls.

She stood by the telphone for about five minutes. She did not doubt that he was doing the same. Then, very slowly, she walked to the window, through which a cold draught was blowing. It had been an unseasonal autumn, windy, not light until about eight o'clock, dark again a bare ten hours later. She shivered in her thin suit, remembered the girl—Patience—in her crumpled blouse and flowered skirt, as if carelessness could in no way detract from her beauty. As it had not. She remembered a tanned cheek, that abundant hair, the downturned eyes, as if modesty forbade her to acknowledge his hand. Neither was eating. That fact, as much as his hand on her hair, argued the strength of the attraction. Although she could have asked him whether he had been alone when he telephoned she had not done so, had been suddenly frightened. She now realized that she had been frightened of him for the last few months, since she had last seen him, in fact. She had recognized a defence against encroachment, masked by a constant smile. She acknowledged her fear, too late for it to do her any good.

Lower Sloane Street was black, quiet, so quiet that when a late-returning couple walked past she could hear the man speak quite clearly. 'We'll know more tomorrow,' he said. 'No doubt the office . . .' and then he was out of earshot. She wondered why anyone should be having this sort of desultory conversation, in the dark, so late at night. On the opposite side of the road no lights showed. She supposed that she should go to bed, thought it a waste of time. To go to bed meant sleeping, and worse than that, waking up in the morning, facing a new day. She would doze off where she was, although she had never done such a thing in her life. A meticulous person, she appreciated the rituals of preparing for the night, the face wiped clean, the cotton nightgown cool against her legs. Sleep was not normally a problem, but latterly her dreams had been vivid, admonitory. In all of them she was found wanting, failed to find her way in an unfamiliar landscape, knew that to ask directions would meet only with scorn, with harsh hilarity. On such occasions she would remind herself on waking that she was healthy, solvent, independent. But she could not face up to the risk of being found wanting on this particular night, saw her health and her independence as derisory, the lonely endowment of one obliged to count her blessings. One should come by blessings naturally. One should not be obliged to manufacture them, to invoke them at every adverse turn of the wheel. She wished now only to drop her guard, but knew that this would be dangerous. Eternal vigilance was the price of liberty, she had read. It was now more than ever true.

She thought of Beatrice, whose vigilance had never matched her own, might even have been willingly discarded in favour of romances, of romance itself, read about, savoured luxuriously, but without expectation. She had not made that endearing mistake. Perhaps she should have behaved differently, demanded a meeting. But she had known that it was over, whatever it had been. Even now she saw that the experience had been authentic, even saw that it was appropriate that it should be ended enigmatically. There was a finality about that telephone call. She would eventually return to normal. Normality meant looking calmly at the facts. No one was guilty, or perhaps they both were. She would give up self-examination, would telephone Tom Rivers and apologize. She owed that not so much to Rivers himself as to his own manifest lack of culpability. He had been decent. Decency was what she would now admire.

When the doorbell rang she forgave him instantly, forgot, genuinely forgot his absence, the scene in the restaurant, forgot Tom Rivers. Yet when she opened the door it was to Max Gruber, a curious hat held to his chest, in an attitude suggestive of ardour, or devotion.

'Max,' she said hopelessly. 'It's very late.'

He glanced at her in surprise. 'It's only just after ten-thirty. May I come in?'

'I was just going to bed,' she lied. 'Is anything the matter?'

He followed her in, turning the brim of his hat between his hands, gave a quick appraising glance to her living-room, which, he noted automatically, was not to his taste.

'It's Beatrice,' he said. 'I'm a little concerned. Have you seen her lately?'

'Not for about ten days, no. Why, what is the matter?'

'I took her out to dinner,' he said. In retrospect this action seemed to him virtuous, in view of what had happened. 'She doesn't look too well to me, Miriam.'

This was a careful understatement. His usual soliloquy had been interrupted by a shocking incident. Beatrice had dropped her fork, upset a glass of wine and—the worst thing of all—had not noticed that she had done so. Within a few minutes she had returned to normal, had looked about her in a dazed manner, had laughed a little uncertainly, then had said, 'Do go on,' although he had been watching her in consternation, had noticed her missing fork, then had pushed her plate away, as if she could not bear the sight of food. He had summoned the waiter to remove the stained tablecloth, had demanded the bill and had sat there with an attentive expression on his face, his mind racing.

He had seen it all before, had commiserated at too many bedsides, had attended too many memorial services to quell his inner conviction. And this was not even a memorial service, which he was usually in a position to enjoy, seeing old friends, fellow survivors. He thought of memorial services as cocktail parties for the elderly, and preferable to other social occasions in that one could sit down. But this manifestation was the sort that preceded memorial services; this was the introduction to a long period of decline, at which he had no desire to be present. Events had outrun him. He had had a gentle, a very gentle period of informal friendship in mind, himself looking in periodically until invited to stay on. He was an old man; he could not tolerate any other outcome. His own heart had beaten uncomfortably in the restaurant, aware of all the other diners turning away tactfully as the waiter stripped off the tablecloth and replaced it with another. A little of the wine had splashed on to Beatrice's blue jacket. She did not notice this at the time, but when they got up to leave—and he had helped her to her feet—she had uttered a cry of distress and dabbed at it repeatedly, so that the table was once again strewn with stained linen.

He said none of this to Miriam, not wishing to involve himself further. He knew, with a sense of shame, that he would now bow out of Beatrice's life. He would telephone from time to time, assure her of his undying devotion, and say that he was going away for a while. Maybe he would even do so. The weather was colder than he remembered it from his days in London, when he had always been bustling, busy, too busy to notice the temperature. His busyness had created its own microclimate. Now he thought almost nostalgically of the concrete panorama from his windows in Monaco, wondered if this might not be a good time to try and redeem his flat, or one like it. He had no ties, or rather he no longer had any ties. His dream of a new home had been only that, a dream. And if there were to be bad news, as he knew there would be, he might be better off out of reach. He felt deeply depressed at these thoughts, which had entered his head with magical suddenness as he manoeuvred Beatrice into a cab. He had seen her into the flat, had raised his hat and kissed her, but had not ventured further. He had done what he could, had survived the embarrassment in his usual worldly manner, but had felt frightened, and when he was alone in the street took a few minutes to regain his equilibrium. Bad news was fatal to men of his age. This was not the convivial atmosphere of a memorial service but the real thing, a glimpse of an altered state. Such as might befall him at any moment, he reminded himself. He had done the best he could, and now he handed the whole problem over to Miriam. It would be her business to do the nursing, the encouraging and eventually the mourning. The more he thought about it the less he wanted to see either of them again.

But Beatrice! That that once lovely girl, with her intriguing air of helplessness, should have come to this, and so quickly! Apart from his sister he knew no other ill people, was careful to stay away from them after the one obligatory visit, felt a sense of relief once they disappeared. His duty now, he reasoned, was to himself, yet he realized sorrowfully that he was not man enough to deal with a situation that held so much grief. Therefore the younger sister, whom he had apprised of the facts (but not all of them), must assume the task as of right. He eyed her carefully: she looked pale, older. He felt a moment's compassion, to which he surrendered, reached out and patted her hand.

Miriam thought that she had advanced beyond mere irritation, but the sight of Max's freckled hand provoked her to an almost enjoyable exasperation. She thought him ridiculous, this whole visit an intrusion. She had early written him off as an inveterate but harmless tease of the old school; her animosity was only just concealed by her carefully neutral expression. 'Max looked in,' Beatrice had said recently, on more than one occasion, taking the style for the substance. Max, they both knew, was not a suitor; he was a courtier, and they had no illusions that this man, or any like him, could make a genuine commitment. There was no loyalty in him. His flowery manner hid so many genuine feints that it was as well to take nothing he said seriously. Therefore it was in order to give an ear to his protestations and to discount them at once. This masquerade was guaranteed to please him, or to please his vanity, which was considerable. He liked women, took every opportunity to cultivate them. In the company of women he rediscovered something of his youth, at home, when he had been adored by his mother and sister, by clucking aunts, even by a remote grandmother. Few spoiled him nowadays. Only Beatrice was gentle enough to play her part.

'Why exactly are you here, Max? Couldn't you have telephoned?'

'I don't sleep very well,' he confessed. This at least was the truth. 'I wasn't in a hurry to get home. And you are so near . . .'

He thought she might have offered him a cup of coffee, made more of an effort. He was affronted by her cross expression. So great was her annoyance that he could see that she had not fully understood what he had been saying. He was saying that Beatrice did not look too well. To Miriam there was nothing new in that. Miriam thought that for a woman with all the time in the world to fuss about minor ailments Beatrice managed rather successfully. This was clearly written on her face.

'Beatrice has always worried about her health,' she said.

'I think she has reason to.' His tone was sharper than he had intended. It was some years since he had issued an order (although that had usually come out in the form of a request). Now he was prepared to arrange matters, in so far as this was his responsibility. Yet he felt a reluctance to inflict a burden on this slight tense woman. He knew exactly what he was handing on, knew almost squeamishly why he was doing so. But this was his chance. He was not duty bound to Miriam, only slightly more so to Beatrice. She had looked quite preoccupied when he had said goodnight, her earlier hospitality in abeyance. He had waited until he heard the door close, had made his way slowly down the stairs. Now Miriam, who suspected him of fraudulence, was quite clearly, and not too politely, waiting for him to leave.

'If you could keep an eye on her,' he suggested.

'Of course. I have always kept an eye on Beatrice.'

'I say all this because I may have to go away.'

'Oh?'

'Back to Monaco. Some trouble with the flat, you know.'

'I thought you had sold it.'

'Only on a short lease.' He thought how disagreeable she was.

'I'll look in tomorrow. I can't do anything tonight, can I?'

'Well, Miriam,' he said. 'It was good to see you again, however briefly.' With the prospect of departure his usual manners returned. 'Goodnight, my dear. Oh, and give my love to Beatrice when you see her.'

Outside in the street, he replaced his hat carefully, conscious of an onerous task accomplished, though not with honour. He shrugged. He had done his best. He was only human, he sighed, and there, in the dark, there was no one to express the slightest shadow of disapprobation.

CHAPTER FOURTEEN

_W_hen the girls were young, when the house was becalmed, and no visits could be expected, they walked, on Sunday afternoons, round the silent streets of their suburb and sometimes as far as the scrubby woodland that surrounded it. Though berating the silence, the inactivity, they experienced a certain peace as their steps took them past the houses of neighbours who on any other day they would greet politely. They were on the lookout for signs of a domesticity that was foreign to their own circumstances, as if they could glimpse not only other lives but a life which they might live if fortune favoured them. Were those curtains on an upper floor still drawn at three o'clock in the afternoon? Then the couple who lived there were still in bed. They looked at each other, hardly daring to imagine such a thing. The two schoolteachers who shared a house could be seen talking through an open window, cups and saucers raised genteelly to their lips: they too must be bored. The elderly man in the cardigan was, as usual, tending his garden, raking up the fallen leaves, for it always seemed to be the same time of year, that uneventful time before the dark days imposed their own curfew, and it was cold enough to send them home early, grateful that the day had been more or less dealt with.

That was the function of those walks, which were accepted as a sort of ritual. In retrospect they took on an aura of tradition, in a family which had no traditions. They leaned towards each other; sometimes Beatrice took Miriam's arm. To an outside observer, but there were few, they presented a picture of maidenly rectitude which was not entirely incorrect: the quiet weather cast its own spell on them, and for brief moments they savoured the innocence they were so anxious to lose. They were in that mood of heightened receptivity that enables one to ponder the shape of a leaf, flattened on the pavement by a recent shower, or to stand quite still to watch a squirrel bound past. They breathed in the semi-rural smells, almost in love with this place where nothing happened, and where they were still safe. One day they would leave it all behind and discover with some surprise that they remembered it with a sort of tenderness. It was only human presence that was disconcerting. Finally, the domesticity of others, or what they imagined of it, failed to impress them with its desirability. Their own could be postponed. For the moment this brief interval was enough.

They would sigh as they discussed their present discontents, but by the end of the afternoon their expressions would be clear of irritation or of longing. They were both subject to the same decrees, the same circumstances; though they might groan at the prospect of another Sunday they knew that such Sundays would always be re-enacted, knew too that the peculiar spell of such Sundays would somehow work on them, disposing them to calm and order of a kind unfamiliar to them on any other day of the week. In this way they learned that acceptance is not always a matter of resignation but of recognition. The very air was uncontentious. Their aspirations, confused and urgent, their longing to

escape, to live as fully as possible, seemed far away. They sensed
that such moments prolonged their childhood, which was after all
safely in the past. It was just that at such times adulthood was
equally safely consigned to some vague period in the future. It
was often dusk when they turned their steps towards home. The
tea would be made; their father would say, as always, 'Did you
have a good walk? Where did you go?' knowing that they would
not tell him, and for once accepting their brief replies as a sign that
nothing had changed, before turning back to his paper. Neither
parent lived long enough to witness their emancipation, for
which they were sometimes grateful.

Contemplating their present lives they agreed, but silently,
that this had been a blessing. These days they avoided those who
had formerly known them, ashamed of, but again accepting, their
tenor of life, much as they had once accepted the silent Sundays of
their youth. These days they walked cautiously round their much
more affluent streets, finding them lacking in incident, comparing them unfavourably with their earlier surroundings. Once
again Beatrice took Miriam's arm, no longer out of inclination but
from necessity; her right leg dragged slightly after one of those
episodes which neither of them was brave enough to name, but
which brought a certain solemnity to Mrs Kinsella's demeanour.
She became as much of a friend as they were prepared to admit,
even looked forward to the sound of her key in the door. But Sundays they had to themselves. On Sundays they were amazed to see
traffic still active in the streets when they themselves were so con-
templative. They walked up to the park or down to the river.
They preferred the river prospect, but here the cars rushed past
them more ferociously. 'George Eliot lived here,' Miriam would
say. 'And Henry James had a flat a little farther along. He was
quite poor. You can see how rich George Eliot must have been.'
Beatrice would reply vaguely. She no longer read as much as she
used to, preferred to sit in her chair and dream. Miriam knew that

if she had not moved back to Wilbraham Place Beatrice would have got up later and later and gone to bed earlier and earlier. There would have been no harm in this, but it was best postponed. Full knowledge comes soon enough.

But mostly, on these walks, they gravitated to less pretentious streets, where men were not ashamed to be seen collecting their newspapers in carpet slippers, where boys romped with dogs, and women carried washing to the launderette. They would take a taxi to the end of the long main road, past the council estates and the petrol station, and discover unknown small houses in terraces hidden from the public gaze. The whine of cars could still be heard but they felt safe, protected from all that urgent traffic, silent and ruminative. It was in Beatrice's nature these days to prefer the small to the great, to value the diminutive—an ornament glimpsed through a window between two loops of nylon curtain, a child's doll's pram in a tiny front garden, a ball abandoned on a doorstep—as if such humility was a protection in itself. She said nothing, not wanting to alarm Miriam. By the same token Miriam no longer criticized Beatrice, blamed herself for having done so in the past, on so many occasions. She found herself reading Beatrice's newspaper, not with annoyance but with genuine curiosity, studied articles on liposuction and hormone replacement therapy. 'My husband left me for another man,' she read. Was this what women discussed these days? In the same way she watched late afternoon television with some of Beatrice's own gravity, before listening to the shipping forecast on the wireless. 'Mallin Head rising today' was sometimes the only comment that passed between them. Their meals were light. Beatrice would have eaten from a tray, but Miriam insisted on laying a table, just as she insisted that Beatrice dress herself every day. When Beatrice went to her room, and to bed, Miriam would fetch her briefcase and settle down to work. She worked late into the night, glad of the reprieve but with a sense of urgency, as if this translation must be finished before worse befell them. This outcome was never specified, but came to form one unified impression, along with the child's doll's pram, the elderly men in carpet slippers, the monotony of their days and the shipping forecast.

Rubbing her aching eyes in the early hours of Monday morning Miriam longed for the usual sounds to begin again and life to return to the streets. On Monday morning proper she would go out, join the stream of those going to work and look curiously at the faces of the smart girls with briefcases, the young men with sports bags, as if they were a different species. How was your weekend, she wanted to ask them. Did you stay in bed till noon, go out to lunch, buy the papers and read until it was perhaps time to visit the in-laws or drive over to friends? She could not have described her own Sundays with any degree of conviction: the ride in the taxi, the slow progress through the recreation ground, the checking of small landmarks, perhaps a timid smile of acknowledgement from one of the people they were likely to pass. She knew that Beatrice was endangered, that she herself might be at risk. The risks were enormous. That most of them had already been taken was no safeguard for the future.

Since moving back to Wilbraham Place she had given her telephone number to no one but Tom Rivers. He had called quite frequently in the early days, seemed puzzled by her unavailability, and unconvinced by explanations which he thought were excuses.

'My sister is not at all well,' she had said. 'I don't like to leave her, particularly in the evenings.'

He had asked what the doctor had said, had been impatient when she explained that Beatrice did not want to see a doctor, or rather no longer wanted to see a doctor, since the young man who had originally turned up in response to a call from Miriam to the emergency service had mentioned the possibility of a slight stroke. Horrified, she had shut the bedroom door behind her,

afraid that Beatrice might hear him. But Beatrice had heard, and
had embargoed further visits.

'He was too young,' she had said, almost normally. 'What
could he possibly know? Where did you get him from, anyway?'

'From that outfit the chemist told me about. Medcall.'

'There you are then. Probably not long registered, out till all
hours to earn some money. I won't have anyone here again,
Miriam. And you can forget that nonsense about strokes. It was
more likely a panic attack. I used to have them, do you remember,
when I was young?'

Miriam thought it prudent not to question this: the explanation would serve them well enough. And Beatrice seemed not to
have suffered any decline in perception or intelligence. But when
she was tired her speech was a little unclear, and she winced when
she got up from her chair, as if her leg were numb. All this Miriam
had tried to explain to Rivers in hushed telephone calls, and finally, since she did not wish to be overheard, over lunch. He
seemed to think that the whole matter could be dealt with ratio-
nally, that a housekeeper could be engaged, or a nurse.

'There is no need for that,' she said. 'I'm there.'

'But Miriam, you will be ill yourself! Why this sacrifice?'

'Beatrice is all I have in the way of family,' she said helplessly.
She did not try to explain their wary complicity, each protecting
the other. She was not sure that she could explain it, could dissi-
pate the puzzled frown on his healthy face, assure him of her own
equilibrium. Nevertheless she turned down his further invitations, insisting that she had to be home by two, when Mrs Kinsella
left. That was why she went to the London Library in the morning these days. She felt ashamed. How could she entertain him
with reports from Wilbraham Place, where she discovered, on
her return to the flat, the main topic of conversation had been
Anne Marie Kinsella's change of job, from the record shop to the
supermarket? How could she tell him about the odd communion

of their Sunday walks, of their prehistory? What could he know
of women like herself, even if he were anxious to find out? He de-
vised meetings for them, coffee, lunch, but these delayed her too
much. Work, and the money thus earned, were too important to
be relegated to second place. She tried, once again, to explain all
this, heard her voice growing shrill, and stopped, abashed. He too
had heard the rising note of exasperation, was reminded of her
behaviour when they had last had dinner together, and had concluded that she was moody, moody being his euphemism for difficult.

'You mean you think I'm being hysterical?'

'I think you're over-reacting, certainly.'

'Oh, Tom, Beatrice has no one.'

'That's very sad, of course. But must she have you?'

'Yes. I think she must.'

'I see,' he said stiffly.

She remembered that tone of voice—formal rather than
hurt—from previous attempts she had made at self-justification.
He was not a man to indulge irrational feelings, hers or his own.
If he were disappointed it would be because he was a little tired of
her increasingly fraught expression, and, more than that, of the
lost look in her eyes, which were surely larger, as if her face had
grown thin. He would have liked to see her more often, fully intended to do so, but was not quite so keen on having the same conversation all the time. He could see that she was frightened, but
failed to understand that her wordless confession of fear was her
only relief from the stoical common sense that served her so well
at home. He could not give full weight to her kind of suffering,
having seen the real thing at too close quarters, in Malaysia, in In-
donesia, where he conducted his own investigations into abuses
by the state. His own work seemed to him more interesting than
Miriam's problems of domestic organization. She could see this,
knew that he wanted to trust her, but did not want to shoulder

these particular burdens. More important: he did not appreciate being held at arms' length. He could make the appropriate noises of sympathy, could feel for her quite genuinely, but would have liked to see her attention directed towards himself rather than un- happily wandering.

'I'm sure your sister urges you to go out,' he said.

'Oh, yes. Yes, she does.'

'Then what about coming out with me next Sunday? You said you liked to walk . . .'

'But you see I usually take Beatrice for a walk on Sunday. It's become a routine. It's really the only time she has a change of scene.'

'I see,' he said again, and summoned their waiter for the bill.

She saw with despair that she had nearly ruined something of value, even in that moment admired him for not flinging down his napkin, admired the courtesy he still showed her, and recog- nized her own inability to convey to this attractive and normally constituted man, to whom fortune had probably been kind, her own particular brand of sadness. This defeat had been preceded by the one she could not talk about, least of all to Tom Rivers, and if she saw him clearly, saw the set of his shoulders and the firm- ness of his jaw, she could still see clearly, too clearly, the graceful figure of the one who had proved even stronger than she had thought herself to be, and whom she now saw in her mind's eye as poised for escape. Recognition of her signal failure added to her shame: she too retreated into courtesy. He kissed her cheek as usual, but it was now she who wanted more. Sadly she turned away, knowing that this was an impossibility. He watched her bent head, was sure that he had lost her.

She also knew that Beatrice was aware of her fear, yet was still strong enough not to share it. Miriam found it difficult these days to know what Beatrice was thinking or feeling. What was never referred to was the fact that their mother, and indeed their father, had both suffered strokes, from which they had subsequently died. But Beatrice appeared to have retreated into a form of serenity into which it would have been unkind to intrude. Of the two of them, Miriam thought, Beatrice was decidedly the more composed, which did nothing to lessen her own sense of failure, failure of heart, of nerve, even of intelligence, for she did not see the way ahead, or rather saw it only fitfully. Her duty, she knew, was to continue, but she sometimes doubted whether she could continue for very long. She put her condition down to justifiable fatigue, promised herself a break from her present habit of working late, placed her hopes in momentary recovery and grew wistful, as sleep continued to elude her. In her mind much information had become elusive, obscure. For this reason, perhaps, she became wordless. In any event, she had never been any good at unburdening herself. She had only to look back on her recent conversation with Tom Rivers to realize how she misunderstood the whole process.

Beatrice was more aware of Miriam's disarray than of her own. She knew that for all Miriam's studied impassivity and frequent disapproval her sister was tender-hearted, knew without asking or being told that something irreversible had taken place, that last hopes had been relinquished, that disappointment had set in. She did not entirely blame herself for this; in fact her own state of mind was curious, almost resigned. But she also knew that without her Miriam would have a better chance. This thought glanced across her mind from time to time, without dismay, as if she had read it in a book. But she did not read much these days, preferring to go through the biscuit tin of old photographs, which she examined attentively, as if looking for clues to her own history. Here were her mother and father on their wedding day, her father smugly smiling, her mother with a faint crease of doubt on her still pretty face. That doubt had become endemic, as though her husband, who continued to smile, but whose smile increasingly embodied exasperation and possibly genuine unhappiness, even before the birth of the children, somehow declared that he was let down, misunderstood. He had thought, no doubt, that his own faults should have been dealt with sympathetically, rather than angrily repudiated. There were no more photographs of their parents together, only one of their mother, anxiously smiling, one hand on the railing of the steps leading down into the garden. A widow then, she had accepted widowhood gratefully, but still that smile was anxious, as if there were no one there any longer to tell her what to do. Anxiety was the key to the whole family, that and the knowledge that there were no guides, no one to advise them how to achieve a better life, better than the one that had so badly let them down.

Here was Miriam, aged three or four, her eyes already dark with apprehension, seated on the obligatory cushion, her hand on a large ball. She was wearing an uncomfortable-looking pleated silk dress, and her hair was long and brushed fiercely back. Another one of Miriam, the most disturbing, showed her clasping a doll, and not doing so naturally, as if the doll had only been lent to her and could be reclaimed at any minute by its rightful owner. She had cut off her hair as an act of defiance when she was fourteen. Beatrice remembered how their mother had shrieked and wept, pressed her hand to her heart and threatened to faint, while their father had trembled with rage. It was Beatrice who had taken her to the hairdresser and had watched while he tidied it up, until a small pretty head had emerged, and her face had taken on a tentative smile. But when they returned home their parents had pretended not to notice, and the matter was never referred to. Miriam had worn it short ever since: sometimes Beatrice could trace the abstracted expression of the child on the plain clever face. No one had said, 'Well done.'

Here was Beatrice at her piano, smiling that discreet smile that accompanied all her performances. She had long ago discarded the childish photographs, as if all she cared about, and cared to have recorded, was the finished person, the musician, seated at the piano, directing that winning smile at some unknown listener, who would ideally be more watcher than listener, keen to study the graceful figure, keen to believe that she was playing for him, or so she hoped. He had never revealed himself, however. There were studio portraits of her which interested her far less. These had in common the strenuous upward glance, the strained throat and parted lips that had been de rigueur for this kind of display. One or two of them had even appeared in the newspapers, on her retirement, which she had announced bravely. 'I'm going before they tell me to go,' she had told an interviewer. No one knew the story behind that retirement, or rather that dismissal. No one had said 'Well done' that time either.

Faced with the glossy almost continental smiles of those latter-day portraits (someone had remarked at the time that she resembled Elisabeth Schwarzkopf) she could hardly believe that she had endured her career for so long. It had in many ways been a mistake, a misadventure, although at the time it had seemed like the card of identity that would permit her to enter the adult world. She had never felt at home. Her rising tide of panic at being so exposed she had fought down successfully, but sometimes, on her way to the concert hall, she had had to stop and force herself to breathe slowly. That was what she now remembered: the fear. So that for all her brave words, and her burning feeling of shame at being so disposed of, she was not really sorry when her career had been taken away from her, had come to terms with her invisibility which had been experienced as a relief, had almost enjoyed playing at being the kind of woman she envied, idle, homeloving, self-indulgent, no further efforts required.

Ideally she would have chosen an alternative career, as a kept woman, perhaps, like those women in Colette's stories, which

Miriam had once urged on her. They had been so close then. Now they no longer confided in each other, as if unwilling to confess to the burden of failure that they both carried. Beatrice even found it restful not to speak, conscious as she was of her faintly lopsided mouth. She preferred to dwell on the remote past, that time before the bright hopes faded. She dated their emergence into adulthood from the day that Miriam had cut her hair. How well she had dealt with that incident, had commanded the hairdresser to delay another appointment, had supervised carefully as the scissors crept round Miriam's newly naked ears! Her triumph on that occasion was the only undilutedly happy memory she could dredge out of a past marked mainly by half measures. But Miriam had known; Miriam had always known. It was another matter of which they never spoke.

The immediate past did not detain her, although there was a photograph of Max among the others. She had asked him for one, like a neophyte at the stage door, when he had got her her first engagement. He had appreciated the request in a way he never entirely forgot, much as she remembered Miriam's haircut. Was it true that she had intended to go away with him, to live some entirely fictitious life in the south of France? She could no longer believe in her own folly, which had been prompted by desperation. She had always had a tendency to invent alternative lives for herself, lives which had come to nothing. And word had reached her that Max too was unwell, had developed a tremor that convulsed his face from time to time. So that the retirement in the sun that she had planned for both of them would have been a geriatric affair. She was glad that it had come to nothing.

Her own life, she knew, was finished. At some point she would be removed to a hospital or a nursing-home, as Miriam had once removed their mother. She would prefer to die at home, or even to linger on indefinitely, but she knew that this would be too hard on Miriam. Neither of them, she thought, had deserved their premature reclusion. She sometimes dreaded Miriam's return to the flat, when both would have to pretend that they were more cheerful than was the case. This almost evangelical cheerfulness grated on them both. It must, she thought, be even worse for Miriam, whose cynical nature had hardened somewhat over the years. In a sense both were broken-hearted, but for different reasons. Of the two of them only Miriam could be saved.

'Do you want your coffee?' asked Mrs Kinsella above the noise of the kitchen radio. 'Only we're out of milk. Shall I pop out and get some?'

For she hated being alone with Beatrice, only felt comfortable when she could complain to Miriam. Yet she had behaved well, Beatrice reflected, had remained loyal, even when she could have found a more agreeable job, one where she could vent her own grievances and worries—Anne Marie going out on Saturday nights with her new mates from the supermarket and coming back the worse for wear—without having to hover anxiously over another. It was Mrs Kinsella who wanted coffee, not Beatrice, who, conscious of her unsteady mouth, pretended that she was never thirsty.

'No,' she said. 'I'll go.'

'Are you sure? You're not supposed to go out when Miriam's not here.'

'It's only over the road. And I haven't been out since Sunday.'

'Come straight back, then. And cross by the lights.'

'I will, I will.'

Out in the air she felt better, although the noise of the street confused her. She grasped her stick, measured the distance to the other side of the road, waited for the lights to change, and to change again. Marooned on the pavement, her courage left her. When the young man from the hairdresser's darted across the road with his plastic cup of coffee from the delicatessen she followed in his wake. Miriam, she thought, her last cogent thought.

She heard the car approaching, felt her stick slip away from her, fell, and allowed herself to fall. Across her mind flashed the message, I have been killed. She sensed rather than heard the voices. 'Don't move her,' said one. 'Leave her down until the ambulance comes.' And a more familiar intonation: 'That's Miss Sharpe. I do her hair.' The crowd that had gathered relinquished her gratefully to the ambulance men, and she had a vague notion of being hoisted aloft, as if on the swing that had been in the garden when they were children. Then she knew nothing.

When Miriam returned from the London Library, her briefcase in one hand and the day's shopping in the other, she was met by a tearful Mrs Kinsella, who told her that Beatrice had been taken to hospital.

'They found her details in her bag,' she told Miriam. 'They rang up. I said I'd wait until you came home. I'm afraid it's bad news.' Her eyes darted away from Miriam's face; she was overwhelmingly anxious to leave.

'You go,' said Miriam. 'I'll see you tomorrow. I expect I'll be here.' She had known what to expect, had known it ever since the slow year had turned its face towards the spring.

'Philip Treadgold,' said the man in the white coat. 'I was here when your sister was brought in. I'm afraid there was nothing we could do. I expect you'd like to see her.'

He led her to a small side ward. Then she sat staring at the bed, wondering how to continue now that the worst had happened. When, after fifteen minutes, a nurse came in, Miriam was conscious only of the newly admitted noise of the ward. Of that, and of Beatrice's once beautiful hair clinging to her own wet cheek.

CHAPTER FIFTEEN

On the morning of the funeral Miriam was touched to see Anne Marie Kinsella accompanying her mother. Both were carrying bulging shopping bags.

'Why, Anne Marie,' she said. 'How nice of you to come.'

'That's okay. We get a day off for a funeral. And we've brought some stuff from the shop.'

'You can pay me later,' said Mrs Kinsella, tying an apron over her black dress, and looking askance at Miriam's grey suit. 'They'll be coming back here, won't they? I don't suppose you thought of that. You've got sherry, haven't you? And whisky for the men.'

'Oh, I don't suppose there'll be any men. Only us, I should think.'

She had put a notice in *The Times,* but had not expected it to be singled out from more important, more lavish deaths. She no longer scanned these every morning, fearful of seeing her own name. And it had only taken a couple of lines. 'Beatrice Sharpe,

musician,' it had said, with the dates of birth and death and details of the funeral, at Golders Green, which she did not suppose
anyone would attend. But in fact she was astonished to see a sizeable group of people, all chatting amiably, outside the small
chapel. She was greeted by men and women she had never met,
who assured her of their sadness over the death of 'a dear friend',
'such a lovely artist', 'so sad when she retired so early'. These were
figures from Beatrice's past, glad of a chance to meet up again, to
exchange professional gossip. And the occasion was guaranteed
not to be too melancholy: few of them had seen Beatrice recently,
none, despite their protestations, had known her too intimately.
The exception was Max, who was, she could see, badly shaken,
holding a handkerchief in readiness with a hand that seemed
palsied. And on the edge of the crowd was Tom Rivers, who
stayed discreetly where he was, finding the enthusiastic gathering
not to his taste. As they filed in he grasped her hand.

'I read it in *The Times,*' he murmured. 'I came to offer my
support. If you need it, that is.'

'I shall do. You'll come back to the flat afterwards, won't you?
Forgive me if I concentrate on getting through this.'

The music she had chosen came crackling through the loud-
speaker, but nothing could destroy the haunting Romanian pan
pipes which Beatrice had loved—although Beatrice was strangely
absent from this event, which seemed given over to her erstwhile
colleagues. Only Max dabbed his eyes, moved no doubt as much
by the European character of the melody as by memories of Beatrice, who, perhaps fortunately in everyone's opinion, had not
died at home, but decently, in a hospital. Cheerful as they seemed
to be, they were glad that they would not have to celebrate Beatrice's passing on the actual premises of her demise. Death was sad
enough, seemed to be the consensus, without having it brought
physically to one's notice. Miriam, rigidly at attention, longed
only for it to end, deplored this crowd of strangers. When the

time came for her to touch the coffin she found that she could not reconcile Beatrice dead with Beatrice living. The latter stayed most forcibly in her mind, but it was the Beatrice of long ago, still ardent, still expectant, before the advent of harsh truths. Everyone dies badly, she reflected, as she led the way out into the garden. She was grateful for the warmth of the spring sun on her thin shoulders.

'Is that the sister?' she heard one woman say to her companion. 'Not much of a resemblance, is there? Beatrice was lovely. When she was young, of course.'

As she waited politely for all these people to disperse Miriam realized that she was responsible for them until further notice. A procession of cars, headed by Miriam, Mrs Kinsella and Anne Marie formed: at the last moment she beckoned Max forward, moved despite herself by the trembling hand, still clutching his handkerchief, and the sunken eyes. He seemed grateful for this attention, which she afforded him only reluctantly; he, in his turn, was glad of the presence of the other two women, whom he took to be relations. Without them, Miriam knew, he might have been encouraged to dwell on his own sadness, which she did not doubt was genuine. But what did it comprise? Remorse over his flight, shame at his own very slight and convoluted warning, the night he had recognized the inevitability of Beatrice's death? Miriam had had time to think about this, to read the signs. She bore him no malice; what had happened had not been Max's fault. It could not be said to be anybody's fault. But she still did not like him.

'You're living abroad now, I heard,' she said, to break the silence.

'Yes. I went back to Monaco. I managed to buy back my flat. The chap I sold it to only wanted it for the Cannes Festival.'

'And will you stay?'

He sighed. 'Yes, I expect I'll stay there now. My brother comes out from time to time. My sister doesn't know me any more.' His

voice was monotonous, no longer the voice of a confident man.
'There's nothing to keep me in London. Those people at the funeral: I used to know them well. Now I hardly know them at all.'
He swivelled round from the passenger seat of the car. 'Old age is
a terrible thing, Miriam. Live while you can. It will all be taken
away when you least expect it. You too, young lady. Make the
most of your life.' Miriam saw Anne Marie's eyes dart towards her
mother, saw the minute defensive lift of the shoulders, was glad
of the girl's robust scepticism. This event—the Kinsellas' contribution to the proceedings—must be celebrated in due form. She
did not yet know what form this would take, supposed that long
discussions were in order, that she would have to stay at home for
several days to give their conversations due weight. She was
rather glad of this. She was now trembling, and, worse, yawning
with hunger. When the car reached Wilbraham Place she looked
up at their building, expecting to see Beatrice's face. Latterly she
had been greeted in this way. She had a moment of faintness
when she saw that the window of the sitting-room was empty.
Then she forced her expression back to neutral, and unlocked the
door to admit all these kindly strangers, whose names, she was
sure, would be offered in due course. What would she say to
them? What did one say? 'Thank you for coming' would be in
order. But that was the formula usually offered to the departing
guest, and she surmised that their departure would be delayed for
some time.

'Will there be a memorial service?' asked a woman in a smart
black hat.

'Oh, no, nothing like that. Beatrice was a very private person.'

She wondered if this was true. What was certain, and unde-
niable, was that Beatrice was not anyone's wife, mother or grandmother. That was what had made the death notice in *The Times*
so brief. Few women remained unmarried, yet Beatrice had done
so. At the same time she was so intensely romantic that it was hard

to see how marriage had escaped her. In fact, Miriam reflected, the two conditions rarely went together. The true romantic fell in love all the time, as Beatrice had when young, disastrously susceptible to a handsome face, a lingering glance. Very private? One would have to be if one harboured such vulnerability. In retrospect Miriam congratulated her sister on having kept so much hidden. Her real feelings could be detected only by a look of perplexity in the round still childish eyes, or by a blush which she concealed by bravely animated conversation. She was an expert at concealment, or perhaps had become so after years of naïve disclosure of the most common, the most archaic enthusiasms. 'Isn't he good-looking?' she would remark wistfully, as a photograph of a well-known person appeared in the newspaper. For like all romantics she responded more to outward appearance than to a consideration of worth or merit. She had discounted Miriam's husband completely on account of his indifferent looks. His more serious shortcomings had barely registered.

What was sad about being a very private person, as she had described Beatrice to this unknown woman, was that the condition was usually forced on one, or at least ascribed to one by others. Few doubted that it was sad, although Beatrice had been valiant, had not shown signs of self-pity, had deplored the sort of compromise entered into by their friend Suzanne, who, Miriam was surprised to see, was present, together with her predecessor's mother. No doubt they would make for Harrods when their duty was judged to be done. Nor had Beatrice ever sought the company of other women, for fear of their questions. Her feelings were too deep, and no doubt too unhappy, to be shared. When she reached the age at which most women had small children she had felt the shame of loss, although again she had kept this to herself. It was detectable only in the bewilderment that overtook her from time to time, as if she did not fully understand why she had been left alone. Thereafter she tried even harder to perfect her mask of

smiling serenity, worldly enough to know that this particular expression was rarely challenged publicly, although speculation
would not be halted by it. But Beatrice would know nothing of
that, or rather would choose to know nothing. She had smarted at
her exclusion, but humiliation had soon turned to a genuine sadness, of which only Miriam was aware. But Miriam also knew
that Beatrice was likely to be beguiled by so many potential lovers
that a certain pleasure resided in the reveries they inspired.
Miriam had seen her intense gaze on that horrible evening when
Simon Haggard had first appeared, and had just as appropriately
disappeared, only to reveal himself in another guise in Bryanston
Square. For that reason neither referred to his visit, since each
complicity cancelled the other out. When the affair that followed
had revealed its limitations Miriam had wondered whether Beatrice had not chosen the better part. An unshared life, though not
necessarily innocent, is at least allowed to cherish its original expectations.

'All right?' said Tom Rivers, touching her arm. 'Shall I try to
move them on?'

'Soon,' she replied. 'But everyone has been so kind. I don't
want to seem ungrateful.'

For there, amongst all the unknown faces, was one she did
recognize, altered by age but still wearing the glad smile with
which she had once greeted the girls in their now distant youth.

'Mrs Oliver!' she said. 'How lovely to see you again. How
long has it been?'

'Oh, many years, dear, since I saw you two coming home
from school. I wanted to pay my respects, as much to your mother
as to Beatrice. I was away when she died; I felt badly about that.
We were quite good friends, you know.'

For Miriam remembered now. Their friendless mother had
accepted this little woman as a friend, or rather had recognized
that it was in order to respond to a neighbour who had shown
such exceptional signs of friendliness. Mrs Oliver, who helped out

at the local primary school, was a kind of genius, eager, unpretentious, always happy to lend a hand in an emergency, without any
sign of reluctance or hesitation. She was the only person whom
their mother, no doubt subject to ferocious inhibitions, admitted
to her company, would not go so far as to invite her, but was
happy, or more than happy, when Mrs Oliver dropped in and
could be offered a cup of coffee without loss of face. Beatrice and
Miriam had been grateful for Mrs Oliver's assiduity. She had had
the true instinct of friendship, or maybe it was love: she did not
recognize stiffness or discouragement, merely attributing them to
shyness, which was accurate in a number of cases. The blaze of
Mrs Oliver's unselfishness broke down all barriers. She shopped
for neighbours, knew their children, presented the same eager
face to strangers as she did to acquaintances of long standing.
Even now the face was turned to Miriam as if Mrs Oliver were
longing to perform some service. Miriam noted two teeth missing
and reflected that Mrs Oliver must be well over eighty. But she
looked hardy: good works had replenished her energies. Miriam
was reminded of statues of river gods she had seen in Rome: stone
water pouring from an inexhaustible cornucopia, and no possibility that the arrested but continuous movement could ever be subject to change.

'We very much appreciated your kindness to our mother,' she
now said.

'Oh, we put the world to rights, Celia and I,' laughed Mrs
Oliver, who was a stranger to sadness and who probably took funerals in her stride.

Celia? Miriam had not known that their mother had allowed
such intimacy. She too had kept her own counsel, a gift she had
transmitted to both the girls, her only gift, perhaps. Miriam now
saw how her mother would have delighted in the company of this
woman, would have taken a timid pride in playing the hostess on
such terms of affability.

'She was very proud of you two,' said Mrs Oliver cheerfully.

'Will you be all right, dear? I'd love to help you clear up, but I've quite a long journey, as you know.'

'Thank you for coming,' she said, as she was forced to say many times to the departing guests. Mrs Kinsella was already removing the plates and glasses, signalling to Miriam that she and Anne Marie were anxious to leave. In the kitchen Miriam took them both in her arms. This was the only time she felt tearful, as, apparently, did Mrs Kinsella. They smiled shakily at each other.

'Do you want me to come in tomorrow?'

'Oh, no. You deserve a day to yourself. You've been wonderful. Anne Marie too. I shan't forget your kindness.'

'I was fond of her, you know,' said Mrs Kinsella, depositing her empty shopping-bags in the pedal bin. 'I'll see you the day after tomorrow, then. Take care.'

When she returned to the sitting-room it was to find Max seated in Beatrice's chair nursing a glass of whisky. 'I was the last of that crowd to see her at all recently,' he said. 'What was it? Six, no, seven months ago. I tried to warn you, Miriam.'

'You did. I thought you were exaggerating at the time, but when I moved back I saw for myself.'

'I knew the signs,' said Max, who seemed disposed to stay. 'The mouth. That tells you everything. But you say she was run over?'

'Yes.'

'Should she have been out on her own?'

'Probably not.'

In that case, he reflected, there was no one to blame but Beatrice herself. He tried a last shot. 'You weren't here, I suppose?'

'No. I wasn't here.'

'I loved her, you know,' said Max, looking into his glass as if surprised to find it empty.

'Of course you did, Max. Everyone loved Beatrice. She hadn't an enemy in the world.'

'She had that gift of putting herself out to please, making herself agreeable. Women don't do that any more.' He became belatedly aware that he was talking to a woman. 'She always did. I dare say you do too, Miriam.'

Miriam wondered if they were thinking of the same person. Her Beatrice was a rather more immovable character than the pliant hostess whom Max evidently had in mind. Her Beatrice was a person with whom she had shared a deep but tacit bond, but whose compliance could not always be taken for granted. She wondered if that Beatrice would ever come back to her, or whether she would be changed for ever into the stereotype so recently celebrated by her former friends. That was it: they had changed Beatrice into somebody else. Perhaps it was the function of funerals to distance the dead from the living, to turn them into unknown people to whom strangers had access. And worse: to make sure that they were never again entirely knowable. This thought frightened her. What if she were now to lose sight of Beatrice, who had kept her company for so long, and whose reliance on her watchfulness had not always been easy to shoulder? She wanted to be alone, so that she could sit quietly in Beatrice's bedroom, and, if possible, call her back to life.

Tom Rivers came back, bringing cool air from outdoors. 'They've all gone,' he said. 'All sent on their way. You must be exhausted, Miriam. Shall we leave you in peace? Or would you like me to come back later and take you out for a meal?'

'Anything,' she said desperately. She suddenly felt that more words were beyond her. Her mouth was sour from the sherry she had drunk and her head ached.

'Can I give you a lift?' he said politely to Max, who had poured himself a small whisky.

'You shouldn't drink any more,' said Miriam sharply.

Sharpe by name and sharp by nature, he reflected, hauling himself out of his chair. She had a married name but he had never bothered to remember it. Disagreeable as ever.

'You'll stay here, I suppose?' he asked.

'Of course. Where else would I go?'

Pity about the flat, he thought. But in truth he was not sorry. London had become alien. And those old friends: not one of them had issued an invitation. He did not blame himself, but his age, and, once more, his appearance. His ugly face no longer had prestige behind it, nor any vestige of sexual energy. He longed to be in Monaco, where no one could witness his fall from grace. He would leave immediately, he decided, or rather when he had had a rest. That was the one advantage of staying once more with his brother. There was no need to explain the facts of ageing to him. He knew them well enough. All those trim fifty- and sixty-year-olds had annoyed him. They'll find out, he thought vengefully, as he allowed himself to be led from the room. He collected his hat from the hall table, glad now of this stranger's arm.

Alone, Miriam walked through the flat, opening all the windows, then went into Beatrice's room and leaned over the iron railing that did duty for a balcony. It had been a beautiful day, and the evening was clear. She could hear the sounds of home-going traffic and longed to be out in the street, sharing the hour at which it was legitimate to think of pleasure. She supposed it would not be appropriate for her to wander out, simply to savour the beautiful evening. Beatrice had been the expert on appropriate behaviour: now, newly exposed, she imagined onlookers expressing surprise and mild admonition if she were to pick up her keys and walk into the park. She looked round the room: all was neat, undisturbed. At the sight of Beatrice's slippers she faltered. But the tears, so near the surface, still did not come.

In her own room she surveyed the manuscript on her desk and knew that tomorrow, or the next day, she would settle down to work again, would keep her regular afternoon hours at the London Library, was now free to go there all day, with nothing or no one to call her home. That, surely, was the point: there was no longer anyone to welcome her home. It would be hard now to live alone, with no conversation, however mild, to punctuate the evenings. And the evenings would now be getting longer, more beautiful, so that, alone, she would measure their poignancy. Beneath her sadness, which she had managed to keep under control, she identified another feeling: disappointment that Simon had not thought to attend the funeral. There was no reason why he should have done: one did not attend the funerals of those whom one had met only once, yet something—compunction, perhaps— might have prompted another kind of person to pay his respects to one whose career had ended by his decree. For she now saw that it might not have been Max who made that final decision, but had left it to a younger partner, newly appointed, to go through the books, to examine the returns, and to suggest that Beatrice Sharpe was no longer an asset. It was usually young people who made brutal decisions, and Max, for all his double dealing, might have adopted indifference as his strategy. He had been on the verge of retirement; besides, it was not in his nature to wish the firm well when he was no longer there to take the credit. He might even have, quite enjoyably, anticipated a few problems for his successors. Simon's confusion had been appealing; no doubt it was genuine. But the fact remained that both she and Beatrice had been comprehensively let down by him. Her own disappointment had lasted longer, might last for ever. Love, arriving at this late stage, had ruined her life.

And yet she did not want to see him again, was too afraid of revealing her lack of comprehension of so agile a character. For his slipperiness had something legendary about it. He was the sly hero of a fairy tale, who is unaware of his own slyness, but who nevertheless relies on it to get him out of trouble. As it had done. She had not reproached him, but now she was troubled by her own discretion. He had simply moved on, out of her reach. And Beatrice too had been left behind, to live out the rest of her days being polite, rather than angry, as she might have been. 'Silence is golden' had been their father's favourite maxim; no doubt he would have been proud of them. And 'Humility in all is an essential virtue. Dr Johnson,' he would add, as if they had not grown used to hearing it. By that time he had almost proudly given up exchanging information with anyone. So in effect they had all been barred from communication, not only in that silent house, which she now saw with surprise as the home they had both lost, but later, throughout their lives.

Beatrice had adopted this silence with some grace. Miriam saw that though her life was unfulfilled she had not complained, understanding that women complaining made an ugly sound. The irony was that she would have made a perfect consort for a certain type of man, someone dignified, formal, but susceptible to charm. And Beatrice had remained charming; that had been her victory. She had not declined in an unattractive way. One was aware of her sadness, but also of her imperturbability. She had been beguiled, all too predictably, by Simon's striking looks, to the extent of forgiving him his message. She had known of Miriam's affair, but had had the grace never to question her. That too was a victory. By the same token Miriam had never confessed the extent of her enthralment—for that, surely, was what it was. That too had been a danger avoided. She supposed that they had both behaved well. But now that Beatrice was no longer present she longed to discuss the whole matter with her, would now be fascinated to hear her judgements. Beatrice was a romantic, certainly, but her feelings had always been governed by some sort of moral code, even if that code were one of chivalry, of acts and gestures offered out of a high understanding of worth, of honour. That code had proved misleading. But at this moment Miriam longed most painfully for her to be present, and to defend that code, which now, perhaps, she might be in a position to respect.

She moved away from the window, overcame her reluctance to enter her own room, took off her clothes and ran a bath. The grey suit would be consigned to the back of the wardrobe, and would probably not be worn again. She washed her hair, brushed her teeth, contemplated going to bed. But strangely, after such an exhausting day, she was not tired. She dressed in a soft printed skirt and a silk shirt, wandered back through the flat, closing the windows. She could no longer detect Beatrice's presence. What she felt was an immense stillness, as if she were living in the aftermath of some natural disaster, an earthquake, a volcano. There was no fear in this, only a sort of recognition. This was how it would be now, a life without company, without surprises. Even this silence was appropriate, Beatrice's last gift to her.

When Tom Rivers rang the bell she snatched up a jacket and met him on the doorstep. For some reason it was important that he did not come in: she wanted the flat to be inviolate. And yet he too had behaved well. But he had never met Beatrice, could only comment politely on her loss, which he probably thought could now be consigned to some distant point where it would give no further pain. She would make no mention of it, nor would she embarrass him in any way. If she desired one thing it was that a certain mutual politeness should prevail.

'I hope you're hungry,' he said. 'I dare say you've eaten nothing all day.'

'No, I'm not hungry. Tom, could we go for a walk? You promised me a walk.'

'One of many, I hope.'

She ignored this. 'We could go to the park. It seems to be a lovely evening.' She yawned in an effort to break the tension. 'I think I need some air,' she said.

'All right, but you'll have to eat at some point.'

They walked up Sloane Street in silence, against the roar of traffic. When they entered the park the noise fell away, as it always did. She was glad of his company, although there were no dangers in this peaceful scene. Strangers walked past them, taking a short cut, avoiding Park Lane. She was aware of the apparent anomaly of their walking the other way, into the centre of town. But she wanted to contemplate movement, even the movement of Oxford Street, wanted to gaze at it, this humdrum commercial activity at the end of a working day, the sort of working day from which she felt excluded.

'We were outside the norm, Beatrice and I,' she heard herself say. 'We had too much time to ourselves. We got things wrong.'

'I hope you're going to have more time to yourself now,' he said, misunderstanding her.

'Oh, yes. I'll have plenty of time.'

'Because I shall want to see more of you. Where exactly are we going?'

'There's a pizza place in Baker Street,' she said. For this was a valedictory journey, cancelling out that earlier itinerary, on a Christmas Day now distant enough to be thought safe.

'You were so kind today,' she said later, raising a cup of coffee with a hand that shook. 'I can't thank you enough.'

'Don't cry,' he said gently. 'You don't want that food, do you? Leave it. I'll take you home.'

'Am I to be allowed in this time?' he questioned her in the taxi, looking straight at the back of the driver's head.

'Not yet,' she replied. Perhaps not ever, she thought, but she took his hand, not knowing which of them she wished to console. An embrace was somehow out of the question.

'Goodnight, Tom. And thank you once again.'

'I'll be in touch,' he said, a little formally, as he did when disappointed. She watched him as he strode away into the night.

In bed she lay awake for a long time, sensing the loneliness of the flat. But when she slept it was without dreams, so that she woke easily and calmly, to another day.

CHAPTER SIXTEEN

That year the summer was exceptional. Every day Miriam rose at five, rejoicing in the light. She made tea, wandered through the flat in her nightgown, then took a bath, put on an old cotton dress and went out into the radiant morning to buy the papers. She had no work, and supposed she was on holiday; in her room the dictionaries had been put away until they were needed again. She was conscious only of the beauty of the weather, as if not to succumb to it were a solecism, an offence against nature.

Her days fell into a pattern. When the shops opened she would buy a sandwich for her lunch, put it in a bag together with the book she was reading, and make for her usual bench in the small stony memorial garden at the foot of the church opposite the river. There she would sit quite peacefully until the clock struck midday, when she would eat her sandwich and go in search of coffee. After that the blaze of the afternoon sun would drive her back home. In the afternoon she would lie on her bed, reading. Already she had got through _What Maisie Knew_ and _The_

Awkward Age, and was about to start on *The Tragic Muse.* She marvelled that Henry James knew so much about women and children, yet had remained a bachelor, and by all accounts a man of the greatest integrity. She liked that about him, that and his reputation for modesty. He had deferred to worldly friends, as if he were not more worldly than any of them. There was nothing cheap about Henry James.

Her second excursion would take place at about five o'clock, when she would go out and buy her supper. Here too she made a long detour, thinking any shop near to hand too feeble an attraction. The year was at its zenith, the trees heavy and immobile, the grass dry, the earth cracked. There had been no rain for over three weeks, a fact deplored by the weather forecasters but enjoyed by everyone else. She liked to see the returning workers, their jackets over their arms, their shirts damp with sweat, trudging along to their first drink of the evening. And the girls, more and more skimpily dressed, their bare feet at ease in their sandals. There was little slackening in the fierce temperature; now as in the early morning her sense of holiday was complete.

It seemed to her that the day had been full of incident. The major event, of course, was the extraordinary power of the light, which made human activity seem otiose. And there were lesser diversions, to which she gave her full attention. She had made several acquaintances among those, who, like herself, came to eat their lunch in this little enclave. There was the highly respectable-looking man, whom she suspected of having lost his job, and who read the *Financial Times* from cover to cover. When he stopped by her to drop his newspaper in the rubbish bin she revised her opinion: he was honourably retired, tasting freedom and, like herself, with nothing or no one to keep him at home. 'Good morning,' they said to each other. 'Another lovely day.' And then, unexpectedly, the breakthrough. 'How are you getting on with that?' he asked, indicating her book. 'Sad stuff, isn't it? And yet it stays in

the mind. Well, I won't keep you. Have a pleasant afternoon.'
'You too,' she replied. Truly one made more friends among
strangers than among familiars.

There was the woman who singled out Miriam as her particular confidante, a decorative widow, who twitched her floral
skirts and adjusted her earrings all the time she was talking, her
agitation politely concealed but slowly rising to the surface. The
talk was of her dead husband, her son who was doing so well in
the computer business, of a holiday she was about to take with a
woman friend. Miriam saw that this prospect was upsetting her,
accounted for the restless hands, and at the same time the great
care given to her appearance. 'Just because I have no man in my
life,' her attitude seemed to say, 'just because I am forced to go on
holiday with my friend Betty, whom I do not particularly like, do
not assume that I am beyond pleasing. I can still attract a second
glance, and am keen to do so. That is why I spend the evenings
ironing my clothes for the following day, or regilding my hair in
my tiny bathroom. I am not finished yet. I see you have got to
know that man reading the *Financial Times*. Just my luck.' When
her still pretty mouth turned down at the corners Miriam would
offer, 'Portofino, you said? It should be lovely.' A sad smile was
her response. 'I miss my husband so much at holiday time. But life
goes on, doesn't it?' 'Yes indeed,' Miriam would say, although her
own life did not seem to be advancing in any recognizable direction. She was mildly interested to note that this stasis did not displease her.

Sometimes, to their delight, a stout baby, always the same one,
would do the honours, standing before them on unsteady legs,
while his young nurse or au pair sank down on a bench and gratefully lit the first of a succession of cigarettes. The widow was better at entertaining him than Miriam was, yet it was to Miriam's
blue cotton skirt that he stretched out his hand. At once she would
cover it with her own, while pretending an interest in other mat-

ters. The hand would be withdrawn, to be tentatively replaced, again to be imprisoned. The small face would split into a smile that revealed even smaller teeth. His name was William; they learned that from the somnolescent au pair, whose eyes were now closed as she tilted her yearning face to the sun. He did not come every day, but when he did they were rewarded by a waving hand as he was wheeled out of sight. On such occasions she and the widow were in perfect accord. 'I'll bring a drink for him tomorrow,' one of them would say, already busy on his behalf. But then it grew even hotter and they deduced that he was being kept at home. They both missed him, smiled understandingly at each other when it was time to leave. Such perfect accord was rarely arrived at with those on whom long acquaintance had already built up a considerable dossier of information. All she desired to know about the widow was her name. When she was able to greet her as Helen she was content merely to accept what she was told, without asking a single question. This relationship was so restful that she wondered why it had eluded her in the past. Like or dislike no longer entered the equation. Attention, observation, were all that were required.

She tried to explain this to Tom Rivers when he telephoned in the early evening. She had made an interesting discovery: he was as solitary as she was. This was a great weight off her mind; she did not doubt that he felt the same. She imagined him as one of those fearless explorers featured in old-fashioned children's books, the sort she had read when she was small, men in goggles and close-fitting helmets, tracking across Arctic wastes, with a pack of dogs in tow.

'I see you setting off for places unknown to civilized man,' she said.

'I am in fact off to Jakarta next week. I rang to remind you.'

'You should be trekking across the Polar regions.'

'I seem to be in those with you already.'

'How long will you be away?'

'About three weeks. That will give you time to read *The Wings of the Dove*. There will be a short examination on it when I see you again.'

'You are very nice to me, Tom.'

'Yes, I am, aren't I?'

'Am I nice to you, or shouldn't I ask?'

'You're all right, I suppose. Tedious, unpleasant, unattractive . . .'

'Tom!' she cried, horrified.

'Don't be silly, Miriam. You are my friend. It was your decision, remember.'

'You mean . . .'

'Precisely.'

She did not ask him what discreet alternative arrangements he had made when she had declared herself unready to become his lover. He had accepted this with good grace, presumably detecting in her not reluctance but evidence of that same curious stasis. She was confident that he remained fond of her, loved him for still expressing interest in her life.

'How was Helen today?' he would ask. 'How many ensembles is she taking to Portofino?'

'Don't mock, Tom. She is really unhappy about going. She is quite frightened.'

'She should stay at home, then. There is no harm in staying at home. You let nobody down. I spent the day at home and I was perfectly content.'

'What did you have for lunch?'

'A tin of sardines and a tomato.'

'I see. And will you eat out tonight?'

'Yes.'

She detected, with her new perceptions, a very slight change in the tone of his reply. A woman, she assumed. Her own feelings on this matter would have to be examined, but not yet. What she appreciated about the present situation was his acceptance of her unpreparedness, even her childishness. Even though she was aware that in time these qualities would cause his interest in her to wane she was content not to anticipate that day, the day when she would lose him. That would be difficult, perhaps unbearable. But she had too much respect for the passage of time to violate her present contentment, to offer a sacrifice before one was due. Indifference was a release after months of painful feeling. She was unwilling to relinquish it.

'What time is your plane for Jakarta?'

'Eight-thirty next Monday morning.'

'May I see you off?'

'I'd like that.'

'Unless . . .'

'No, no, that'll be fine. I'll pick you up.'

'Will you ring me on Sunday?'

'Yes. Are you going out again?'

'Later, no doubt. Take care of yourself, Tom.'

'You too.'

Still the amazing weather continued. It was mid-August, and already the evenings were lengthening. But the days were so filled with a strange plenitude that it was easy to dismiss thoughts of autumn, and impossible to think of winter. She took up her position in the garden as if she had always done so, since the beginning of time, greeted Helen and the man with the newspaper as if they were fellow students in some secret seminar. Once three boys came and kicked an empty Coke tin around but were discouraged by the uninflected stares directed at them and made off, leaving the tin spinning on the ground. This was eventually removed by the man with the *Financial Times*. Once a small cloud passed over the sun and they looked at each other, concerned. But the sun soon reasserted its rights, and Helen sighed, twitched her skirts and went on with her story.

'She wanted us to share a room, but I put a stop to that. I felt mean, but it's not as if she were short of money. And it takes me so long to get ready in the morning . . .'

'You were quite right. I never shared a room with my sister.'

'Oh, I didn't know you had a sister.'

'She died,' said Miriam briefly.

'Oh, I'm so sorry.'

'There's no need.'

For Beatrice had left her in peace. There could be no ghosts in such a summer. She thought of her every evening, when she went through the flat, but her thoughts were quiet, accepting. Proper grieving, on which she had turned her back, could be postponed until she had time for decent reflection. Because she knew that this process must be gone through, and that she would in due course give it her full attention, she put it off, feeling quite easy about doing so. At some point, she knew, their alliance would reassert itself: Beatrice would once more keep her company, as she had done in the past. And as she grew older the past was lengthening, was no doubt more weighted than the future. Quite simply she had decided to enjoy these days that had been given to her. The great sun cancelled out any incipient darkness within. For this she was grateful.

There was a slight infraction of her marvellous new regime when Helen, at the end of one afternoon, when they had both stayed longer than usual, invited her home for a cup of tea. Miriam did not want this, did not want intimacy of any kind, but it would have been impolite to refuse. Looking round Helen's tiny immaculate sitting-room she could see why the holiday seemed such an alarming prospect. Helen fitted in here, her full skirts as much a feature of the place as the pretty china plates in a corner cabinet, and the matching china candlesticks and bonbon dishes on the small octagonal table. In the adjoining kitchen she could hear cups being assembled on a tray, could smell scones or muffins being warmed under the grill. She knew that the feast would be served with the maximum of ceremony, felt unsuitably dressed in her old skirt and blouse. Helen, she could see, had re-freshed her make-up in the kitchen, where she no doubt kept some sort of kit for all emergencies.

'My husband always loved to see me busy,' she said, arranging glass dishes of two kinds of jam at Miriam's elbow.

'And you still do all this? Just for yourself?'

'Oh, yes. I still miss him, you see. That's why going away with a woman is going to be so difficult. I'm not used to the propin-quity . . .'

'Why not tell your friend that you don't want to go?' she asked. She reflected that until recently she would not have been capable, or perhaps guilty, of such a lack of reticence.

'But it's all arranged,' said Helen, who did not seem grateful for the suggestion, but pleasantly excited, as if she were contem-plating a woman of a different species, like the bad girls she had been forbidden to play with on the way home from school.

'She's got two weeks to find someone else,' Miriam went on. 'You don't have to make an excuse. Just tell her you won't be ready in time.'

'But I am ready.'

'No, you're not. You don't want to go. You're not ready to go away with a woman. That's it, isn't it?'

She did not know why she was offering this advice, apart from the fact that it was in the same spirit of glasnost that had dic-tated her actions for the past month. She could see what this was about. Helen, whom she did not know, and might not see again, really wished to talk about her husband, to this stranger, to any-one, maybe to elicit comparable confidences, and thus to be at home in the only way she appreciated. The holiday had been de-vised by a more robust personality in an effort to take her out of herself. To this friend mourning was unseemly. Miriam could al-most sympathize, but in a moment of self-doubt wondered whether mourning should not be given pride of place. She had almost lost sight of her own, but was aware that it lay in wait. She had made a mistake in accepting this woman's invitation. She would have done better to have gone straight home, to have spent a few quiet moments in Beatrice's room, making contact again, although she was not ready to do so. The longer this could be put off the better. Yet she could still appreciate Helen's problem.

'I must go,' she said. 'I'll see you on Monday. Thank you for tea.'

At the door—and she was aware that her contribution was being judged imprudent—she asked, 'Will you go, do you think?'

'Of course I'll go,' replied Helen primly. 'I hope I'm not one to let an old friend down.'

'Good for you,' said Miriam, turning away. The friend, no doubt, was feeling the same way. They would congratulate themselves later on having got through the holiday, or the ordeal, might even consider doing it again. In the dark days ahead they would suppose that they had enjoyed it, only too grateful that the following summer was still a long way off.

But summer was still an eternal now, although a notice in Marks and Spencer said, 'Take comfort in wool.' Dark-coloured clothes were already on display, yet the assistants were pale with fatigue. It was they who deserved their holiday. Suddenly discouraged by the plastic bag bumping against her leg (for even that sensation was familiar) she took a taxi home, longing for the silence of the flat. She closed Beatrice's windows, feeling, for the first time, an edge of loneliness. She was in for the evening, for the night, until the new sun released her again the following morning.

The next day was Sunday, which she always found difficult. Sunday was a day traditionally consecrated to ennui, a day on which it was inappropriate—Beatrice's word—to eat a sandwich for lunch. In Miriam's mind Sundays were situated somewhere in

February, with only a bleak sky to lighten the day. And on Sundays, of course, she took a walk with Beatrice. Now, theoretically, she was free to enjoy the sort of Sunday which she used to assign to other people. She could get up late, read all the papers, spend the afternoon at a museum, if she so chose. But she was too restless to stay indoors, and the papers would contain little of interest at this quiet season of the year. Most people were still away; when she went out Sloane Street was almost silent. It was still very early, barely seven. Quite suddenly she was disheartened, not knowing what to do with her time. Time was the problem, she realized, and would continue to be so as the days grew shorter. And the winter was inevitable, even after so exceptional a summer. *Je redoute l'hiver, parce que c'est la saison du confort.* Rimbaud had said that, and, perhaps wisely, cut his winters short. But death, even when not entirely involuntary, was not the ideal solution.

This Sunday would be no different from any other. And in the morning Tom would be gone for three whole weeks. This, no doubt, was what accounted for her moment of discouragement, and now, perhaps, was the moment to consider the implications of this. She would miss him; in many ways she needed him to be there. She felt for him a secure, an established affection that somehow negated physical love. He was the brother she had never had. So used to her own company, or to the company of her sister, she was newly aware of the attractiveness of men. And Tom was by any standards an attractive man, large, reassuring, with nothing of the original about him. It was true that women responded to that latter characteristic, in which they saw a whole youthful history which excluded them. That, presumably, was why some women went to football matches. Tom was cordial, grown-up. He had always behaved impeccably, had not expressed ill-humour at her refusal. Sometimes she suspected that he was relieved: her comparable gift to him was never to question him, to allude to the possibility of other women in his life. He had no sisters, he had told her, and she thought, or hoped, that she fulfilled that function for him. Friendship with a man was an unfamiliar sensation. She had a sudden desire to hear his voice, but knew that she must not disturb what was probably a private interlude. In any event he had promised to telephone that evening.

She wondered briefly, for it was impossible not to, what kind of woman would appeal to him, and came up with a profile of someone pretty decided, a colleague no doubt, with the same interests and preoccupations. This would be a woman of some quality, shrewd, courageous, undeterred by discomfort or danger, with wide experience of the world's most uncomfortable regions. Miriam saw her in a khaki shirt and trousers, with a fine unadorned face and short red hair. The same sort of background, probably, a family history that could bear the light of day. She was not jealous of this woman. How could she be? She herself had succumbed to more corrupt attractions which still aroused in her a mournful excitement. She was not good enough for Rivers, that was it. Sometimes she heard a wistful note in her voice when she was speaking to him, but only because her respect for him was so great. If she were unavailable, and had made herself so, it was because she judged herself to be unsuitable. Her earlier love affair had disqualified her, made her unsure. The distance she maintained between them was not tactical. It was the natural expression of a profound remorse.

The day would be filled, but, she suspected, with difficulty. For the first time since Beatrice's death she felt fretful, unoccupied, yet at the same time resentful of restraints, real or imaginary. She knew that her own deeply receptive nature would be adequate to the task of measuring her loss, of allotting future time to its perusal, of reaching some conclusion about the conduct of her own life. She had obliged some law of nature and let the season govern her moods. It would have been unwise to disregard the compelling power of the sun, but it would now be wise to proceed as if the sun were unlikely to shine for ever. Already there were minute signs that autumn was on its way: a stillness in the heavy trees, as if they were longing to shed their leaves, asters and dahlias beginning to arrive on flower stalls. As she walked along the Embankment she brushed imaginary cobwebs from her face: there were more spiders about than usual. She did not have the confidence to sit down in her usual place, now empty of its familiars. Tomorrow, for a little while longer, she would recapture the spirit of what she now saw as a blessed hiatus, almost like the interval between sleeping and waking. Now she did not question the impression that that interval had expired.

The walk was perhaps a mistake. Disconcerted, she turned back towards home, busied herself with minor household tasks, half wanting to be rescued, yet too unprepared to go in search of rescue. In the afternoon she would go to the British Museum, or to the Wallace Collection—it hardly mattered which. The advantage of the Wallace Collection was that it would be empty; on the other hand it was in that problematic part of London that had been the scene of her most shameful encounters. She marvelled at the strange coincidence that had placed Simon and Tom on the same trajectory, could not quite face retracing those steps, though the Wallace Collection was innocent. It would have to be the British Museum, she thought with a sigh, but was in fact disinclined to leave the flat, and wished only to sit quietly with a book in her lap, even though she knew that the book would remain unopened.

She waited restlessly for Tom's telephone call, and yet was startled when it came. No sound had been heard in the building all day.

'Tom?' she said cautiously, conscious of the fact that he might not be alone.

'Everything all right?'

'Yes, fine. I'm seeing you tomorrow morning, aren't I?'

'Can you wait outside for me? I'll be coming by cab, rather early, I'm afraid. Is seven o'clock too soon for you?'

'Quarter to, if you'd prefer it.'

'Yes, that might be preferable.' He sounded businesslike; there was definitely someone there. He could be having this conversation with anyone. She felt the slightest bit uneasy at the thought.

'That's better,' she heard him say in his normal voice. 'My brother stayed the night. He's just gone, I'm glad to say. I love him, but I need some time to myself. You're all right, I trust. All well out there?'

'What will you be doing in Jakarta?'

'East Timor, actually. Keep that to yourself.'

'Is that dangerous?'

'Unsavoury, certainly.'

'Will you be safe?'

'Of course.'

In the morning, seeing him in the first beautiful light, she did not doubt that he would be safe. What troubles could befall this splendid representative of the established order, in a cream-coloured suit that hinted at England's colonial past, his hair sternly brushed, his expression benign? He took her hand and raised it to his lips, then relinquished it and gazed interestedly out of the car window.

'I always think this is the worst part,' she said, as they sped down Cromwell Road. 'This is the point at which I know I'm never coming back. That my home is only a memory. That London is irretrievable. This is worse than the flight itself. The flight is fantasy. This is the wasteland. This is reality.'

'People live here too, you know. All the way to the airport. Cleaners, mechanics, useful people.'

'I know I'm not useful, Tom.'

'Oh, don't start.' But he looked at her quizzically, indulgently, took her hand again. 'What will you do while I'm away?'

'I'll get down to some work, I think, although there's nothing urgent. Will it be hot out there?'

'Oh, yes.'

'It will be autumn when you get back.'

'Oh, hardly. Still time for a holiday. I've been invited to join some friends in Sardinia, as a matter of fact.'

She felt briefly alarmed, as though she were losing him. This feeling intensified as he strode into the airport building, as if he could hardly wait for her to catch up with him. Strangers eyed him with respect, not so much for his height and vigour as for his air of being in his element, of being in control of circumstances. The light-coloured suit emphasized his strong, suddenly over-whelming physical presence.

'Do you want coffee?' he asked, but absent-mindedly.

'Yes, I think so. And you should eat something. You've a long day ahead of you.'

In the cafeteria he was clearly preoccupied, his lips pursed, his fingers playing with sachets of sugar. She felt that they had be-come distanced, as though the journey to Heathrow, about which she had felt so superstitious, had separated them. When they stood up to leave she saw that he looked suddenly older, as if an anxiety had surfaced.

'You'll be all right, won't you?' she asked.

'Yes, yes.' Then, turning his full attention on to her, 'Don't wait, Miriam. These places are so horrible. Take care of yourself.'

It was what he always said. She watched him walk away from her, felt his kiss on her cheek. When he comes back, she thought, but did not know quite what she thought. On the return to London she imagined meeting him again, fulfilled merely by his renewed presence. This impression kept her company throughout the rest of the day and even into the night. But when she switched on her radio on the Tuesday morning it was to hear that his plane had come down in the sea and that there were no survivors. Sab-otage had not been ruled out.

CHAPTER SEVENTEEN

*W*inter reconnects one with one's losses. Christmas, celebrated in the shops from October onwards, is dreaded by the bereaved, and perhaps even more by the bereft. Miriam, bereaved of Beatrice, still looked up at the window when she returned home at the end of the day, expecting to see the white oval of a face, a lifted hand, and still, when the telephone rang, wondered whether someone—the police, the Foreign Office—were trying to contact her to tell her that Tom had been recovered from the sea. She maintained a strict control of her emotions; nothing of her dismay appeared on her face. She felt an immense confusion, was almost grateful to the monotony of her daily routine for consuming her time, which was a continuous problem. Waking early, she dreaded the extra hour thus afforded her: what to do with it? She was not easy until she left the flat and joined the crowd at the bus stop. There some commonality of purpose asserted itself; she was disguised as an honest wage earner. Only she knew that no conversation, of an idle casual tenor, such as she imagined among colleagues, would enliven her day; only a muted greeting from a custodial figure would signal her arrival at her place of work. Thereafter the silence would be unbroken.

These days, though still in thrall to her original discipline, she loitered, lingered, looked into windows. If she were lucky there would be a picture in a small commercial gallery to detain her, or she might make a short detour to the French tourist office and pick up some timetables. This was satisfactory as far as it went, but she missed the random, the intimate nature of small shops on unfrequented streets, with their more humble displays, that she and Beatrice used to appreciate on their Sunday walks, in areas where shopkeepers still lived on the premises. She did not know whether what she felt for such places was homesickness or some more recent nostalgia; she only knew that all the components of loss were there. Their hard-earned sophistication, Beatrice's and hers, the determination with which they had faced the world, were no longer of any use, were, for quite long periods, genuinely unavailable. She knew that this was how Beatrice had felt at the end of her life, when the support of her own character was beginning to falter. Miriam now sensed that she was united with her sister as never before, imagined her reactions to those tiny incidents which sometimes furnish a life more readily, more accessibly than major events, birth, marriage, even death. She no longer had any desire to question Beatrice on what she might now be qualified to discuss but rather to induct her seamlessly into humdrum everyday banality, to comment on a passing occurrence or a striking face, to link arms again, to walk slowly down uneventful streets on misty silent Sunday mornings, mornings which were the proper repository for that great abundance of time which she now had in her gift.

As for Tom Rivers, she quite simply mourned the fact that she would never see him again, that he was beyond recall, had died in so abrupt and definitive a manner that she could not admit him into her daily life, as she could her sister, was unable to imagine taking a walk with him, as they had once anticipated. Her keenest regret was that this walk, or these walks, had never taken place; with their disappearance, with the impossibility of their now ever taking place, she felt as if her own life had been interrupted, as his had been. She had no faith, was unable to console herself with visions of Beatrice and Tom in the hereafter, conversing affably: the idea was ludicrous, although she knew that they would have been compatible. She felt something more unexpected, an impression of some not quite conceivable harmony in which men and women, their differences forgotten, were at last able to meet without prejudice, without preconception, not in some problematic next world but in an ideal world, as this was meant to be. In a state of Edenic honesty, but with all their worldly experiences still to inform them, the dead would at last confess as they had never done in life, could at last bestow praise, affection, love, not for some absent Deity but for one another. She did not know whether this impression was theologically correct, rather thought not, since everybody qualified for a place. Simply she knew that the dead were composed of the same material, that there were no more differences between them, and that had these differences not been perceived earlier, in life, as it were, it was because the living were so frequently in error.

This was almost a consolation, but not quite. Sometimes, in that strange passage between sleeping and waking, she would see Tom, in his light-coloured suit, or Beatrice, in her black dress. Tom would seem to be striding away from her, as he had done at the airport, and it was easy to imagine his stride continuing without loss of impetus, as if he were some mythical character whose brief life comprised endless journeys, purposeful wanderings, missions undertaken in obedience to promptings, compulsions, of which she, earthbound, knew nothing. Once she had a sense of Tom, still in his suit, striding off into regions with no geographical boundaries, which her own scepticism would not allow her to identify. Whereas Beatrice was always turned towards her, smiling discreetly from behind her piano, with none of the disappointment that had clouded her gaze as life let her down. This Beatrice, she could see, was possessed of some secret knowledge she had not formerly apprehended; there had been some sort of reconciliation. So that whereas Tom's energy could not be stilled, Beatrice was all acquiescence. Fully awake, she marvelled that these images were so exact. Eternity had made them immortal. She had no need to fear that they would vanish. Their posthumous presence was assured.

She saw that these two people, who had never met, held the keys to her own life, were her completion, her fulfilment, whereas more ephemeral characters, such as Simon Haggard, were simply made of inferior material. Once he had passed her in a car; at least she had seen a hand waving and had identified it as belonging to him. The only surprise was that she felt no curiosity about him. His physical splendour was no longer a memory; it was as if he had become a dead star, a random fragment of astronomical matter, beyond usefulness. Naked, as he always was in her memory, he had less physical presence than Tom in his pale suit, as if his nakedness had been inopportune, ill considered. Yet she had loved the one, not quite loved the other. Both partings had been unnatural, yet no one was entirely to blame. She saw now that shame and guilt were otiose; only regret was permissible. And defensible. Miriam saw that she too deserved regret for the manner in which she had been forsaken. One's life is not always in one's own hands. That is why it is so convenient to blame outside forces. But in fact one's secret self makes certain choices, rejects others. This is a matter for reflection, not for self-castigation. But it is apparently easy to explain to others: 'That was where I went wrong. That was where I made my mistake.' It was in fact more sensible to contemplate destiny. Just as it was Tom's destiny always to be walking away, and Beatrice's to smile loyally, it was hers to appreciate their closeness, in death as in life, and, almost as important, to see them as persons of worth, deserving of praise. Her younger self—but she had not been so very young—had mistaken the external envelope as an indication of excellence. This, in retrospect, struck her as delayed childishness, or the sort of awestruck impressionability with which she had so often reproached Beatrice. Yet for all his splendour Simon had dematerialized, and his absence left her almost indifferent. Quite simply, other considerations now held sway.

Occasionally, at this misty season of the year, when the light began to fade at three o'clock, and sometimes earlier, she allowed herself to go home, packed up her books without compunction, knowing that the same steady stream of words would be faithfully present when she returned on the following morning. It was not quite a day's work, but it would have to do, for the time being at least. Just as she was anxious to leave the flat, she was anxious to get back to it before the evening set in properly. The lightless days, which she found difficult, were followed by nights of a depth which she had almost forgotten. Once she had lit the lamps in the sitting-room and in her bedroom the flat seemed welcoming, as it had not done for a very long time, although she still found the approach to the building in Wilbraham Place unrealistic, unconvincing, unlike the homecomings she envisaged for happier people. Those characters she had seen only in pictures, images of other lives, so superior to her own ruminative progress towards an empty evening. She would make tea, sit demurely, reflectively, as Beatrice must have done. Beyond the windows all was dark. When a light came on in the building on the opposite side of the road she would know that someone else had reached home. This other light was the only sign that distinguished day from the very nights which she found so conducive to the thoughts and memories that she now cherished. This was her dream time, infinitely preferable to those more disconcerting dreams, over which she had no control, and which would sometimes startle her out of the black sleep on which she had almost come to rely.

On one such evening, unsignalled, no different from all the others, she was astonished, and not a little annoyed, when the doorbell rang. She was even more annoyed, when she opened the door, to see Jonathan Eldon, her former husband, whom she had mentally consigned to an earlier life, a life before life, standing there. He looked no different, although his hair was grey. Such was her stupefaction that she could find no words with which to greet him, merely gazed at him uncomprehendingly. He exuded a kind of haphazard prosperity; she was obliged to concede him a certain presence. His bulky overcoat concealed his thinness, which, as far as she could make out, the years had not modified. Otherwise he looked like an aged boy, although he had never been boyish. The grey hair was the only clue to the authentic old man he would eventually become.

'Hello, Miriam. What are you doing here?'

'I live here.'

'Oh, I didn't know. I came to see Beatrice, actually. I thought she might know where you were.'

'I'm here. And Jon, Beatrice is dead.'

'Good God. I am sorry. Heart, was it?'

'It was an accident.'

'What a shame. I mean, what a terrible thing. Well, I've found you at any rate. Aren't you going to ask me in?'

Resigned, she led the way into the sitting-room, gave him a drink, wondered how soon she could send him back to Canada. Unless, terrible thought, he had returned to England.

'What are *you* doing here?' she asked rudely.

'Well, I'm back, you see.' He picked up her book. 'Henry James. What do you think of Henry James?'

'Not now, Jon. Tell me about yourself. What brings you back?'

'I'm doing some work at Imperial College. I'll be there for a year or two. They may ask me to stay on.'

'And where are you living?'

'I've rented a place in Gloucester Road. Useful for the College. Not very nice, though.' He looked round the room. 'This place hasn't changed. Neither have you. You're older, of course. Did you marry again?'

'No, I didn't.'

'I did.'

'Yes, I remember you were going away with someone. Your lab assistant, I think you said.'

'Christina, yes.' His face fell.

'What happened?'

'Well, she left me, didn't she?'

'For another man?'

'Another woman, actually. Don't laugh, Miriam.'

'I'm so sorry,' she said, composing herself. 'I'm sure it was very painful.'

'It's always more humiliating for a man, when that happens, though I gather it's getting quite common. She joined this group, you see. They met every week to denounce male power.'

'How very old-fashioned of them.'

'One night she came home and said she was moving in with her friend Linda. I didn't know what she was talking about. Then she said she now felt free to explore her own sexuality, not merely to be an accessory to mine. I didn't understand. Do you?'

'No, I don't. But then I haven't met Linda.'

'I'm glad I've managed to amuse you at last.'

'Dreadful of me,' she said. 'Unforgivable. Do go on.'

'Well, I divorced her. She didn't expect that. But I don't hang about.'

'No, you certainly don't do that,' she agreed. 'And are you living alone now?'

'For the moment,' he said cautiously. 'It's worse for a man, you know. Being left, I mean.'

'I doubt that. It's bad for anyone. Everyone.'

'The thing is, Miriam, can you think of any reason why we shouldn't get back together again?'

'I can think of quite a few reasons. We were quite incompatible, as you well know.'

'I don't mean sex, if you don't want it,' he went on. 'Though as I remember it that worked rather well.'

'Yes, I suppose it did.' Her tone was polite, not particularly friendly.

'I could move in here. It makes perfect sense, actually. I mean we're both getting on. You must be what? Fifty?'

'Forty-nine. Be honest, Jon, the idea had only just occurred to you.'

'Well, what's wrong with it?'

'Quite a lot, as it happens. For instance you haven't asked me how I feel about it.'

'Well, go on,' he said, shrugging himself out of his overcoat. 'I'm listening.'

'I've been in love,' she said slowly.

'I'm not talking about love.'

'No, you're not, are you? I am. That's the difference between us. I've known both kinds of love, the kind based on desire and the kind based on esteem. Both are incomparable. Nothing comes after. Nothing could.'

'And did they love you, these men?'

'Neither said so, certainly. But yes, I think they did.'

Suddenly she knew this to be true, and the clouds in her mind dispersed. What she had felt had been shared, in one way or another, had even been anticipated. The spark had not landed on stony ground. Indeed that ground had never been stony, and once again felt fertile, with movement under the earth, as if spring were breaking through.

'So you see, Jon, an arrangement such as the one you suggest would simply not do. I'm sorry. I'm sorry for both of us. But as for myself I'm better off alone.'

'Contemplating your lost loves? I take it they're both in the past?'

'Oh, yes. And yes, I shall probably contemplate them, as you say, for the rest of my life.'

'You've been reading too much. That was always your trouble.'

'My trouble is that neither of these characters came out of a book. There were no happy endings.'

'Well, why not be practical? We know each other. We lived together for five years. Doesn't that count for something?'

'Of course it does.' Astonishingly little, she thought.

'So you're going to spend the rest of your life sitting here alone, like patient Griselda . . .'

'Oh, but I'm not waiting for anything. Or for anyone. I just know what I have to do. What I want to do.'

'I can see that you're lonely without Beatrice.'

'I should be lonely anyway. I've always been lonely. Beatrice was lonely too. But loneliness can be acceptable, you know. Even companionable.'

'And what am I to do?'

'I don't know. I can't tell you that. How could I? I no longer try to arrange people according to my own ideas. People do what they must. You'll settle down to your work, I suppose, and you'll become absorbed in it. Don't underestimate the importance of work. I've sometimes been guilty of that.'

'I think I know the importance of work.'

'Of course you do. Perhaps that was one of the reasons why

we shouldn't have married. Neither of us understood what the other was doing. Or understood each other, come to that.'

'Why did you marry me, then?'

'Because I'd known you a long time, and because I wanted to be married. There, that's an honest confession. It doesn't do me much credit, I know. I thought I should be happier if I were married. I thought you would be too. But I didn't love you, any more than you loved me. Why did you marry me?'

'For the same reasons, I suppose. I was contented enough, but I knew the difference. I loved my wife; Christina, I mean. I dare say I'll fall in love again.'

'What makes you say that?'

'Because I find life rather dull on my own.'

'You've always been restless. You were with me.'

'I found you rather annoying. So silent, so disapproving. You never seemed to back me up. Never wanted a discussion.'

'The sort of discussions you wanted belong in a university seminar, on a chosen subject. I simply don't have any views on the things you were so interested in, world historical figures you seemed to have come to rather late, if you'll forgive my saying so. No, Jon, we couldn't live together again, not ever. I've become even more silent, you see. I'd drive you mad. And it's not just you. I want to live alone now. I've a great deal to think about.'

'So you're saying it's not on, then.'

'That's what I'm saying, yes.'

'You won't find anyone else, you know. You're still quite a nice-looking woman, but most men want something a bit livelier.'

'You mean, you do.'

'Well, possibly.'

'I understand. I'm sorry, Jon. I think it better if you don't come here again. This is the sort of conversation that one only has once. Don't you agree?'

'Do you want me to keep in touch?'

'Of course. It's a terrible thing to lose a friend at my age. At our age,' she corrected herself. 'It seems such a wilful thing to do, so artificial, even after an argument. Telephone me from time to time, let me know how you're getting on. Ring me on Sundays. Sunday is always a long day. I'll be glad to talk to you. But it's possibly better if we don't meet.'

'You were always hard, Miriam.'

'There you are, then. Not the right person for you to live with.'

'These men of yours . . .'

'I don't intend to talk about them.'

'They're both in the past, I take it?'

'Yes, both in the past. But still very present.'

She saw the faces of Simon and of Tom Rivers quite distinctly, as if both were dead and had appeared to her in a dream. That Tom was dead she did not doubt, and Simon living, yet now they seemed to have come together in some mysterious conjunction, as if she were the link between them. She understood then that she had had meaning for both of them, and was glad of it. There were to be no more inequalities, no more inadequacies: praise and blame were irrelevant. The stories were not unfinished. On the contrary: they were still potent, like books so important that one read them over and over again. Simon was now as legendary as Tom Rivers; she saw his lethal grace as a quality she could never bring herself to condemn, almost smiled with indulgence as she remembered him. Tom she saw as a sacrifice on the part of the gods, jealous as always. Both assumed hieratical status in her eyes, and she knew that she would always see them as she had seen them in life, untouched by age or discouragement. For that reason she was somehow their guardian, for ever in possession of their unaltered selves.

'I'll be on my way, then,' said her former husband. She saw that like all mortal characters he was marked by the passage of time. The grey hair sat oddly above the long eager face, still eager even after her punishing remarks. But his overcoat seemed too big for him. That was what she now saw.

'How is your health?' she asked, although she had never known him to be ill.

'I'm fine,' he said, surprised. 'I'm always fine. Until now, that is.'

'We're both going the same way, Jon. I'm not getting any younger either. You'll telephone me?' she asked, placing a hand on his arm.

'I might,' he said. 'I haven't exactly been welcomed home, have I?'

'No, and I feel badly about that. But what I had to say had to be said at once. You do see that, don't you? In time we'll be able to talk about something else.' She doubted this, knew that he would return to the subject if she let him. She had no intention of allowing this, felt unmoved. His practicality repelled her. She could never countenance the sort of arrangement he had in mind, thought up on the spur of the moment, to accommodate his own sudden feeling of displacement.

'Let me know how you are,' she called after him, understanding him all too well.

'Actually,' he said, turning round on the stairs, 'I always found you very difficult to get along with.'

'There you are, then.' But she had to allow him the last word.

When she could be quite sure that he had gone—for she knew that he was quite capable of coming back and arguing his case all over again—she took their glasses through to the kitchen, tidied the sitting-room and saw that it was eight o'clock. There was no reason why she should not go to bed. As she had told Jon, and had newly realized, she had plenty to think about, and no one was likely to disturb her again that evening. Nevertheless she must put a stop to this habit: she was not old and infirm. She resolved that this would be the last evening of her reclusion, her last long night.

She thought that she had fallen asleep at once, but woke again after a few hours. During those unknown hours she had had a marvellous dream, which came back to her in vivid colour, the colour of a summer morning. In the dream she had been travelling by train to an unknown destination. She thought that the train was headed for the coast, but was quite content not to be sure. The man in the seat beside her was heavily asleep, his head on her shoulder. The fact that she did not know him did not make her feel uncomfortable. At some point all the passengers—for this was some sort of tour—were issued with a light lunch, consisting of a biscuit and a glass of Armagnac. The sleeping man woke up abruptly, rubbed his eyes, and said, 'I'd forgotten you were there.' She merely laughed agreeably: she seemed to be in excellent spirits, enjoying the excursion. When the train stopped she left the others behind, but she could still see groups of them, in the distance, and somehow in front of her. They were mostly elderly women, in modest hats and plastic mackintoshes, although the weather was exceedingly fine, and there was no hint of rain. The resort, or whatever it was, stretched before her in a vast panorama, apparently empty; this was unusual, as she was given to understand that this was still the holiday season, somewhere in the region of late September or early October. She was aware of newly washed sands, flocks of seagulls, and everywhere the radiant light. She debouched on to a broad esplanade, of vaguely octagonal shape, with white railings, against which several people were leaning. Prominent among them were three old women, looking concerned and unhappy. She herself, wearing a light blue suit which she did in fact possess, advanced joyfully towards them, breathing in the brilliant air.

At this point she woke, with a feeling of extreme gratification, as if she had recently returned from a successful journey. She must have fallen asleep again shortly afterwards, but the strange thing was that the dream recurred, or perhaps only seemed to. At several instances she could see that octagonal esplanade, a platform or promontory, as it now seemed to her, could see the worried ladies with their old-fashioned hats and their glistening shrouds of plastic, could see her own untrammelled advance, the white birds wheeling above her head. She thought that she had never tasted such freedom, never enjoyed such weightlessness, but did not seek to understand the reason. Were they all dead? But no, the man in the train had woken up. Were they all then sleepers, glad to be released from their painful waking lives? She could not answer that, but thought that something more benign had been intended.

When she had woken again properly it was not to light but to darkness, the darkness of a winter morning. She groped for the radio and switched it on. 'Three hours,' announced the usual grave tones, a little before her usual hour for waking. All seemed to be in order. She would make her tea, take it back to bed, until the shipping forecast released her into the day's activity. A blessed pause ensued. 'Ronaldsway,' she heard. That meant the bulletin was nearly over. 'And finally Mallin Head,' said the careful voice. 'Falling very slowly.' How pleasant these people seem, she thought, opening the curtains onto silence. All at once the thought occurred to her: she would give up the room in the Avenue des Ternes, which belonged to a past which was now remote. She could go to Paris for the day, as she had done before. Maybe that was the meaning of the train in her dream; certainly she had stepped lightly, easily. Once more she saw the figure of Tom, in his pale suit, so paradoxically at home in that anxious place, all low ceilings, and, in the cafeteria, sugar spilled by nervous fingers, saw him stride off, away from her. He had not thought about her in those last moments, but she knew that he might have done so, before the end. She repaid him now, with love and gratitude, even though she knew he would not come back.

If her courage faltered a little she accepted that this would always be the case. She sighed, standing in the flat, her briefcase in her hand. She had a long winter to survive. It would not be easy. But she saw, for the first time perhaps, that if careful attention were duly paid, it might, it could, be managed. Once again, eternal vigilance was the price of liberty. Now, at last, she was ready to proceed.

ANITA BROOKNER is the author of eighteen finely crafted novels, including *Visitors, Dolly, Fraud, Altered States,* and *Hotel du Lac,* which won the Booker Prize. An international authority on eighteenth-century painting, she became the first female Slade Professor at Cambridge University. She lives in London.

A B O U T   T H E   T Y P E

This book was set in Granjon, a modern recutting of a typeface produced under the direction of George W. Jones, who based Granjon's design upon the letter forms of Claude Garamond (1480–1561). The name was given to the typeface as a tribute to the typographic designer Robert Granjon.